PLEX PRESENTS:

CRUMBS TO BRICKS

By Christopher "Capo Cat" Freeman

Can't Stop! Won't Stop!

I0680493

CRUMBS TO BRICKS

Copyright 2012 by: Christopher Freeman
Written by: Christopher Freeman
Cover Design Created by: Christopher Freeman & Cedric "Ckillz" Killings
Graphics by: Cedric "Ckillz" Killings
Book Design by: Pamela L. Quigley
Edited & Perfected by: PLEX

A Plex Presents Book Published with permission by Badland Publishing
PO Box 11623
Riviera Beach, FL 33149-1623
(561) 892-4746

ISBN: 978-0-9839123-4-7

First Edition

www.badlandpub.com

ACKNOWLEDGEMENT & DEDICATIONS

This book is dedicated to my son Christopher L. Freeman, Jr. You can be anything you want to be son. The sky is the limit.

I would like to thank the man up above. Without you I wouldn't have been able to write this story. To my main man PLEX. They don't make them like you anymore. You gave me a chance and held my hand throughout this entire project. I am forever grateful. Special thanks to my mom, grandmother, and dad. You guys raised me and I know that it was no easy task. To my Lil bro Jacoby aka Beam aka Killer. Bro you held me down through everything. I love you. To my other two brothers Ebony and Mitch. Yall two niggas did what yall could also. Thanks. I love you niggas.

For my niggas that I have did time with from all over the country. This is for yall. I'm going to start with my Gunshine state niggas first. What up Tiger Spark, Tank, Monkey E, Jelly, Stanka, Big Keith, Bulldog, Dre Goldy, Big Al, Fat Cat, Dixie, Ball, Eight Ball, Ty, Fat Ruben, my girl Star, my girl Bookie, YaYo, Sammie Wilson (All three of 'em out of Duval), Jarvis Mitchell, Chris Blair, Convertible Burt, Boss, Big Mook, Suge, Bino, Wax, Eric Carpenter, Big Corey, Bunkie Brown, Mark Bell, Champ, Mike-Mike. Man it's too many of you niggas to name so I'm gonna switch states. GA: Montana, Coffee Man, Two, Dan Marino, Pimp. West Coast, Dookie Dave, Eat 'em Up, Fluff, Twin, Shawn Craine, Chris Alexander. DC, DC Mike, Fat Rat, Lil Mike, Slob, Yank, Jay Fields. All you niggas need to buy my book. I want to shout out Duval County. I fuckin' love my City! Black Pine, May Port, Jax Bch, Atl Bch, Out East, Southside, Northside, Westside and all the hoods in between. Shout out to my cuz, Lavaughn Brown. You a real good nigga. I love you. To my girl Trice, Amber, Keisha Black, Katrina Taylor, Ebony Bogins, Tylitha, Reecy, Lynn, Starlette, and to everyone I forgot I got ya next time.

OFF DA' RULER'S DESK

Yo Kim! Tracey! Bruh-Bruh [Mike Harper & Cedric Killings]! Pam! Junior [Big Gemo]!!! Break out the good sh#@ 'cause we 'bout to get poured up and celebrate the second biggest day in BADLAND history. The first being the release of STREET RAISED: The Beginning, and now two years later we're dropping CRUMBS TO BRICKS, the first release on BADLAND by a free author. All of our releases have been special to me, but this by far is the specialist to me. Because not only is this a fire ass book, but it shows the growth and strength of our brand. Capo's a business man with freedom and supreme hustle, so he could've taken this project to anyone [or simply done it himself] and probably received more money, yet he trusted me and the BADLAND/PLEX PRESENTS/BOOK GANG team to make this sh#@ happen. Yo Capo! You're a real ni#@a and I take my hat off to you, bruh –bruh! You made the right move, now let's get a million!!!

Niko Thompson, Al [outta Louisiana], Pimp [outta DC], Troy Cannon [my real ni#@a and financial chief], J-Roc Carter [my under-boss], K-1 [the ni#@a behind the trigga], Jimbo [I couldn't do it without you!], Pookey, Big Joe Hollywood, Gangsta [my lil' home outta Chi-town. Yall look for his novel TURNED OUT], James Hairston [my homie and author of FEDERAL NIGHTMARE], Lisa Banks [I'd be f#@ked in the game without you! Thanks for everything!], Summer Rose [where would I be without you?], Flaco [slim, I seriously f#@ks with you! You're my dog for life and love you, boy!], my dog Brad, and everybody over at URBAN EXPOSURE [If yall reading this yall need to cop an issue or two!!!], and everybody that buy and read our books. WE LOVE YALL and we THANK YALL!!! We'd be NOTHING without yall...Erma Mitchel, Kawannah Rouland, Pam Little [I love yall!]...

G'z up! Suckas down! G'z keep their word and provide for their own. Suckas fake moves and suck the life-blood outta the people...what do you do?!

ONE LOVE, PLEX

Capo Cat

CRUMBS TO BRICKS

BOOK 1NE

For those who are not incorporated into the system, for whatever reason, [capitalist] society provides its own alternative – organized crime. In the ghetto this alternative is legitimized by the fact that so many people are forced to engage in at least petty illegal activity in order to secure a living income. The pervasiveness of the lucrative numbers racket, dope peddling [car thievery, pimping, prostitution, and murder for hire] further enhances organized criminality in the eyes of ghetto youth. Social scientists have observed that the role of criminal is one model to which such youth can reasonably aspire. It provides a realistic career objective, certainly more realistic than hoping to become a diplomat or a corporation executive…

■ From: On Transforming The Colonial/Criminal Mentality
■ [Statesville Prisoners Organization]

CHAPTER 1

"U.S. Marshals...we have a federal warrant for your arrest...please don't make a scene. The DEA will explain everything once we reach headquarters," the tall blond U.S. Marshal explained as he blocked Goldie's only possible escape.

Goldie sighed heavily and looked to his wife Kismet, who sat opposite him in their booth. He knew that this time was coming. He'd been having eerie feelings every since his partner Alex had gotten arrested in that reverse sting. So for that reason Goldie had been spending as much time as he possibly could with his wife. On this night the couple had decided to eat out and catch a late movie. However, from the looks of things the movie was definitely out of the question.

"Mr. Jackson, please, could you come with us?" asked the other marshal, whom was short, pudgy and had red hair with freckles covering his pale face.

Goldie winked his eye at Kismet and silently mouthed the words, *I'll call you later*, before he rose and was escorted out of the high-end sports bar by the two marshals.

All sorts of thoughts raced through Goldie's mind as the marshal's van sped through traffic. In no time at all they were parking at DEA headquarters.

Once inside the huge modern fortress, Goldie was taken to a large room with a big conference table in its center. The room was cold and sparsely decorated. In the far corner of the room there were two small holding cells. Wanted posters plastered all four walls.

"Have a seat, Mr. Jackson," instructed the short, pudgy marshal.

After Goldie had found himself a seat, the marshals left the room.

What the fuck is up wit' this? Goldie questioned himself as he sat, waiting. Thirty minutes passed before two more men entered the room. They introduced themselves as DEA Agents, Hogan and Ricks. Goldie eyed them. They looked real familiar. *These look like the same two crackas I seen in Savannah,* he thought to himself.

A pregnant silence hung over the room as the three men stared off. Agent Ricks was the first to speak.

"We've been watching you, Jackson. We've been watching you for quite some time...and I must admit, you're a very impressive individual...have the marshals informed you of your charges?" he asked, pausing to allow Goldie to answer. Goldie said nothing so Ricks continued. "Well, for your information you've been indicted by a federal grand jury for conspiracy to distribute 1,500 kilos or more of cocaine."

Goldie's head fluttered and he began to sweat. "Man, I want my lawyer," he was finally able to say.

His request seemed to have fallen on deaf ears, because Agent Ricks continued to talk to Goldie as if he'd never mentioned *wanting a lawyer*. "We want your connect, Mr. Jackson. We already know—"

"Fuck you, cracka!" Goldie snapped. "Get me a muthafuckin' phone so I can call my muthafuckin' lawyer," he barked, standing to his feet.

Agent Hogan, who'd been quietly listening up until this point, sprang into action. He grabbed Goldie from behind and forcefully slammed him face down onto the conference table.

Ricks took the opportunity to further antagonize Goldie as his partner held him down on the table. "I thought you were smart...but you're nothing but another dumb-ass-nigger," he said, bending to eye-level with Goldie. "Now I'm going to tell you what I want. We, my partner and I, want your black ass in prison *for life!* You goddamn stupid son-of-a-bitch." He grabbed a handful of Goldie's long dreadlocs and yanked them as he spoke. "I knew you had those two marshals and our informants killed...you better give me Jesus Diez or I'll personally stick the needle in your arm when you get your *death sentence*."

"Cracka, fuck you! I don't give a fuck what you want or what you do. I ain't got shit to say."

With that being said, Hogan relaxed the pressure that he'd been applying to Goldie's face and neck, allowing him to sit back in his chair.

"Fuck this piece of shit, partner. He'll wish like hell that he'd talked to us before it's all over with," Agent Ricks said as he and Hogan exited the room.

A long while later the marshals returned with a phone. "Make it quick, superstar," said the tall blond marshal as he placed the phone in front of Goldie.

Goldie quickly snatched the phone up and started punching in numbers. It rang a few times before a smooth confident voice came across the line.

"Yes, Marquis Wimberly, how may I help you?"

"Aye, Marquis, this Goldie. Man, I got a muthafuckin' problem."

The spit-fire attorney sighed heavily. "This better be of colossal magnitude, Sultan. Because it is 11:00 p.m. and I'm scheduled to be in a Texas courtroom by noon tomorrow."

"Man, look, I got picked up on a muthafuckin' conspiracy. These crackas talkin' 'bout 1,500 keys, man."

"Goddamn, Sultan. Where are you?"

"I'm at the muthafuckin' DEA building in Jacksonville."

There was silence as the lawyer thought. "Okay, listen, you'll be going to a detention hearing in the morning. I'll have my jet landing in Jacksonville before I'm off to Texas...the different time zones should compensate the closeness in schedule, but I'm really cutting it close."

"Aiight, man. Just please *be there!*"

"I'll see you tomorrow, Mr. Sultan," the lawyer replied and hung up.

¢   ¢   ¢

Goldie felt a helluva lot better knowing that Marquis Wimberly would be there with him in court. The marshals had taken him to the Duval County Jail after his phone call. There he was booked, processed and assigned a cell. Once inside he began pacing back and forth. He was restless. *I can't believe I done got jammed up by the muthafuckin' feds,* he kept telling himself. Yet the fact remained that he had *gotten himself jammed up by the feds.* The realization landed on him like a ton of bricks...*I remember when there was only crumbs,* he thought to himself.

Finally realizing that his pacing was counterproductive, Goldie got on his bunk and began to recount the events that led up to this whole big mess...the *Crumbs* that led to *Bricks.*

CHAPTER 2

Sultan Jackson, known on the streets of Duval County as Goldie, grew up in a dilapidated home in Atlantic Beach, FL – a city seven miles outside of Jacksonville. His neighborhood, Black Pine or DA Pine as its inhabitants affectionately called it, was the most predominately black neighborhood in Atlantic Beach. It was full of drugs and violence. Who needed cable TV in DA Pine when they could regularly watch an *action packed, R-rated* movie play out in the very streets they called home? *BOYZ-N-DA HOOD, NEW JACK CITY, JUICE, BELLY, BLOOD LINE, AND STREET RAISED* were just everyday living in DA Pine.

Although there was lots of love in the Jackson home, it was inevitable that Goldie would succumb to the street life. Reason being, criminologist have noted two popular theories as to *why some people are more prone to commit crime than other.* Yet society has not moved to better the conditions that support their findings, which are: *a person's environment greatly influences his or her behavior, thus giving merit to the saying that 'people are products of their environment'.* Another theory suggests that *criminal behavior is predetermined in an individual through hereditary traits in their DNA.* Factor the two scientific studies together and you're sure to come up with Goldie or another troubled black youth just like him.

Born the oldest of four boys, raised in a single parent home – his father was doing 30 years in prison – Goldie was always more ambitious and mature than most of his peers. For even though Mrs. Jackson did her best, she could not keep enough food on the table for her four growing boys, nor could she keep them out of the streets, especially with two jobs occupying the majority of her days.

¢ ¢ ¢

Goldie was a born hustler. At school he pitched quarters, sold candy, shot dice or did whatever it took to get paid. His situation dictated his actions. And at the tender age of fourteen he was already displaying natural adult-like leadership skill. Skill that, had he been placed in a better environment and provided the proper guidance, could've sat him atop the corporate chain.

Goldie had at least four other young teens working for him in his candy-dealing enterprise, along with numerous other hustles that he indulged in. And because he possessed good money management skills, Goldie kept close to $700 in his stash.

Everyday on his way to school, Goldie and his next oldest brother, Cashman, would have to walk through the early morning drug-traffic that filled their block. Often he'd stare at the crack-fiends and wonder *what made them go so crazy over those little rocks?* It was that same curiousity, combined with another's misfortune, that afforded him his entry in the dope game.

¢ ¢ ¢

One day a small time drug dealer named Snake was running from the police. In his attempt to dodge the cops, he ran past the Jackson home and dropped a bag of rocks as he jumped their back fence. The police were dead on his ass, but did not see the bag fall. However, young Goldie did. As soon as the police were over the gate and the coast was clear, Goldie snatched up the bag and went straight to his room. His brother Cashman was right behind him.

"Aye bruh, what's that?" Cashman asked, watching Goldie as he emptied the bag's contents onto the dresser.

Damn! Goldie thought to himself as he looked at the hundred-something rocks that laid before him. *I bet a nigga can make two stacks off this shit,* he continued thinking, totally ignoring his brother's questions. He was only fourteen and two grand was a lot of potential profit to him.

"Man, is that crack-rock?" Cashman asked, seeing that his brother had ignored his first question.

"Damn sho' is," Goldie answered, smiling at the possibility.

"Man, I know you ain't gonna sell that shit," Cashman replied, shaking his head and causing his dread-locs to swing back and forth.

"Shittin' me!" Goldie bassed on his brother. "I'ma sell everyone of these shits. I mean, why wouldn't I? The shit can't be that hard. I know all the bassers in the hood. All a nigga gotta do is let a few know that I got it and it's on."

Their entire block was a drug infested trap. So Goldie had been watching the dope-boys do their thing since he was a kindergardner. He knew how they operated. He'd also peeped a lot of their mistakes. So he wasn't going to chase cars like he'd seen them do. *Nah, that's stupid,* he surmised. *I'ma just hug the block until I get me a few good customers. Then I'ma buy me a phone and give them my number. That way I ain't gotta be out there.*

After concluding his plan, Goldie put all of the rocks back in the bag except for ten.

"Dig, lil' bruh. If you keep your mouth closed I'll throw you a few dollars."

Cashman looked at his older brother crazy for a minute, then agreed.

¢   ¢   ¢

After hiding the bag Goldie hit the block. On his way to the park he saw Dirty-D. Dirty-D was an old school baller turned crack-fiend. Approaching him, Goldie informed him he had some fat stones. Goldie also told the crackhead that he'd *look out for him if he would bring him some business.*

"Well, let me get a blast, then," Dirty-D stated, extending his open palm. "Yall young niggas runnin' 'round here sellin' that *Haitian.* So I needs to see whatchu workin' wit', youngblood."

Goldie looked at dirty ass Dirty-D real hard for a minute, knowing that the fiend was running game. Still, he relented and gave him one of the ten rocks that he had brought out. A *straight-shooter* materialized in Dirty-D's other hand like magic. Shamelessly, he slammed the rock into the glass pipe and put a large flame to it. Right there in the middle of the street, Dirty-D inhaled the strong poisonous crack vapoers. His eyes bulged as he exhaled the smoke above his head.

"Pa-partly cloudy...strong chances of rain," Dirty-D whispered. "Youngsta, this shit you got here ain't that bad."

"So you gon' help a nigga?" Goldie asked, proud that his product had passed the test.

"I'll brang you some business." Dirty-D paused. "As long as you keep yo' word and look out for me like you said. Where you gon' be at?"

"I'ma be in the park. I ain't tryna be by all them other niggas, so just come through there."

Goldie went over to the park and found an empty bench. Within twenty minutes Dirty-D came through, followed by two other friends. One spent $50 and the other wanted to spend $100, however, Goldie only had four rocks left.

"Look, I'ma run over to my people and get you six more, aiight?!" Goldie said excitedly, clutching the crackhead's money. The crackhead looked around nervously, lips and hands shaking, and was about to ask for his $60 back, but Goldie cut him off. "Look, buddy, my people live right 'round there. I be out here all the time, so I ain't gon' run off witcha money. Plus I'ma throw you one extra for waitin'."

The man looked at Dirty-D and Dirty-D nodded his head yes. With some reluctance, the man agreed and Goldie shot off home to re-up his bomb. Goldie had made $150 just that quick. He could not believe it. *Selling candy ain't never been this sweet,* he said, smiling to himself.

After grabbing some more rocks, Goldie went in his back yard and jumped on his bike. When he made it back to the park Dirty-D had two more fiends standing there with him and the other guy. Goldie served them quick and got them on their way.

"That's another hundone' I done made you, youngblood," Dirty-D stated, a greasy smile etched across his face. "I'ma brang you all the money, long as you –"

"Here, Dirty-D, my nigga." Goldie cut him off, passing the older drug addict three fat rocks. Dirty-D upped his *straight-shooter* and blasted off.

¢ ¢ ¢

It was 10:00 p.m. and eight trips later when Goldie finally came in the house for good. His mother was due home from her second job and Goldie knew that Mrs. Jackson *was not going for it.* The street lights had been came on, so he was supposed to have *been in the house.*

Once inside Goldie shot straight to his room and pulled out his stash. He'd already had $800 in *candy money*, but after counting up the dough he'd just made in the park, Goldie was now $1,700 strong. *Damn!* He wanted to shout. It had taken him months and months of hustling to get $800, but the rocks had doubled his stash in a few hours. *Boy, I gotta get some more of that shit!*

"Ay, Cashman! Let me holla atchu, boy!" Goldie yelled from his room.

Cashman entered the room and his young eyes almost popped out of their sockets. He'd never seen that much dough before.

"Damn, bruh!"

"Here," Goldie said, handing his little brother $50 in all ones and fives. "This yours. Now keep yo' fuckin' mouth shut."

"Thanks, bruh!" Cashman said with a proud look in his eyes. Goldie had always been his hero. To him, Goldie could do anything. And holding what felt like a million dollars to him only further proved his thoughts.

¢ ¢ ¢

The next day Goldie left school and went up to the Jap's store and copped a pre-paid phone. The *Japs* really weren't *Japs*, they were Chinese, but niggas in the hood weren't hip to nationality. Everybody that had fair skin and slanted eyes were *Japs*. And as long as the niggas from the hood were spending dough, the *Japs* didn't give a fuck what they called them.

The store had everything from food to drug scales. If niggas needed it, the Japs had it. The area that the store sat in was drug infested, so the owners simply capitalized off of it. *Beer, blunts, straight-shooter, baggies, scales, phones, razors, no-taste no-smell, etc* ...The Japs were killing them.

From there Goldie went home and wrote out his new phone number. Every fiend that bought a rock from him would also get his number.

"You ready, Dirty-D?" Goldie asked as he approached his bench.

"Wake me up, youngblood."

Goldie handed Dirty-D two rocks and his new number. Dirty-D pocketed the number and smoked both rocks before running off to drive-in business.

Things pretty much went the same as the day before, which meant that Goldie's little drug stash was getting low fast. *Shit,* he thought, realizing that he needed a plug to score more work from.

On his bike, on the way back to the park with the last of his stones, Goldie spotted John Boy sitting nice on the hood of his Lexus. John Boy was an official big-boy in the hood. He sold weight to all of the dope-boys in Atlantic Beach, as well as some cats in Jacksonville. Word on the street was that John Boy was playing with millions and that niggas who played with his money found themselves *dead.* He'd been arrested three times for homicides in the last two years. However, the cases were always dropped.

"Ay, D!" Goldie began, taking some money from Dirty-D's hand. "Man, a nigga runnin' low on stones...and, well, I was wonderin' if you could help me find some."

Dirty-D thought for a moment and then asked, "How much you tryna spend, youngblood?"

"'Bout $1,500, depends."

"$1,500? That's a lot of money for a lil' nigga yo' age. But I'ma holla at John Boy and see what's up. I'll hit yo' phone when I know something."

¢   ¢   ¢

"Yeah, what's up?" Goldie answered his phone about an hour later.

"Yeah, Sultan, this Dirty-D. I talked to ole boy and he wanna meet you. Can we swing by yo' crib?"

Capo Cat

"Yeah, come on through," Goldie said, knowing that his mother would not be home from her second job until about 11:30 p.m.

Goldie went and sat on the porch. Things were really coming together. In just a few days he'd made major progress. Now he was about to secure a plug to further facilitate his rise. Goldie was doing the numbers in his head when John Boy's Lexus pulled up. Dirty-D motioned for Goldie to come to the car.

"What's up, youngblood?" Dirty-D said as he lifted the seat to allow Goldie to slide in the back seat.

Once Goldie was seated, John Boy began speaking. "What's up, my nigga? Dirty-D said you tryna spend a lil' money...he also said he been bringin' you a lot of money."

"Yeah, I gotta lil' something I'm tryna spend. What's up?"

"What's up is, where you got the dope from that you been sellin'?" John Boy questioned.

"I found it. Now I need some more. So is you gonna serve a nigga or what?"

John Boy smiled. He liked Goldie. The kid had heart. "Aiight, lil' nigga. Whatchu want?"

"I got $1,500."

"Damn, you been bammin', huh?" John Boy said, looking over at Dirty-D with surprise.

"He sho' have," Dirty-D chimed on. "Everybody I smoke wit' been brangin' they money to young Sultan. He treat us wit' respect and he don't be on no corner actin' stupid. He smart."

"Aiight, lil' nigga. I'ma do that for you. And I'ma give you my number. But listen, *this game ain't for the weak.* Only the strong will survive this shit," John Boy preached.

Goldie nodded his head and passed John Boy the money. After counting the money, John Boy passed Goldie a pack containing 200 juggler-dimes. John Boy sold everything from *crumbs to bricks*, and Goldie was destined to follow his course...

CHAPTER 3

During the months that followed, Goldie's cash stash increased significantly. He was booming! He'd gone from spending $1,500 on his re-up to copping $5,000 worth of crack every two days.

One day, after buying a new package, Goldie decided to count his stash. He had cash hidden all over his house. Gathering it all up, he placed it on his bed. When he finally finished counting he couldn't believe it. $57,000 was sitting before him. Not to mention the 600 rocks he'd just bought.

Goldie decided to treat himself since he hadn't made any major purchases. But first he counted out $6,000 and placed it in his mother's bedroom. He wanted her to buy herself and his brothers something nice. He then called John Boy.

"What's up, my nigga?" John Boy answered, recognizing Goldie's voice when he answered.

"Ay JB. A nigga need a favor."

"What's that?"

"Man, I need you to take a nigga to buy some golds."

"Shit, when you ready?"

"I'm ready now…How much them shits cost, anyway?"

"They two-hundred a piece," John Boy answered.

"Cool, come get me," Goldie said before hanging up.

Goldie went back to his room and counted out $3,200. In Florida it was a must that every dope-nigga have gold-teeth. Before a nigga even bought his first car he had to have some golds.

¢ ¢ ¢

John Boy arrived at Goldie's house twenty minutes later. Goldie hopped in the Lex and they headed to Solid Gold Dental.

"So you finna get a few golds, huh lil' nigga?" John Boy

asked as he zoomed in and out of traffic. "How many you tryna get?"

"How many you got?" Goldie asked John Boy, knowing the answer but asking anyway.

John Boy looked like the poster boy for the Florida thugs. He had 18 big, long, wicked dreads that sprouted from his scalp like palm trees. His edge-up was always fresh because his barber, Drew, cleaned him up every other day. And his mouth was full of 22k gold.

"Twenty," John Boy replied.

"Well, I'ma get sixteen," Goldie said.

"Damn! Boy, you got money like that to spend?" John Boy questioned, shocked. He'd just sold Goldie 600 rocks. So he figured if Goldie still had $3,000 to spend after that, then the young nigga was truly smart with his money.

John Boy had taken a liking to Goldie the first day he met him. The other dope-boys in the hood wanted to rob Goldie, because they knew that he was making a little money. But John Boy was protecting him by keeping his business out of the streets. However, John Boy decided at that moment to tempt the wolves. He wanted to see how Goldie would react to pressure.

"Mr. Jackson, we're ready to see you now," said the dental assistant.

Goldie followed the dental assistant to the back and had the work done to his grill. When the dentist was done Goldie paid him, then walked back up front so he and John Boy could leave. Goldie felt like he'd reached a milestone in the drug game by getting his golds. There was no turning back now. He was all in.

"Today is the day that the world is gonna know that I'm in the game," Goldie said to himself. In his mind he'd made his bones. So he knew he'd have to tell his momma what he was up to. He'd left $6,000 on her bed. Yes, it was definitely time he came out of the closet.

When Goldie entered the reception area of the dentist office John Boy was waiting, looking like a proud father. "Smile, my nigga! Let me see them thangs," he said.

Goldie smiled, showing all sixteen.

John Boy walked over to Goldie and gave him some dap.

"Boy, I just came up with a nickname for you. I'ma call you Goldie."

John Boy drove Goldie home and dropped him off. He then drove over to Lewis Street and posted up on the block. The dope-boys were out in full effect. And whenever John Boy graced the block with his presence, like Jesus Christ, a crowd surrounded him. "What's goin' on out this bitch?" John Boy asked no one in particular.

"Man, shit been dead as fuck," replied DJ, a petty hustler by nature.

"Shit, Goldie gettin' all the money," John Boy said, throwing the bait out into the water.

"Who the fuck is Goldie?" Lil Ben asked, looking perplexed.

"Man, you know Lil Sultan. That's what they call him now. The lil' nigga got a sixteen pack in his mouth now," John Boy answered.

"Damn, that lil' nigga doin' good," replied Snake. Snake was a grimey ass nigga. He was the kind of nigga who'd rob his own grandma and pistol whip her if she took too long giving up the cash. He'd already been watching Goldie. And now he'd made up his mind to go ahead and rob him.

¢   ¢   ¢

When Mrs. Jackson got home from work she went straight to her room. She must have been real tired, because she usually spoke to her sons as soon as she walked in the door.

"Sultan!" Mrs. Jackson yelled from her bedroom. "Come here, right now!"

When Goldie entered his mother's bedroom she was holding the $6,000 he'd left, searching his eyes for answers.

"Where did this come from?" she asked.

"It came from me…I been out there doin' my thang and I wanted to give you a lil' somethin' so you could buy yo'self and Cashman 'em somethin' nice."

"Boy, what thang? Whatchu mean, doin' yo' thang?"

"Ma, I been sellin' drugs…"

"Oh, no, Sultan! I can't believe you," Mrs. Jackson stated in a harsh whisper. "I've been bustin' my ass, workin' two jobs to keep food on the table, and you go and sell drugs? How much money is this anyway?...and what's that you got in yo' mouth?"

"I got gold-teeth now, ma. And that's six grand."

"Six grand? Boy, this is a lot of money...and how much that stuff you got in yo' mouth cost?"

"Three grand."

"Boy, you got money like that?"

"Yeah and I got a lot more. For real, you can quit one of them jobs, because I'ma pay the rent. You just take care of yo'self and my bruthas. I gave you that money to go shoppin' wit'. So don't worry about me, I'll be okay."

"Baby, I don't know what to say. I mean, I should be mad, but Lord knows I'm tired."

"Well Ma, don't say nothin' then. Just pray for me and take care of yo'self and my lil' bruthas."

"But son, the drug dealers are either killed or get life in prison."

"That ain't gonna happen to me, Ma. I'm gonna stack my money and get out of the game. I'm gonna start some businesses once I get what I need and yall won't want for nothin'."

Mrs. Jackson had tears in her eyes. Sultan was her first born and she knew that she'd lost him. She knew that he'd gotten a taste of a lifestyle that was as addictive as the drugs he sold. Knowing deep in her heart that her son would never change, Mrs. Jackson decided that the best thing for her to do was to pray.

¢ ¢ ¢

The buzzing sound from Goldie's phone as it vibrated on the floor grabbed his attention. He'd just woke up and was about to get ready for the day. Retrieveing his phone from the floor, Goldie answered "Who this?"

"This Spit Fi'," answered the fiend on the other end of the line.

"What's up, Spit Fi'? Whatchu need?"

"Man, I'm tryna spend a stack. This dumb cracka-bitch

gave me half of her income tax check and I'm tryna smoke my back out. Can you handle that?"

"Yeah, I got you," Goldie replied, trying to hide the excitement in his voice.

"Aiight then, come through. And hurry up if you can. I need a blast bad."

Goldie hung up the phone and grabbed his bag of rocks. He counted out fifty stones, then hopped on his bike. Arriving at Spit Fi's house eight minutes later, Goldie knocked on his door. Spit Fi' wasted no time answering. As soon as Goldie crossed Spit Fi's threshold, Snake stepped from behind the door pointing a pistol. "You know what it is," he snarled.

"Snake, man, what's up? What's the gun for?" Goldie asked, scared to death. "Spit Fi', what's up wit' you, man? I thought we was cool?"

"Fuck-nigga, didn't I say give it up?" Snake barked, pressing the barrel of his gun harder to Goldie's head.

"Aiight man, you got it," Goldie said, handing Snake the bag containing fifty $20 rocks.

"Now getcho bitch-ass from 'round here fo' I buss yo' ass," Snake threatened.

Goldie ran out of the house and jumped on his bike. He damn near broke the pedals off that bitch trying to get out from around Spit Fi's house. When he made it home he called John Boy.

John Boy answered, "What's up, Goldie?"

"Man, I just got robbed!"

"What!?" John Boy asked, faking surprise.

"Yeah, that nigga Spit Fi' set me up and Snake robbed me."

"Damn, that's fucked up."

"Ay, let me hold a gun?"

"A gun? Whatchu need a gun for?"

"Man, is you gonna let a nigga hold one or not?"

"Yeah I gotchu…I'ma be at yo' house in a hour," John Boy said before hanging up.

After the call, Goldie went to his mother's bedroom and took one of her bandanas. He went back to his room and removed a black Raider's cap and some dark clothing from his closet. Placing it all on his bed, he sat and waited on John Boy to arrive…

CHAPTER 4

John Boy whipped his Lexus into Goldie's yard an hour later. He hopped out and knocked on the door. Cashman let him in. When John Boy entered Goldie's bedroom he was sitting on his bed staring into space.

"What's up, boy? You aiight?" John Boy asked.

Goldie looked up at John Boy and the look on his young face told John Boy that murder was on his mind.

"Man, I hope yo' ass brought the gun."

Noticing the dark clothing that lay on the bed beside Goldie, John Boy answered his little homie, "Yeah, I got it...but Goldie, whatchu finna do?" he asked, removing the black Glock .40 from his waist. Of course, he already knew what Goldie was about to do. At that instance he felt guilty, because it was truly his fault that Goldie had gotten robbed. However, being the nigga that he was, John Boy shook off the bad feelings just as quickly as they had set in. *Shiid, fuck it!* John Boy thought, *he gonna have to handle a lot worse shit than this if he plan on playin' in this game...he might as well start now.*

¢   ¢   ¢

Goldie waited until everybody in his house was fast asleep. He then got *blacked-out*, bandanna, cap and Glock, and eased out of the house. Goldie crept behind cars and houses until he was on the side of a house that faced the corner where Snake and a few other niggas hustled.

Snake stood in the midst of the crowd of niggas running his mouth. Goldie caught bits and pieces of the conversation and it had him *heated*.

"Yeah, that lil' bitch shitted on his-self when I stuck that fi' to his head. Mmaannn, that shit was stank as fuck!" Snake said, cracking up laughing. Everybody around him was also laughing at the humorous twist that he'd put on the story of how he'd robbed Goldie.

Goldie was on fire as he pulled the black Raider's cap down low and tied the bandanna around his face. Heart beat pounding, Goldie was scared to death! Yet he knew that this had to be done. After slowly cocking the .40, he took three deep breaths and ran out into the crowd of niggas.

"Yeah! Fuck-nigga! Shit this, bitch-ass-nigga!" Goldie yelled as he started letting loose with the pistol.

Snake heard the words, followed by the *Blocka! Blocka! Blocka! Blocka! Blocka!* Of the Glock .40 and pissed on himself. Throwing his hands up, Snake tried to surrender to the approaching man in black. "You got it, bruh! It's in the –"

A slug ripped through his hand and crashed into his forehead. The exit-wound in the back of his head leaked blood, brains and bone fragments. His body hadn't even hit the street yet, but his audience had scattered like roaches with the lights on. Goldie bussed at their asses for good measures.

Goldie ran back home and hid the gun under a house at the end of his block. Once he made it inside he stripped out of his clothing and jumped in bed. Goldie had killed his first man, but instead of him being scared or remorseful, he felt powerful. He felt like God, because he realized for the first time in his life, that he had the power to choose who lived or died. Goldie went to sleep with a smile on his face.

¢   ¢   ¢

The next morning homicide detectives were still in the neighborhood looking for witnesses. However, they were left holding their nuts because nobody in the Pine talked to police. Not even the old people.

Goldie got a call from John Boy. He told Goldie that he'd be over to his house in fifteen minutes. John Boy pulled up in Goldie's yard not a second later than he said he would. When he did so, Goldie was sitting on his porch drinking some Kool-Aid.

"Damn, nigga you murked Snake?" John Boy asked when he was within Goldie's earshot.

Goldie didn't answer, but John Boy looked into his eyes and knew the answer. A killer could always look another man in his eyes and tell if he'd killed before. A baby face couldn't hide it. It was always in the eyes.

"Niggas is sayin' you murked snake. I don't thank a nigga gonna say shit to the police, but the next time you put in work, don't do the shit in front of people. Masked up or not," John Boy schooled.

"Yeah, I gotcha," Goldie dead panned.

John Boy now saw Goldie in a different light. He felt confident that Goldie was cut out for this. Goldie was so young, yet he was on top of his game. By now the whole hood had heard about Goldie murking Snake, so niggas would think twice before trying the young nigga again.

At the same time, the South was getting too hot for John Boy. There wasn't a day that passed that he didn't see the Feds following him…or at least that's what he thought. John Boy knew that he was getting too big to be in one place. He had to move. The only problem was the money. It was just too good to let go. John Boy needed someone to run shit for him while he moved elsewhere.

"Goldie, have you ever thought about selling weight?" John Boy asked.

"Nawl."

"How much money you got saved?"

"Damn dog, what's up wit' all the questions?"

"Nigga, I'm tryna put yo' lil' ass up on somethin'. So how much you got?"

"I got about fifty grand put up."

"You got fifty grand!?" John Boy exclaimed. He didn't think Goldie had money like that. He'd given him credit for $10,000, but $50,000 was out of the equation. "Oh, you ready, my nigga. I'm definitely about to promote yo' ass…I'm about to move, and since you my lil' nigga I'm gonna let you run shit for me down here."

"Where you movin'?"

"I'm thankin' 'bout New Jersey. I gotta lil' hoe up there. She say niggas payin' twenty-eight stacks per brick up there."

"Well shit, what I gotta do?" Goldie asked, loving what he was hearing.

"Aiight, the first and most important thang is that you can only buy from me. I'ma give you all of my people. I'ma show you how to weight, cook and cut coke, but you can only buy from me. Now how you love that?"

"Shit, let's do it!" Goldie exclaimed, showing his whole grill.

¢ ¢ ¢

Arriving at John Boy's 6000 sq. ft. home, Goldie was in awe. The home was located in a subdivision called Queen's Harbor and compared to Black Pine it was as close to heaven as Goldie ever thought he'd get. Every yard in the upscale neighborhood was carefully manicured. The streets were litter free and there wasn't a basser in sight.

John Boy pulled his Lex up in his circular driveway. The driveway stretched all the way to the back of his house. Using a remote control, John Boy opened the three car garage. Inside were two cars that Goldie had never seen John Boy drive before, a 600 convertible Benz and a Porsche 911.

They entered the house through a door in the garage that led to an elegant kitchen. Marble floors, marble counter tops resting on solid oak, and expensive modern appliances. The kitchen cost more than an average home.

John Boy stopped in front of one of the kitchen cabinets as Goldie ventured on. Pausing at the threshold of the dining room, which also offered an excellent view of the living room, Goldie stared at the crystal chandelier, oak dining room table [which seated eighteen people] and a large grandfather clock adoring the spacious room. The living room was laced with a 70 inch flat screen, white leather sections and white wall carpet.

Both rooms belonged in the pages of The Better Living magazine.

"Ay Goldie, come check this out?" John Boy called out.

When Goldie walked back into the kitchen John Boy held the pantry open. Young Goldie couldn't believe his eyes. Every shelf was stacked with kilos of cocaine. There had to be one hundred of the individually wrapped squared.

"Got damn! That's a lot of shit," Goldie declared.

"Yeah, my nigga, but it can always be more," John Boy replied modestly. "I run through 'bout two hundred of them shits per month. Every brick you see here," he said, pointing into the pantry, "I get for $12,000 a piece and I let 'em go for $18,500. Now what I'ma do for you is let you get 'em for $14,500 and you give 'em to the people I turn you on to for $18,500. I'ma also leave you this house and that Porsche…Nigga, can you drive?"

"Yeah I can drive," Goldie answered.

"Aiight, then. This shit is gonna be a big responsibility for you, but if you listen to me you gon' be good."

John Boy walked over to one of the cabinets and grabbed a scale, baking soda and a Vision Ware cooking pot. Placing it all on the marble countertop of the kitchen's island, he then withdrew a kilo from the pantry. John Boy took a hammer out of the drawer and began beating on the kilo until he was sure that the cocaine inside was broken up good. Reaching back into the same drawer, he retrieved a razor and cut two long lines from the top corner to the bottom corner of the kilo wrapper, forming a large X on its face.

Goldie smiled as he watched John Boy open the work from the middle of the X, peeling it back, exposing the flaky white cocaine. Cutting on the scale, John Boy removed chunks of cocaine from the open wrapper, placing them upon the scale until its digital screen displayed 125 grams. "Goldie this a eighth of a kilo," he said, gesturing at the chunks of coke on top of the scale. "It's eight of 'em in a key. Each eighth you gonna sell for $2,325. Now double that and you got 250 grams, which goes for what?" John Boy asked.

"Um…$4,650," Goldie answered.

"Yep." John Boy smiled. "Okay, 500 grams is a half-bird and 1000 grams is the whole thang. It's really all math."

John Boy ran water into the Vision Ware pot, adding fifty grams of coke and fourteen grams of baking soda before placing it on the stove and cutting it on medium high. When the cloudy mixture started to boil, he waited until the water cleared, which meant that the baking soda was almost cooked out.

Taking the pot off of the stove, John Boy placed it in the sink, cut on the water, then using his hand, he splashed water into the pot until all of the cocaine dropped to the bottom. Next he poured off half of the water and splashed more water into the pot, replacing what he'd poured out. After that he placed the pot on the counter and raked the cocaine-gel that had settled at the bottom of the pot with a fork. He did so to rid the gel of air bubbles and also to even it out. He let the pot of cocaine sit on the counter until it hardened.

When John Boy was satisfied that the work was ready he poured off some of the water in the pot and gave it a twirl, causing the cookie of crack to detach from the pot. The results were beautiful. John Boy laid the cookie on the counter and put a Tweet razor on it. He came up with 170 fat-ass slugs. "These are the rocks that I sell to you for ten dollars a piece," John Boy said, holding up the bag of rocks.

"But John Boy, why you sell 'em for ten dollars to the hustlers when you can let the fiends get 'em for twenty and make double?"

John Boy looked at Goldie and explained. "Because it's all about the fast flip. Why run 'round all day sellin' rocks to make five grand when you can flip one key to a nigga and make four grand in one sale? Remember Goldie, it's about math and the fast flip. Now let me see you weigh up fifty grams and cook it."

Goldie did good on his first try. His only mistake was that he poured a little of the cocaine-gel down the sink when he poured the water off. But by the time he'd cooked up two keys he was a pro.

CHAPTER 5

Three years later John Boy and Goldie were on top of the world. John Boy had moved to New Jersey and expanded his operation into other northern states. He'd became a major distributor and his connect, Jesus Diez couldn't have been happier. John Boy was supplying major players in at least seven different states and was so far up the food chain that the Fed's nicknamed him Johnny Ghost.

Goldie, on the other hand, was moving a lot of weight in the Jacksonville Metropolitan area, as well as a few other southern cities. He was 18 years old and already considered a kingpin. While John Boy relied on the gift of gab and business prowess to advance in the drug game, Goldie had taken a more sinister route: Murder and Mayhem. He'd participated in over five murders in a two year time span.

Goldie was a baller's baller. For his 17th birthday he spent over $200,000 on his birthday party. He even bought his mother a house out in Queen's Harbor, larger than the one John Boy had given him. A 600 Benz was parked in the driveway with a red bow on its roof when Goldie first took his mom to her new home. He'd taken special care of the women in his life. There were only two.

Mrs. Jackson and his wifey Kismet.

Goldie met Kismet when he was seventeen. By then he'd all but dropped out of school because of all the kilo's he was serving. They met at a high school football game. And from the first time Goldie laid eyes on Kismet he knew that she was the one. At their first encounter they exchanged numbers and began spending a lot of time talking on the phone.

Kismet had an idea what Goldie was doing in the streets, but she didn't really know to what extent. Her father was a narcotics detective for Atlantic Beach Police Department. And if he ever found out she was fucking with a street nigga he'd have killed her.

Goldie would pick Kismet up from school and drop her off a few blocks from her house everyday. No matter what Goldie was doing in the streets he never forgot to pick up his girl. He'd buy Kismet expensive gifts that she'd have to hide from her parents. She was the most popular girl at her school. Even the teachers would comment on her, in the staff dining hall amongst themselves, because she wore clothes that they couldn't afford.

All of the guys at school wanted to holla at Kismet, but thought better of it because they all knew who her man was. They'd all heard the stories about how Goldie had murked this nigga and that nigga. They'd heard how he was flooding Duval County with enough bricks to dam the St. Johns River.

Kismet had heard the rumors also, but to her Goldie was harmless. She'd even heard her father speak of Goldie. It seemed like everytime a nigga got killed in Duval County, be it Atlantic Beach or Jacksonville, he always blamed Goldie. She wanted to defend her man, but she knew her father would never understand so she said nothing.

Kismet would always keep her ears open whenever her dad's cop buddies would come over. One night Kismet's dad and one of his fellow officers were downstairs discussing a bust. She overheard them talking about Goldie.

"After tomorrow we won't have to worry about Goldie's ass anymore. He's going to get a life sentence for sure. And I can't wait to see it," Detective Martain said to Kismet's father, David Kato. "And that was some good work you did with that snitch, Detra. Once that motherfucker opened his mouth I thought we was gonna have to get a muzzle to shut him up."

Both officers shared a hearty laugh at that one. Then the talk turned serious again. "Martain, do you really think the deal is going down tomorrow? I mean, I didn't know Alex Brooks was buying that much coke. Thirty keys, Jesus Christ!"

"Detra knows not to play with me. I've got his ass by the balls. He said the deal is gonna go down tomorrow and that's what better got-damn-it happen. Now let's go over this thing one more time," Detective Martian said, opening the notebook that was on the table. "Okay, Alex is supposed to pick the drugs up from a mini-storage on the 1100rd block of Mayport Road in a Uhaul. He is to do this after Detra meets Goldie with the cash at the Dick's Wings on the 2500rd block of Mayport Road at 2:30 p.m. Once Detra gives Goldie the money, Goldie will give Detra the storage number and combination to the lock on the unit where the cocaine is stashed. Detra is to then text message the info to Alex's phone."

"Okay, that all sounds good, but why won't Goldie just sell Alex the dope himself? He's been dealing with the guy long enough," Kato stated.

"I guess he thinks that if he doesn't actually sell to a person, and it's a set up, he can't get the charge. Maybe he doesn't know about circumstantial evidence," Martian answered.

Kismet had heard enough. She went back to her room, locking the door behind her, and called Goldie.

¢   ¢   ¢

The next day Goldie was at the Dick's Wings. And just as they had planned, Detra arrived at 2:30 p.m. with the cash.

"Man, when Alex gets this shit he gonna really be in power," Detra commented. He was wired for sound. The detectives were listening and recording the conversation from a van a block away.

"Yeah, my nigga, I'm givin' Alex some good shit. You know I pay top dollar for only the best imported shit."

The detectives were loving what they were hearing. "We've got his ass now," stated Detective Martain. He then turned back to the conversation taking place in the Dick's Wings.

Goldie opened up the duffle bag and checked the cash. "It's all there," Detra said.

"Aiight, text Alex and put in the numbers 211, followed by 34-9-15."

"Team one, do you have a visual on the Uhaul?" Kato spoke into his walkie talkie.

"Yes sir," answered team one's commanding officer.

"Good, wait until he loads the drugs into the Uhaul. As soon as he tries to leave, stop him."

"Roger," team one's commanding officer responded.

Detra left the Dick's Wings at 2:40 p.m. to meet with Officers Martain and Kato.

"Team two?" Martain said into his walkie talkie.

"This is team two," team two's commanding officer answered.

"Team two, I want you to take Goldie down as soon as he walks out of the restaurant. Do not let him reach his car."

"Copy."

Kato hit the talk button on his radio. "Team one, what's going on?" he asked.

"Alex and an unknown black male are loading furniture into the back of the Uhaul."

"Furniture? What the hell are you talking about?"

"The cokes in the furniture," Martain cut in. "It's got to be."

"Okay, team one, the coke's in the furniture. Stop them when they try to leave."

"Ten-four, Detective."

Just then there was a knock on the van's door. It was Detra. They let him in.

"I did, good, huh?" Detra asked, smiling like it was fun to fuck over his friends.

You would have thought that he'd hit the lotto as happy as he was and it pissed Kato off. Even the police hated rats, yet they needed them to get the job done. "Yeah, you did real good," Kato replied.

Goldie paid for his food and walked out the door of Dick's Wings at 3:15 p.m. Before the doors of the restaurant could shut behind him, DT Crown Vics came from everywhere. "Get down you son-of-a-bitch!" an officer yelled, gun drawn and aimed at Goldie's head.

¢   ¢   ¢

Goldie dropped the duffle bag and did as he was told. Just as Alex put the Uhaul in gear, DT Crown Vics came from everywhere, blocking his path. He and his cousin Harold were snatched out of the truck and forcefully handcuffed.

¢ ¢ ¢

Once Goldie was cuffed, Detective Martain and Kato drove to the scene with Detra hidden in the back of the van. The tint on the van was too dark to see through, which was fine with Detra, because he knew if Goldie could see him he was as good as dead.

When Martain parked the van, Goldie was already in the back of one of the Crown Vics. His duffle bag was on the hood of the one he was detained in.

Detective Kato opened the Crown Vic's door and spoke. "How are you Goldie? I'm Detective Kato, with Vice. It seems that we've got you in a jam. You're going away for a long time, my friend."

Goldie said nothing as he stared at Kato. He looked very familiar. He also had the same last name as Kismet. After a long silence, Goldie finally spoke. "Look, Mr. Kato, you ain't got shit on me. All I was doing was getting somethin' to eat."

Kato started to laugh. "Oh yeah? Well what about the money in the duffle bag?"

"What money? Man, ain't no money in my bag."

Kato called to Martain. "Hey, look in that duffle bag, will ya?"

Martain did as he was told and was shocked. "Kato, there's nothing but clothes in this bag."

"What the fuck do you mean, clothes?"

"Come see for yourself."

Kato walked over and looked in the bag. "Fuck!" he yelled, then ran back over to Goldie's open door. "Where is the fuckin' money, you son-of-a-bitch!?"

Goldie was silent as he thought about Star. She was a waitress at Dick's Wings and had left with the cash in her backpack when her shift ended at 3pm. Goldie had been fucking her on and off for the past six months.

"Team one, check the furniture in the Uhaul," Kato barked into his walkie talkie.

"Copy sir."

Thirty minutes later team one chirped back. "There's nothing, sir."

"What do you mean, nothing?" Kato barked.

"We checked everything. We even cut the sofas open and ran the dog around them. There's nothing, sir."

Kato threw his walkie talkie to the ground, shattering it. "Got-damn-it! Martain, the Uhaul's clean!"

"See, I told yall pigs I was gettin' somethin' to eat."

"Why, you drug dealing motherfucker!" Kato snarled, storming back to the open door that Goldie was cuffed in. "You're a slick son-of-a-bitch, but I'm gonna nail your ass to the wall if it's the last thing I do!" he spat, saliva foaming at the corners of his mouth.

"Ten thousand a month to back off?" Goldie whispered to Kato.

Kato frowned and slammed the car door in Goldie's face. They had to let Alex, Goldie and Harold go. Kato was pissed! There was going to be hell to pay for his fuck up. And Detra was due for a good ass whipping, compliments of David Kato and Lonnie Martain.

¢   ¢   ¢

The night before, Goldie and Alex had met up at Six Pockets. They decided to fake the deal the following day in order to identify the detectives on their asses and attempt to bribe them. They also wanted to make sure Detra was indeed a rat...he was.

CHAPTER 6

"Kismet, baby I need to know the truth?" Goldie stated as he zoomed through traffic in his Porsche 911. He'd just picked Kismet up from school and was taking her home. It had been two days since the botched bust and the suspense was killing him. He'd fought the urge long enough to question Kismet about the source of her information.

Kismet sat quietly, staring out of her window. She knew exactly what Goldie was asking her. And although she never wanted to hide anything from him, she'd been too scared to tell him that her father was a cop. Slowly, Kismet turned to face Goldie. Her heart sank. His hazel eyes seemed as though they were looking right through her. He was so cute. His eighteen fat, wicked, dreads hung a little past his shoulders. They were sun kissed, so they matched his skin complexion and gold-teeth.

"Goldie, you know I love you, right? I'm gonna tell you how I found out about that set up, but please understand that I never lied to you. The only reason I never told you what I'm about to tell you now is because I thought that if I did so you'd leave me alone." Kismet paused and took a deep breath. "My father is a narcotics detective. His name is David Kato. Everytime he and his friends talk about doing a bust I listen to see if your name comes up...I'm sorry, Goldie."

"Damn," was all Goldie could say. He knew that Kismet had to be related to Kato, but he didn't think that he was her father.

Kismet had tears in her eyes as she sat facing Goldie, searching his eyes for answers. But Goldie's eyes said nothing, causing Kismet's tears to flow faster.

A few moments of silence passed before Goldie uttered, "Baby, you could've told a nigga about yo' ole boy. But this shit ain't gonna change nothin'. You still my baby," he said, reaching over and pinching Kismet's cheek.

Kismet felt like she could breathe again after hearing Goldie say that nothing had changed between them. She had been so scared of how he'd react to the truth. But now she knew Goldie loved her no matter what. Kismet went on to divulge what she'd overheard her father and Detective Martain discussing the night before. "Goldie, they were talking about raiding one of your tracks…or traps, on Friday. They were talking about busting the one on Lewis St."

Goldie looked over at Kismet and smiled. She'd just saved him about thirty grand worth of work, and God knows how much cash it would have cost him to bail his workers out of jail.

¢   ¢   ¢

Three Weeks Later
The house located at 315 Agave Drive was identical to all of the other single family homes on its block. The only difference was the police car parked out front. After the botched bust, Detra Green was stashed away at the residence under 24 hour protection. It was supposed to be a safe location; however, that all changed when Kismet stumbled across its whereabouts while snooping around her father's home office.

Kismet had snuck into her father's home office and went through his file cabinet. There she found a folder marked Detra Green. She recognized his name immediately. Flipping through the papers inside, Kismet discovered that Detra Green had been arrested for molesting his girlfriend's ten-year old sister. Then, in exchange for leniency, he agreed to set Goldie and Alex up. Kismet found the address to the safe-house on the bottom of Detra's cooperation agreement. She was so appalled after reading the police report detailing the sexual battery on the little girl that she told Goldie what Detra had done and gave him the address to the safe-house where Detra was being kept.

¢   ¢   ¢

Harold brought the black cargo van to an abrupt stop next to the

Capo Cat

police car parked in front of 315 Agave Drive. The side door of the van was already open, but the startled officer inside of the police car never got a chance to see the face behind the muzzle flash that ended his life. Two dark figures emerged from the van, stealthly advancing on the house. They were carrying assault rifles. One of the masked men went in through the rear of the house, while the other kicked in the front door. Moments later they found Detra cowering in the hall closet.

Detra trembled like a wet rat as he was led out of the house at gun point and forced into the back of the van. Once inside, Goldie took off his mask and struck Detra's bitch-ass on the side of the head with the stock of his Choppa, knocking him out cold. The van sped off into the night.

Thirty minutes later a loud noise awakened Detra out of his slumber. He opened his eyes and his worst nightmare stood before him holding a chainsaw. He tried to scream, but he had duct tape covering his mouth. Running crossed his mind, but he was duct taped to a chair. Looking around, Detra took in his surroundings and realized he was in a desolate wooded area. He began to sweat.

Goldie killed the chainsaw's engine once he noticed Detra had woke up. He snatched the duct tape off of Detra's mouth. "So you just gonna rat a nigga out like that, huh?" he asked.

"Man, whatchu talkin' 'bout? Goldie, man listen." He swallowed, more sweat pouring down his baldhead. "Man, I would never tell on you, man."

"Nigga, do I look stupid to you? Bitch, you ain't thank we knowed it was a set up when you brought that money to Dick's Wings?" Goldie slapped the shit out of Detra before he could reply. "Ay, Alex, get me that box cutter and crowbar out the van."

When Alex returned with the box cutter and crowbar Goldie instructed Harold to pull down Detra's pants.

"Man, Goldie, why you got them takin' my pants?" Detra began to cry. "Oh God! Please, man! Pl—"

"Bitch! Shut up," Goldie spat, slapping Detra's fuck-ass once more. "Damn nigga, what the fuck is that?" Goldie asked, pointing at Detra's small member. "Ay, my nigga," Goldie beckoned. "I ain't gay or nuthin', but Alex, you gotta see this nigga's shit." Alex and Harold both looked and fell out laughing.

"Nigga, is this why you like to fuck lil' girls?" Goldie questioned, grabbing Detra's dick and cutting it clean off with the box cutter.

Detra passed out from shock. Goldie, undeterred by all of the blood, wedged the crowbar into Detra's mouth and used the box cutter to sever his telling ass tongue. Detra woke up screaming, but it only excited Goldie more. Goldie picked the chainsaw back up, cut it on, then slowly beheaded Detra with it.

¢ ¢ ¢

The next day Detra's smoldering body was found in the woods, his head against a tree with his penis stuffed in his mouth.

The following night, Goldie was in bed asleep, dick hard as a muthafucka. He was dreaming about fucking Oprah again. In his dream he had the media mogul bent over on top of his King size bed. He was just about to slide his dick into her fat, rich ass when a thunderous explosion jolted him awake. The swat team was all over his bedroom. He was arrested without incident.

¢ ¢ ¢

At the jail, Goldie was booked on two counts of murder for the deaths of Detra Green and Officer Herbert Forrest. He called John Boy from the holding cell, who in turn called his high profile Miami lawyer, Marquis Wimberly, to represent his young friend at his bond hearing the following day. Marquis was at the State Attorney's office the next morning before their doors were even open. His presence alone made the District Attorney squeamish. Knowing what he knew, Mr. Wimberly had Goldie's bail hearing put off until the afternoon in order to look over the State's evidence. Needless to say, the State didn't have shit. Nevertheless, they put up one hell of an argument, but Mr. Wimberly was still able to convince the judge to grant Goldie a $1,000,000 bail, being as the State's case was so weak.

The bail was posted later that day. And as he descended the ramp on the side of the jail, after his release, he was met by Detectives Kato and Martain. "I know you killed them, you son-of-a-bitch! I'm going to nail your ass to the got-damn wall one of these days," Kato threatened.

But Goldie only smiled as he side stepped the two officers. He walked a short distance and hopped in the car with Alex, who was parked in front of the jail waiting on his release.

"Man, what was them crackas talkin' 'bout?" Alex asked, looking nervous.

"Fuck them pussy-ass-crackas. Them bitches ain't got shit. If they did, they would've got you and yo' cousin ass too. The lawyer said he'll have the case dismissed by next week."

Alex sped out of the jailhouse parking lot, pushing his Benz to Goldie's house, dropping him off. Goldie had decided to stay in a hotel. Walking up his long driveway, Goldie sighed. Police tape was still on his front door. And the inside of his house was trashed. Luckily he never kept work at his house or he would have been finished. The police had been through everything.

Goldie gathered up a few outfits for his stay at the hotel, hopped in his Porsche 911 and was on his way. He called John Boy after checking in and getting situated.

"They done finally let the bird out of his cage, huh?" John Boy answered his phone. He had Goldie's number programmed under the letter G.

"Yeah, my nigga, you know them crackas can't keep a good nigga down. But yo, I need you to do something for me?"

"What's that?"

"I need you to holla at them two dudes that did that lil' cleanin' job for you last month. Man, them two fuck-ass police I was tellin' you 'bout done fucked my house up!"

"Damn nigga, ain't that ole girl peoples? And as big as yo' house is, I know that shit got to be a big mess. Shit, them niggas gonna charge the hi-hi for that job."

"Man, I don't give a damn what it cost. When it comes to my house, it's whatever. I need you to make this shit happen, ASAP!"

After putting a hit out on Detectives Kato and Martain, Goldie called Kismet.

"Hey baby, are you okay?" Kismet asked, answering her cell. She also had Goldie's number programmed in her phone. "I saw you on the news last night. They said you got arrested for killing that snitch Detra and murkin' a policeman."

Goldie smiled at Kismet's attempt to talk ghetto. "Yeah, they had me, but they had the wrong man. Anyway fuck all that, can you sneak out?"

Goldie picked Kismet up an hour later from the usual spot down the street from her house. They stopped by the Waffle House to get something to eat before making their way to Goldie's suite at the Comfort Inn. Entering the room, Goldie was all over Kismet as soon as the door closed. He had her buck-naked in less than thirty seconds.

Laying Kismet on the King size bed, Goldie admired her body. She was bad-to-death! She looked just like DMX's girl, Kiesha, in the movie Belly. They even shared the same skin complexion.

"Bend over," Goldie commanded.

Kismet did as she was told, sticking her ass up in the air. After doing so, she anxiously anticipated Goldie entering her soaking wet love-box from behind. But to her utter delight, Goldie kneeled behind her and started eating her pussy from the back.

"Oh Goldie, shit," Kismet whimpered. Her pussy was on fire!

Goldie continued to feast on Kismet's swollen pussy lips until cum mixed with saliva oozed down her smooth thighs, staining the bed sheets. The more Goldie sucked and nibbled, the freakier he became. He ordered Kismet to open her ass cheeks and when she did so, he inserted his silky hot tongue into her quivering rectum. Kismet shivered uncontrollably from the sensation she experienced. She'd never had her ass ate. Kismet was so overwhelmed with pleasure that she collapsed onto the sweat drenched sheets.

"Girl, I ain't done wit' this pussy yet," Goldie declared, flipping Kismet over. He pulled down his pants and boxers in one swift motion, exposing his rock hard tool. "Suck it," he said, eyeing Kismet as she eyed his one-eye monster. A sexual hunger filled her eyes.

Kismet sat up and began sucking Goldie's dick hard, like she was trying to suck an apple through a straw. When she began massaging Goldie's balls, while trying to swallow his throbbing swipe, he almost blew his load.

"Hold on, baby. Shit!" Goldie said, pushing Kismet back onto the bed. He knew that if he released the huge nut building in his balls, he'd be finished.

Spreading Kismet's thick chocolate thighs, Goldie inserted his engorged cock into her hot love-nest. The act was so passionate that it took her breath away. He started pounding her pussy like a machine.

"Oh, shit I'm 'bout to cum," Goldie uttered after pulverizing Kismet's wet cum-catcher for ten straight minutes.

Kismet pushed Goldie off of her when she felt his dick swell. "Cum in my mouth, daddy!" she begged, grabbing Goldie by his ass cheeks, guiding his fuck-rod into her dick starved mouth.

Goldie released the mother of all nuts into Kismet's jib, coating the back of her throat with thick white ball-juice.

CHAPTER 7

"This is Ted Dallas, reporting live from the scene of a grisly crime," the network news reporter stated. Kismet was watching TV in her bedroom. "Two officers have been mur--. Excuse me, three officers have been murdered, and a fourth has been life flighted to Shans for wounds sustained in a shoot out with unknown assailants. Details are sketchy, but what we do know is that a call about a large drug deal taking place came in and it seems the officers were gunned down while responding to the call. We will have more information as the investigation progresses. This is Ted Dallas, news at twelve…back to you, Bob."

Kismet turned off her TV and ran to her parent's bedroom. The crime scene was just four miles from their home. "Mom, call dad. Some officers were killed tonight," Kismet huffed, out of breath.

Mrs. Kato called her husband's cell phone ten times, back to back, only to go straight to his voice mail box. She then called the police station. "Hi, my name is Shatya Kato, Detective Kato's wife, and I'm trying to get in touch with him."

"Are you at home, Mrs. Kato?" the operator asked.

"Yes, I'm home."

"Okay, you're gonna need to stay there. There's an officer on the way over as we speak."

"For what? What's going on?"

"Mrs. Kato, the officer will speak to you as soon as he arrives."

Mrs. Kato slowly hung up the phone. She looked back at Kismet. Tears began to fill her eyes. She didn't have to utter a word, because her expression said it all – something was very wrong.

Kismet began to cry and ran to her bedroom, closing and

locking the door behind her. Ten minutes later she heard the doorbell ring. Seconds after that she heard her mother's screams, confirming her worst fear. Her father was gone.

Kismet called Goldie from the phone on her nightstand. "Goldie they killed him," she cried into the receiver.

"Wha--. Who killed who?" Goldie asked, feigning shock. He already knew what had happened.

"They killed my daddy. Goldie come over here, please. I need you," Kismet pleaded.

"Somebody killed yo' daddy?"

"Yes, so please come."

"Aiight, baby, but what about yo' ole girl?"

"Don't worry about her. I need you."

When Goldie arrived at Kismet's house he saw the officer's police cruiser parked out front. Something in his gut told him to leave, but against his better judgement he killed his engine. Goldie hopped out of his Porsche and rang Kismet's door bell. Kismet opened the door and let him in. Stepping inside, Goldie was met with strange looks from both the officers and Mrs. Kato. However, the officer's looks were more of a glare.

"Kismet, who is your friend?" Mrs. Kato asked.

Before Kismet could answer the officer spoke. "Sultan Jackson, aka Goldie. Why he's the biggest drug dealer in northeast Florida."

Mrs. Kato was taken aback. "Kismet, how do you know someone like this?" she questioned, gesturing to Goldie.

"Mom, Goldie's not a drug dealer."

"To hell he's not," the officer interjected. "Not only is he a drug dealer, he's a murderer. He was just arrested two weeks ago for killing an informant and an officer."

"Those charges were dropped!" Kismet protested.

Goldie remained silent through the verbal exchange. He wanted to kick his own ass for coming into Kismet's home. The officer's comments, although true, wasn't the type of shit he wanted Kismet and her mom to hear about him.

The officer spoke again. "As a matter of fact, Detective Kato was leading the investigation into Mr. Jackson and his criminal activities. And quite frankly, I don't think he'd approve of his daughter dating a sociopath. You kn—"

"Stop it!" Kismet barked. "Just stop it! I just lost my dad and Goldie's here to comfort me....Please, just lose the conversation about Goldie."

Mrs. Kato agreed for the time being, but she made a mental note to get to the bottom of this shit about her daughter dating a drug dealer.

Kismet led Goldie to her bedroom while Mrs. Kato stayed downstairs and chatted with the officer.

"Goldie, I can't believe my daddy's dead," Kismet sobbed.

"Damn baby, it's aiight. I'm here for you."

Goldie felt a tinge of guilt, being that he was responsible for Detective Kato's murder. But Kato had forced his hand with the constant harassment. If only Kato had taken the $10,000 that Goldie had offered he'd still be alive. *Shit, it costed me fifty stacks to get him killed*, Goldie mused.

"Goldie, I'm pregnant," Kismet whispered.

"What?"

"I'm going to have our baby."

Goldie didn't know what to say. He wanted to have a child but he wanted to be out of the game when he did. "When did you find out?"

"I found out yesterday. I haven't told my mom and da—"

Kismet choked up and started crying again. The thought of her father never knowing or seeing his grandchild was heart breaking.

There was a soft knock on Kismet's bedroom door followed by Mrs. Kato sticking her head in. "Baby, I have to go to the morgue with Officer Bork. You can stay here if you like. I'll be right back," she said.

"Okay, mom, I'll stay here. I wouldn't be able to handle seeing dad like that," Kismet sniffled.

Goldie gave Kismet solace in his embrace as they lay in her bed, each in their own world. Kismet thought about her father and Goldie thought about being a father...

CHAPTER 8

As Goldie pushed his freshly detailed 600 Benz down 1st Street, his cell phone began to vibrate in his pocket. Pulling it out, he glanced at the screen before pressing answer. It was John Boy.

"Dog, I got some problems. I need you to get up here to D.C., ASAP," John Boy explained.

Goldie could tell by the urgency in John Boy's voice that shit was real. He wanted badly to know what had his dog sounding the way he did, but he wasn't about to ask him over the phone. After agreeing to come he told John Boy to book the flight. Goldie then continued on his mission to pick up his freak bitch Lorraine. He wanted some head and she loved to swallow.

¢ ¢ ¢

The Following Day
The flight from Jacksonville to the Nation's Capital was uneventful. Grateful, Goldie silently thanked God when the plane landed safely in D.C. Once off of the large commercial airliner, Goldie strolled into the airport to retrieve his luggage. He was walking toward the baggage claim when someone grabbed him from behind.

"What's up, my nigga?" John Boy asked, releasing Goldie from his grip.

"Shit, what's up wit' you? I can tell you been eatin' good," Goldie replied, giving John Boy a once over.

Although John Boy was still supplying Goldie with enough white to build an Eskimo village, they hadn't seen each other since John Boy moved north three years prior. He'd have the eighteen wheeler deliver Goldie 400 bricks a month in hidden compartments built within the truck's long trailer.

After placing the last of Goldie's luggage in the back of John Boy's 500 convertible Benz, John Boy took Goldie to the condo he was renting on the outskirts of the city.

"So, you gonna tell me what the fuck goin' on up here or what?" Goldie asked. He was seated on a green leather sectional in John Boy's spacious living room.

John Boy sat up in his lazy boy. "I got a meetin' tonight wit' this nigga from New York. Nigga name Tony Bolivia. The nigga been havin' smoke wit' a nigga 'cause I been takin' his business."

"Takin' his business? How long you been out here? You told me you was in Ohio."

"Shiid, a nigga been out here 'bout two months. I ran into this bad-ass-bitch from out this way when I was in Atlantic City a few months back. One thang led to anotha, and here I am," John Boy stated, stretching out his arms for emphasis. He went on. "Man, this spot is a muthafuckin' gold mine, I swear to God! The nigga Tony Bolivia was up her slangin' units for $24,000, killin' 'em. And these D.C. niggas ain't no lightweight hustlers either. They gettin' they paper. Anyway, I cut into a few cats and started lettin' 'em get them thangs for the 18.5. Them niggas stopped fuckin' wit' Tony immediately. Shit, them niggas started takin' some of Tony's customers they muthafuckin' self. Tony kidnapped one of the niggas and put that iron on his back."

"Damn, the nigga shot dude in the back?" Goldie interrupted.

Shaking his head, John Boy answered, "Nawl, the nigga tortured dude. That nigga had dude hangin' from a ceiling in one of his spots and put a hot clothes iron on that nigga back like Penny momma did on that one episode of Good Times."

"Damn! That nigga wild as fuck! Shit, I'ma do me a nigga ass like that," Goldie stated, excitedly.

John Boy shook his head, smiling. "Boy, you stupid as fuck. Nigga, I'm tryin' to tell you what's up and you tryin' to steal a nigga torture techniques."

"My bad, dog...what happened, again?"

Sighing, John Boy continued. "Anyway, that iron got dude mind right. He told Tony that he was gettin' his work from me before Tony blowed his brains out." Staring piercingly into Goldie's eyes, John Boy added, "and can you believe that fuck-ass-nigga started sendin' me threats after offin' dude?"

Goldie grunted. "Damn, that's some hoe-ass shit right there. Whatchu think he want to meet up for, 'specially after all that shit?"

"I don't know, but I'ma tell the nigga to buy from me, and I'll fall back and let him get all the money. And I'ma give 'em them shits for 17.5 so he can drop his price to 23 and still make his lil' fifthy-five hundred."

"Damn, you shoulda been told that nigga that. I bet that's cheaper than him gettin' 'em up in New York," Goldie remarked.

John Boy sucked his teeth. "Man, I did try to tell that nigga that shit. I sent two niggas to holla at 'em and the nigga killed one of the niggas and sent the other nigga back wit' a message tellin' me to take my bama-ass back down south or I'm next."

Goldie bussed out laughing. And John Boy, seeing Goldie cracking up, joined in. When Goldie finally calmed down his demeanor turned dead serious. "Shit, my nigga, whatchu gonna do?" he asked.

John Boy rubbed his chin. "Well, I know one muthafuckin' thang, a nigga ain't finna pack they shit and leave. I'm runnin' through a hundred units a month up here. I'm tryin' to get shit established so I can just pick up and drop off."

"Well, that's what it is then. Fuck them green-ass-niggas. They either gonna roll with us or get rolled on, and it's as simple as that! What time is the meetin'?"

"Six-thirty."

Goldie glanced at his rose-gold Bell & Ross. "That's two hours from now. We need to beat them niggas there."

A hour later John Boy and Goldie arrived at Chocolate City in John Boy's gun-metal-grey Corvette.

"Man, how we gonna get in the club wit' guns?" Goldie asked, subsequent to observing the security guards in front of Chocolate City's entrance. John Boy removed a Glock .40 from his armrest and handed it to him.

"Tuck that shit and follow me," John Boy said, exiting the

car.

Reaching the entrance of the club, John Boy greeted one of the security men with a handshake, inconspicuously handing him five, one hundred dollar bills during their brief contact. The security guard glanced at the cash and nodded, letting his partner know that they were special VIP's.

The club was packed. Hoes were dancing buck-naked on stage. A waitress brought over a complimentary bottle of champagne for John Boy and Goldie to get their drink on. It wasn't long before a couple of hoes gravitated over to VIP, offering lap dances.

¢   ¢   ¢

Meanwhile on the Other Side of Town
Rico received a call from one of the dancers at Chocolate City informing him that two niggas with gold grills and big ockey looking dreads were in the club. He knew that one of the niggas had to be John Boy by the description that CoCo gave.

Rico was Tony Bolivia's enforcer. He handled all of Tony's dirty work. When Rico got the call from CoCo, him and a couple of his goons were at one of Tony's traps gearing up to get at John Boy.

The meeting that Tony Bolivia had arranged between him and John Boy was actually a set up.

Taking out his cell phone, Rico called his boss. "Tony, I just got a call from CoCo. She said two niggas wit' big dreads and gold-teeth at the club right now. It's gotta be John Boy."

"Country-ass-niggas…that nigga John Boy must've went there early. Well, nigga you know what to do," Tony said, ending the call.

For two years Rico had bodied numerous niggas at Tony's command. The last body he'd dropped for his boss was only a week earlier when he'd ran up in a church, masked up, and wacked a nigga during a funeral.

"Yall niggas strap up. We got the nigga John Boy on the scope," Rico said to his two henchmen.

They'd all been snorting coke and drinking for two days

straight. Truth be told, that was all Rico did everyday all day. And being the savage nigga that he was, it was a dangerous combination.

Rico never really thought things out. It was truly a miracle that he wasn't on deathrow awaiting execution. He'd killed plenty, sometimes blasting muthafuckas in broad day light. He was so high off of the coke that he'd secretly scored from a nigga he knew that copped from John Boy, that his only plan to wack John Boy was to run up in Chocolate City, masked up with choppas, and kill everything that moved.

The nigga didn't even have an escape plan.

CHAPTER 9

Pandemonium broke out at the entrance of Chocolate City after Rico and his two thugs hit the security guards up at the door. Everyone in proximity ran for refuge in fear of death.

At the sound of gunfire, Goldie flipped the table he and John Boy were seated at and pulled his mentor down just as the wall mirror behind them shattered into a million pieces. The whole area was being bombarded with bullets as Jim Beam's song, "When Bullets Rain" suddenly stopped pumping out of the club's speakers after the DJ caught a stray .762 to the dome, causing him to fall on top of the turn tables.

"What the fuck?" Goldie muttered, removing the Glock .40 John Boy had given him from his waist.

Rico and his two goons continued to spay the club with no regard. Even CoCo's sheisty ass got blazed as she tried to dive off of the stage.

John Boy whipped out his Desert Eagle and grabbed a piece of the broken mirror off of the floor. He stuck the reflective glass around the table to get the positions of the gunmen.

The shooting suddenly stopped.

Watching intentively, John Boy spied one of the gunmen – the one he surmised was the leader – gesturing for one of the masked killers to check the restrooms. The other he sent to check the VIP area. Pulling back the mirror and resting his back against the overturned table, John Boy tried to steady his nerves while listening to the broken glass and debris crunched under the weight of the approaching gunman.

Goldie started to ask John Boy a question, but was silenced when John Boy placed his pointer finger to his lips, signaling him to remain quiet as his mind raced. Something in his gut was telling him that everything transpiring at that moment was because of him.

And if spotted, he'd be killed on sight.

So with a strong will to live and the instincts of a natural predator, John Boy popped up from behind the table like a jack-in-the-box, squeezing off two carefully aimed shots. Both found their mark. The first shot caught the approaching gunman in his Adam's apple, causing his head to drop after the bullet exited the back of his neck, severing his spine in its wake. The second shot hit him on the top of his head as he went down.

Seeing one of his comrades go down, Rico fired his choppa in the direction that the shots had come from. But John Boy had already ducked back down behind the table. However, Rico didn't care, he just kept firing until he was out of bullets.

Bewildered by the sudden break in gunfire, both John Boy and Goldie peeked around the overturned table as Rico was flipping his AK's banana clip. It was their cue. They came up firing, hitting Rico multiple times in his midsection. The force from the rapid succession of shots backed Rico up, pinning him to the wall. He did the murder-man-dance for 8.3 seconds before crashing to the floor – dead.

John Boy and Goldie made their escape. They ran out of the club and hopped in the Vette, leaving the remaining gunman cowering in the restroom. Police strobe lights could be seen in the distance as John Boy hauled ass out of the club parking lot. The hiding gunman made his escape out of the emergency exit just as John Boy bent a corner one block away.

¢ ¢ ¢

Back at the condo, John Boy and Goldie were in the living room trying to make sense of the shit that had happened back at the club. Then, out of John Boy's peripheral, something on the TV screen caught his attention. "Hold on," he said to Goldie, cutting him off in midsentence. He turned the volume up on his big screen and listened in as the lady reporter told her story.

"Seventeen people were killed tonight in what investigators are calling a massacre. Police have identified a masked gunman who was also killed and believed to be one of the perpetrators of this malicious assault. The man is 20 year old Rico Williams." An old mug shot of Rico flashed on the screen behind the reporter. "We will ha—"

Turning off his TV and facing Goldie, John Boy said, "That fuck-nigga Tony sent them niggas to the club to off me. The nigga who picture they showed was that nigga's partna."

"Damn, that nigga vicious! All them people had to die just to get at you?...where that nigga Tony stay?"

"Shit, I don't know where that nigga stay at."

"Well, we need to get at that nigga, 'cause next time yo' ass might not be so lucky."

The room was quiet for a few minutes until John Boy snapped his fingers, killing the silence. "I got an idea."

"What? Nigga, spit it out," Goldie interrogated, impatiently.

"I'm finna call this hoe I know that do Tony's baby momma's hair. She might know where that nigga stay."

John Boy picked up his phone and called Edna.

"Hello?" A female voice answered.

"What's up, Miss-Good-Pussy?"

"John Boy? Nigga is this you? Why you ain't been callin' a bitch?" Edna asked, knowing damn well that she was a bird-bitch that was lucky to even be late night action for a nigga of John Boy's caliber.

"A nigga been busy, but what's hood? A nigga tryna slide through there...and I got whatchu love," John Boy added enticingly.

"You got some blue dolphins?" Edna anxiously queried. She was a certified pill-animal. She was on everything, painkillers, antidepressants and ecstacy.

"Nawl. They ain't blue, but they fi'."

"Well come on over then. The kids sleep."

John Boy thought about the last time he was over Edna's house. "Hold on...Is you sho' all of them muthafuckas sleep?"

Edna had five kids and they were bad-as-hell! John Boy remembered how they kept knocking on Edna's bedroom door every five minutes, begging for shit while he was balls deep in Edna's large intestine.

"Fuck you nigga," Edna said, angry that John Boy was referring to her children as muthafuckas. However, her anger quickly subsided, thinking about the pills John Boy said he had. "Is you still comin' or what?" she asked shamelessly.

"Yeah, give me 'bout thirty minutes."

John Boy and Goldie arrived at Edna's house twenty minutes later. Edna answered her door in nothing but a thong and six inch heels. She didn't bat a fake eyelash at the sight of Goldie – a complete stranger. Instead, she let them both in, making sure to walk in front of them to showcase her cosmetically enhanced butt cheeks.

"Have a seat," Edna invited, motioning to her couch. "Whatchall niggas want to drink?"

"Hen'," they said in unison.

Returning with two shots of Hen', Edna took a seat between the two men, handing them their drinks. "Alright John Boy, what's up? A bitch ain't heard from yo' slick ass since I turned you on to Lil Jimmy."

Lil Jimmy was Edna's little brother. He was buying ten to fifteen kilos a month from John Boy.

Edna continued. "And I know this pussy good, but I also know that ain't why you over here. So what's up?"

Smiling, John Boy spoke. "You right. I wanted to holla atchu about a lil' proposition I got for ya. You tryna make ten stacks right quick?"

"Hell yeah I'm trying to make that. Shit, what I got to do?"

Thirsty bitch, Goldie mused.

"Don't you be doin' Tony Bolivia's babymomma's hair?"

Edna nodded in the affirmative.

"You know where they live?" Goldie asked, joining in on the conversation for the first time.

"No, I don't know where they live. I do her hair over here, but I know where Mable's sister lives though."

Mable was Tony Bolivia's baby mother.

"Can you get Mable over here so we can follow the bitch," John Boy asked.

"Yeah, I think I can do that…You still gonna pay me the ten grand right?"

"Shit, I'ma give you fifteen if you can make that shit happen ASAP," John Boy promised.

"Okay, yall ain't gonna do nothin' to that girl is yall? You know she got kids."

Goldie heard the fear in Edna's voice and decided to kill her ass too when shit went down.

"Hell nawl," John Boy replied convincingly. "Do I look like the type of nigga that'll kill a woman with children?"

Studying John Boy's face before replying, Edna said, "No, you don't look like the type of foul-ass-nigga who'd do some bullshit like that."

I wonder how I look, 'cause I damn sho' will, bitch! Goldie thought to himself.

John Boy handed Edna two yellow *monkeys,* which she popped with no chaser. Less than a hour later her tonsils were being massaged by Goldie's swollen dick head, while John Boy thrashed her freakishly large asshole like a deranged sadist. They mutted Edna like the dog bitch that she was. They left her laid out on her living room floor with man-milk covering her face, hair and back.

¢ ¢ ¢

The next day John Boy received a call from Edna. "Mable is on her way over. I called her and told her exactly what you told me to say and she said she was on her way," she informed him.

After giving Edna the pills the day before, and prior to them taking affect, John Boy told Edna to call Mable the following day and tell her that she was about to go out of town for a few weeks. He told her to tell Mable that if she wanted to get her hair done before she left she'd best come over before 3 p.m. or be assed out.

"How long did she say it's gonna take her to get there?" John Boy asked.

Edna told him that Mable said she'd be over in an hour and a half. She said Mable had to go buy some hair and a relaxer, then drop her kids off to her sister's since Edna's kids wouldn't be there to play with them.

"Aiight, hit me when she get there," John Boy said before hanging up.

Two hours later, Edna called John Boy back informing him that Mable had arrived at her house. She then got busy with the gossip and Mable's hair. Edna heard her doorbell ring and excused herself, leaving Mable alone in the kitchen, which also doubled as a small hair salon. The thought of earning an easy $15,000 caused a crooked grin to form on Edna's face. When she stepped into her foyer and opened her front door, she received the shock of her life. The barrel of a pistol crashed into her face, knocking her to the floor.

"What the fuck was that?" Mable asked herself upon hearing the commotion emit from the front of the house. "Girl, is you okay?" she called out to Edna.

After a few moments passed with no response Mable stood to investigate the noise. But, before she could take three good steps, John Boy leisurely strolled into the kitchen aiming a pistol at her head. "Don't even thank about it," he said in his thick southern drawl. Mable wanted to open her mouth to scream, but was too afraid.

Subsequent to splitting Edna's shit, Goldie grabbed a handful of her long ass weave and drug her to her bedroom. There, he put one in the back of her head, then walked room to room making sure that no one else was present in the house. Satisfied that there wasn't, he made his way to the kitchen where John Boy held Mable captive.

"Everything scrate?" John Boy asked when Goldie walked in.

"Yeah, my nigga, everythang hood," Goldie answered.

Turning his attention back to Mable, John Boy said, "Check this out lil' momma. This shit ain't for you. A nigga just tryin' to eat. I want you to give me yo' babydaddy number so I can call him. Then I want you to tell that nigga you been kidnapped and it's gonna cost him a hundred stacks to get you back. When we get the cash, we gonna let you go," John Boy lied.

Mable silently nodded her head, signaling that she understood.

John Boy took out his cell and began punching in the numbers as Mable said them. He placed the phone to Mable's ear when the number he'd dialed was answered.

"Tony, some niggas done kidnapped me. They want a hundred grand to let me go," Mable cried into the phone.

"Wh--?" Tony attempted to speak, but was cut off when John Boy snatched his cell from Mable's ear and spoke.

"Look nigga, we got yo' bitch. So get that fuckin' money up or it's a don-dada. I'll call you back in a hour wit' instructions on where to take it. You got one hour, nigga," John Boy reiterated before terminating the call.

John Boy had already decided on how and where he was going to off Tony Bolivia. And since Mable's services were no longer needed, he withdrew his .40 from his waist and put two in her head. They left her twitching corpse where she fell and drove to one of John Boy's mini storages. There, they retrieved two AK's before heading to the warehouse district.

Reaching their destination twenty minutes later, John Boy parked his Benz behind an old building that was once used as a steel plant. Opening his trunk he removed the twin assault rifles and made the call to Tony Bolivia.

CHAPTER 10

Tony answered his phone before the first ring was complete. "Hello?"

"Come to the ole warehouse district. And come by yo'self. Fuck nigga, if I see anybody else witcho ass, kiss yo' bitch good bye. And have that fuckin' cash too."

John Boy ended the call, giving Goldie the thumbs-up before taking up position onside of the building.

Goldie took cover inside of the rusted structure.

Twenty minutes later a sleek new Beamer pulled up in front of the old steel plant. Tony Bolivia hopped out carrying a brief case. When Tony neared the entrance of the building, John Boy stepped from his hiding place, pointing an AK at his head.

"Drop the briefcase," John Boy commanded.

Ignoring the command, Tony asked, "Where is Mable?"

John Boy's finger tightened on the trigger. "She dead! What?...nigga, you thought it was sweet?"

Tony was seething with anger. He couldn't believe the country-nigga standing before him had the balls to kill his fucking baby mother. *Who the fuck do this nigga think he is?* Tony asked himself. Then it dawned on him. *This shit ain't got nothin' to do with money. This nigga wanna kill my ass*, he thought.

Tony had been so fucked up after getting the phone call from Mable, about her being kidnapped, that he couldn't think straight. Even after seeing John Boy with the gun and knowing that he'd just tried to have him killed, Tony still had it in his mind that he could simply pay the ransom and get Mable back.

But now, realizing that he'd walked into a trap, Tony tried his luck.

With the speed of a striking cobra, Tony reached for the pistol concealed in the small of his back. As he did so, he simultaneously attempted to grab the barrel of John Boy's AK.

A glimmer of gold flashed as a wicked grin slowly parted John Boy's lips, caused the hair to stand up on the back of Tony Bolivia's neck.

¢   ¢   ¢

Goldie watched the scene play out with a kind of nefarious amusement. Tony reached for John Boy's weapon. And although the New York drug boss moved with lightening speed, it was too slow. John Boy seemed to move in slow motion. Squeezing the trigger on his modified AK-47, he knocked Tony's top clean off. The sight was bloody and gruesome. Yet Goldie smiled as it happened. John Boy bent to pick up the briefcase that the deceased dealer had dropped, but was interrupted by the sound of screeching tires. Five cars full of niggas turned the corner at the same time that Goldie stepped out of the building.

Aiming his choppa at the lead vehicle, "Get down!" he yelled to John Boy before firing.

Bullets pierced the lead vehicle's frame as easy as an ice pick through cloth. One of the deadly projectiles struck the hitch in the grill of the lead vehicle, causing the hood to fly up. The driver was hit in the chest and lost control of the old Caprice. The car clipped the side of an abandoned fork-lift, flipping over three times before the car burst into flames.

Goldie continued his onslaught of the four remaining vehicles, which all had come to a stop. He watched, still busting as armed men filed out of the cars, taking cover behind their open doors.

¢   ¢   ¢

John Boy dove behind one of the rusted steel beams that littered the condemned steel factory's property. And although it seemed that Goldie was gunning by himself, John Boy was letting just as much lead fly.

John Boy popped up like Rambo – AK on fully. Together, he and Goldie sent so much lead at Tony's men that it was hard for them to shoot back.

"Man, fuck this shit, slim," one of Tony's goons said to another. They were both crouched down behind two separate cars. "One of them niggas shootin' automatic shit, joe. I'm 'bout to bou-"

The scared goon's sentence was cut short when a choppa bullet ricocheted off of the pavement, pierced the fender of the vehicle he was cowering behind, and lodged into his throat.

The dude that the dead goon was talking too gawked at his corpse, horrified as it twitched on the pavement. "Fuck it," he said under his breath and took flight in a low sprint. He ran in the opposite direction of the choppa fire.

Progressively, Tony's mens' cars started to resemble Swiss cheese. Three more of Tony's goons were killed before the rest of them got the point and took flight behind the other goon who'd ran.

John Boy and Goldie continued blasting at the fleeting men until their clips were spent.

"Dog, let's get the fuck outta here," Goldie said.

John Boy grabbed the briefcase and they jumped in the Benz, hauling ass back to the condo.

¢　¢　¢

Two weeks after Tony Bolivia's murder, the Feds were all over D.C. Unbeknowst to anybody outside of the Federal government, Antonio Jones, BKA Tony Bolivia, had been the recipient of a sealed indictment handed down, six and a half months prior to his death.

He'd been indicted under the R.I.C.O. Act.

The Feds picked up everybody they 'thought' had been affiliated with the slain drug dealer, causing a vacuum in the streets.

Turf wars ensued as niggas fought over what was left behind by Tony Bolivia and his crew. And while the turf wars raged on, John Boy was wacking any nigga who wasn't buying work from him.

There was only going to be one organization to reap the rewards of Tony Bolivia's demise, *TEAM JOHN BOY*.

When the choppas finally stopped chopping there was

eighty-six drug related murders in D.C. during that two month period. John Boy was elected the unofficial Mayor of the City. John Boy picked four dudes from four different sides of town to manage their area. He created boundaries that each dealer had to respect or be dealt with. He agreed to give each of the four dealers fifty kilos on consignment everytime they re-upped as long as they bought exclusively from either him or Goldie. Anyone found to be in violation would be murdered – no questions asked.

John Boy gave Goldie a piece of the D.C. action as a gift, because had it not been for Goldie's help, locking down D.C. never would have happened…

CHAPTER 11

Stepping off of the plane into the Florida sun, Goldie inhaled deeply. He was home. Two and a half months away from Duval County seemed like forever.

Entering the busy airport, Goldie spied Kismet and Alex. The wideness of Kismet's hips caused blood to rush to his dick. She looked delicious. The extra weight from her pregnancy only made her that much finer.

Goldie stuffed the last of his luggage into the trunk of Alex's Lexus before climbing into the backseat. Alex sat in the driver's seat and Kismet on the passenger side. Digging in his pocket, Goldie removed a long jewelry box. "Kismet, look what daddy got you," he said after tapping her on the shoulder.

Kismet turned and saw the 10kt diamond and platinum necklace and gasped. "Oh, Sultan, it's beautiful," she beamed.

The necklace was purchased with Goldie's half of the $100,000 that he and John Boy took from Tony Bolivia.

¢ ¢ ¢

The trio arrived at Goldie's Queen's Harbor Mini-Mansion thirteen minutes later. Kismet went inside while Alex helped Goldie with his luggage. When the two men had unloaded everything, Alex filled Goldie in on how things had gone in his absence.

"Yeah, my nigga, shit been doin' what it do out here," Alex started in his slow southern drawl. He continued, "I just sent that nigga Big Woo ten more of them thangs yesterday. And that nigga Brown-eyed Ron outta the sea-poat' came through last week and bought twelve of them shits. 'Round here, shit still jumpin'…Oh, and I almost forgot, man, that nigga Cashman burnt Spit Fi'."

"What?"

"Yeah, that nigga killed that nigga in broad day light."

"Killed him? When?"

"Shit, that was 'bout a month ago," Alex answered.

Hearing that Cashman had murked a nigga was unsettling to Goldie, to say the least. He didn't want his little brother involved in the streets. However, if what Alex had said was true, then Cashman was all in. Goldie knew from first-hand experience the god-like power that any man brave enough to shake hands with the devil felt after taking a life.

"What the fuck happened?" Goldie asked.

Alex sighed. "Man, from what I heard, Cashman fronted Spit Fi' a forty and Spit Fi' ain't pay him when he said he would. They say Spit Fi' kept duckin' the nigga, coppin' from other niggas and shit until Cashman caught his ass in Royal Palms on Amberjack tryin' to cop from another nigga. Niggas say Cashman rocked his ass in the middle of the street."

"Damn! What about the po'lice? Did the po'lice fuck wit' him 'bout it?" Goldie asked, concerned. He didn't know that Cashman sold drugs, let alone toted iron.

"Man, you know niggas ain't crazy enough to snitch 'round here," Alex answered sarcastically, as if Goldie had asked a stupid question.

"Aiight, I'ma holla at that nigga tomorrow," Goldie said before giving Alex dap.

Alex hopped back in his car, chunking the deuces up before pulling off to handle some business.

Kismet was descending the stairs when Goldie entered the house. "Sultan, are you alright?" she asked, noticing the forlorn expression on his face as they neared each other.

"Yeah, I'm good. I miss you, baby," Goldie said, changing the subject. "I know you don't like the lil' weight you done gained," he added, taking Kismet into his embrace.

"No, I don't like the weight, but I'm still fine," Kismet declared, playfully.

A 22k gold grin appeard on Goldie's face. "You sho' is," he said before tonguing Kismet down.

Kismet and Goldie went to the master bedroom and made love until they were both exhausted.

The next morning Goldie was up bright and early. After getting himself together he headed over to his mother's house.

"Hey, Ma," Goldie said when Mrs. Jackson opened her door.

"Sultan! Baby, I'm so happy to see you. Come on in here and give momma a hug."

Goldie gave Mrs. Jackson a hug and kiss, then followed her into her dining room where they both took a seat at her large solid oak dining table.

Mrs. Jackson grabbed Goldie's hand and looked into his eyes, pleadingly. "Baby, you need to talk to Cashman. I don't know what to do wit' him anymoe. The boy don't go to school and sometimes he be missin' for days."

"Is he talkin' back and bein' disrespectful?" Goldie asked, hating the hurt in his mother's eyes.

"No. He done changed, that's all...And he stay in them devilish screets."

"Well, I'ma talk to him. He here, right?"

"Yeah, he up in his room."

Goldie went upstairs to Cashman's bedroom and knocked on his door. He didn't wait on a reply before entering.

"What's up, big bruh?" Cashman said, happy to see Goldie.

They exchanged brotherly hugs before Goldie plopped down on Cashman's bed. Cashman sat down in the swivel chair in front of his computer.

Goldie looked over at Cashman, disapprovingly shaking his head. "Man, what's up? A nigga go outta town for a couple months and you get stupid?"

"Look big bruh, that shit wit' Spit Fi' was outta my hands."

"Outta yo' hands?!" Goldie said, raising his voice.

"Man, that fuck-nigga called my bluff. I couldn't let his bitch-ass owe me money and run 'round tellin' niggas I'm sweet."

"But it was only forty dollars, silly-ass-nigga!"

"It was the principle."

The calmness in Cashman's voice had Goldie heated. "Nigga, you only seventeen! What the fuck you doin' wit dope, anyway?...Who sold you that shit?"

Cashman looked at Goldie like he'd lost his mind. "Damn bruh, you want a nigga to snitch? Shit, I gotta eat too."

Ignoring the snitching remark, Goldie said, "Nigga, you ain't got to do shit. Look around you," he said, sweeping his hand around the room. "Nigga, you got everythang a nigga yo' age could want…What? What, you need money nigga?" Goldie asked, fumbling around in his pocket and pulling out a fat knot.

"Man, I don't need yo' money. I got my own! What I really need though is some work."

"Nigga, is you fuckin' stupid? Do you really thank I'ma give yo' lil' ass some dope?"

"I got money. So you ain't gotta give me shit."

Amused, Goldie said, "Okay, lil' nigga, what you want?"

Cashman stood up and walked to his closet. "I want a halfa brick."

Goldie started laughing. "A half brick? Nigga, that's ninety-two-fifty."

Cashman opened the small safe at the bottom of his closet and removed ten stacks. Tossing the rubber banded bundles of cash onto his bed, he said, "That's ten, keep the change."

"What the fuck? Nigga, where you get this from?" Goldie asked, picking up a banded stack.

"Bruh, a nigga been on the grind. And bruh, I really need that work. I got a lil' team of niggas waitin' for me to put somethin' in they hands."

The whole time that Cashman talked, Goldie watched his eyes. Cashman had a familiar look in them that Goldie had seen in other hungry niggas' eyes in the past. At that moment, Goldie realized that no matter what he said, Cashman was going to continue doing what he was doing.

"Aiight, lil' nigga I see that you gonna be hard headed, so this is what I'ma do. I'ma get you a spot and let you pump out that bitch. I don't want yo' lil' ass in them streets no more. You hear me?"

Cashman was happier than a sissy in a penitentiary packed with lifers when Goldie told him he'd give him his own trap. Before Goldie could get out the door good, Cashman was calling up Ernest – a member of his clique.

The clique, not including Cashman, consisted of three wild ass juveniles out of Atlantic Arms projects. They were all the help Cashman felt he needed to run his trap. Each of the young boys, ranging from ages 15 to 17, were Cashman's most trusted associates.

Mike-Mike was the youngest. At age 15 he was known to slang iron and do whatever it took to get paid. After his father was killed by police, he was forced to be the man of the house and look out for his mother and three sisters.

Ernest was a killer. He was only 16 and already had three bodies under his belt. Truth be told, he was waiting on another nigga to jump out there to become vic' number four. Ernest had just come home off a two year stint for manslaughter. He offed his uncle after finding out that he'd been molesting his little sister. He and Cashman had been good friends since first grade.

Now Jay, he was the most layed back of the three juvenile delinquents. He was mostly on money and hoes, considering himself to be a player. But he was still a vicious ass nigga. At 17 years old he was the manipulating force behind numerous robberies and one murder, Spit Fi's murder to be exact. He and Ernest had played in the sand box together.

"What's up, my nigga?" Cashman asked when Ernest came to the phone. Ernest's little sister had answered.

"Shit. Chillin', watchin' TV."

"Well, get yo' ass up. I need you to hit Mike-Mike and Jay. Tell them niggas we need to meet up for some important business."

"Some business?" Ernest asked.

"Yeah! Big bruh 'bout to give a nigga they own trap and I'm brangin' yall in wit' me."

"Man, get the fuck outta here. Nigga, I thought you said Goldie will kill yo' ass for fuckin' wit' that shit?"

"Dog, I ain't bullshittin'. So hit them niggas and tell 'em we all gonna meet in the park in 'bout two hours."

Two hours later the four youths met in the park.

"Aiight yall, this some serious shit," Cashman said, looking around at the other three youths, making sure he had their undivided attention. "Big bruh done gave a nigga the green light. So we gonna open the trap up on Friday. That's two days from now. We startin' out wit' a half brick of hard. And I ain't talkin' 'bout that whipped up shit either. I'm talkin' 'bout that straight-drop, grade-A shit."

Liking what he was hearing, Mike-Mike asked, "So where the spot gonna be at?"

"That shit gonna be on Ardella," Cashman answered.

"Whoa, hold on…Ardella?" Jay questioned, cutting in. "Ain't Boo 'nem got a trap on Jackson?"

"And?" Ernest said.

"And? Nigga, Jackson is one screet over from Ardella. That's like puttin' two Burger Kings next to each other," Jay retorted.

Ernest sucked his teeth. "Man, fuck Boo 'nem. It's enough money 'round there for everybody."

"Yeah, and shit, wit' the price we gettin' the half for, we gonna have them monkey-nuts and still get paid. Anyway, them niggas pushin' that whipped up shit. Boo 'nem 'round there droppin' ten in the thousand and brangin' it back. Nigga, we puttin' the whole twenty-eight in the six wit' no Dawn," Cashman boasted.

Ardella Road was located on Atlantic Beach in Black Pine – the same neighborhood Cashman was raised up in until Goldie moved them to Queen's Harbor. And although Cashman lived in a better environment, he couldn't get the hood out of his system. Every chance he got he found his way back.

¢   ¢   ¢

Alex dropped the pre-cooked and cut work off to Cashman the next day while Mrs. Jackson and her other two boys were gone shopping. Cashman called up Ernest, Jay and Mike-Mike after Alex left. They met up a few hours later at the park in Atlantic Arms to divide the samples that they were going to pass out to the fiends.

The four youths hit every hood on Atlantic Beach with a venegeance, letting the smokers on every block test their product and informing them of their trap on Ardella.

"Got-damn!" Kenny Cheek said, exhaling crack vapors. "I

ain't had no shit like this since Goldie use to beat the block on that ole beach cruiser of his."

Kenny Cheek was given his moniker because his ass cheeks were forever showing while he rode his bike all day in search of crack. Even the police called Kenny Addison by his nickname, Kenny Cheek. Kenny Cheek had been smoking crack since it first hit in the eighties. He barely had a dime to his name, yet he smoked like a king. This was because of all the rich white clients he'd met over his years of bassing. Kenny's fiend friends all had nice families and where prominent members of society. Scared of being robbed or busted in a reverse sting, Kenny Cheek's white clients gave him their money to buy their crack.

"So you say yall gonna be in the blue house on Ardella, right?" Kenny Cheek asked in his signature whiny voice.

"Yeah, that's right," Cashman answered.

"Bet that up, then. I'ma spend big wit' yall as long as yall keep this same shit. Man, these niggas out here done took the game to another level. Boo 'nem over there on Jackson sellin' that ole whipped up, thin ass shit, fuckin' up my clientele. And to make it so bad, they got the best shit around. The other day one of my crackas gave me eight-hundred dollars to get him a cookie for a party he was havin'. That nigga Boo sold me some shit so thin you could see through it," Kenny Cheek complained.

"Well, you ain't gotta worry 'bout that no more. We gonna keep that grade-A. And you can bet that!" Cashman promised.

The following day, Cashman and company opened the trap at 7 a.m. sharp.

Kenny Cheek stopped through shortly thereafter. "Yo, Cashman, let me get five of yo' fattest dubs?" he requested, handing Cashman a hundred dollar bill.

Cashman gave Kenny Cheek six dubs instead. "Make sure you spread the word that the shop open and we got that grade-A."

"I gotcha," Kenny Cheek assured him before pedaling off.

A few hours later the traffic was unbelievable. It seemed as if Cashman and his clique were giving away free crack by the way the fiends had swarmed their trap. They even let the fiends smoke in the back yard.

By Saturday night the entire half kilo of crack was gone

and the bassers were still coming.

Cashman called Alex and placed an order. Alex informed him that he'd drop the work off the following day and to sit tight until then. The youths took advantage of the down time by counting up their take. They came up with a total of $31,000. Putting $9,250 to the side – for the re-up, the youths split the profits four ways, totaling $2,935 apiece.

"Boy, we gonna be some rich ass niggas if we keep runnin' through halfs like this," Ernest commented, counting his money over for the third time.

"Yeah, we might need to buy the whole thang if we get off the next half this quick. Shit, I know we done missed out on at least ten stacks in the last four hours," Jay added.

Everybody nodded their heads, knowing that Jay had spoke the truth. They had a gold-mine on their hands. Now they had to merely keep it supplied.

CHAPTER 12

Meanwhile In a House One Street Over

"Got-damn-man! Them fuck-ass-niggas on Ardella got a nigga shit lookin' real fucked up right now," David vented to the other two niggas in the room. "Shit, the only reason we made the lil' bread we made tonight is 'cause them niggas dry."

"Yeah dog, you right. Them niggas done took all our business. Shit, we need to start droppin' our shit scrate or somethin', before we be lookin' for a job 'round this bitch," Nick, another member of the trio said, giving his opinion. He continued, "We won't make what we been makin' if we scrate drop our shit, but we won't starve either."

David shook his head and sucked his teeth. "Even if we do scrate drop our shit, them niggas still gonna have all the bassers comin' to them. Them niggas got that glass and they shit big. Did you see the size of them stones Po'kie Fish bought from them niggas?"

"Fuck! Man, why don't both yall niggas shut the fuck up! You niggas been cryin' like lil' bitches for twenty minutes. If yall woulda shut yalls' fuckin' mouth for five seconds I could have told yall what we needed to do," Boo said, speaking up for the first time. He'd had enough of the whining. "All we gotta do is find a new plug wit' cheaper prices, 'cause you know Cashman gettin' that shit for the low. And we all know Henry ain't gonna drop his prices for us no more. He cried the last time we asked. Plus I know that nigga cuttin' our shit to even his losses."

"Okay then, where we gonna find a new plug at, genius?" Nick asked sarcastically.

"If you shut the fuck up I'ma tell you. Yall remember them hoes from Houston that we met in South Beach?" Boo asked.

"Do I," David commented, thinking about Brandi's freaky

ass. Paying for her pussy was the best $1,500 he'd ever spent.

"Man, them hoes ain't got no work," Nick snarled.

Boo sucked his teeth. "Nigga, I know that, but I bet them hoes know where it's at. Shit, them muthafuckin' Mexicans floodin' Texas wit' that work. I hear niggas sellin' bricks for $15,000 out there. And that lil' hoe April who I was fuckin' wit' is 'bout her paper. The bitch told me she can get anything a poe' nigga need. Yeah, that's what the bitch told me when I asked her what she do."

"Well you need to stop talkin' and hit that hoe up then," David encouraged.

Boo took his cell and selected April's name on his speed dial before pressing send. "What's up, ma?" he asked when a female voice answered.

"Who this?"

"Damn, you forgot a nigga already?"

"Nigga, I ain't got time for games. Now who the fuck is this?"

"This Boo from Duval."

"Oh, hey baby! What's good witchu? And what took you so long to call?"

"I woulda been called but you know how shit be. Anyway, I'm callin' now and I need a favor."

"Nigga, I know damn well you ain't callin' askin' a bitch for no money?"

Boo took his phone from his ear and stared at it in disbelief. Putting it back to his ear he said, "Hell nawl, bitch! I get money. I was tryin' to see if you could get a nigga some work. What them bi--. Hello? ... Hello?" Boo looked up at his two partners. "Man that hoe hung up."

"Shit, call that hoe back, then. Bitch probably got a raggedy ass phone," David suggested.

Boo called back. "Hello?" he said when April answered.

"Look nigga, don't be talkin' reckless on my phone. Come to Houston and call me when you get here," April commanded before hanging up.

¢   ¢   ¢

8:00 p.m. The Following Day

"Nigga, we bammin'!" Mike-Mike exclaimed after handing the bassers in front of him three dubs in exchange for $60.

Alex had dropped off another half of kilo earlier that day. And as soon as the word got out that Cashman and his clique were back on, the fiends rushed Ardella like Night of the Living Dead.

"Man, this shit crazy," Cashman said, passing out rocks and pocketing cash.

There was a line of bassers from the front door to the street. The back yard was so crowded with fiends smoking that it looked like a wild fire was burning nearby.

"Dog, at the rate we movin' this shit we definitely gonna need to cop the whole thang next time," Jay commented. "Cashman, gon' and placed the order, my nigga."

"Aiight, I'ma put in the order, but let's wait until we out," Cashman suggested.

All of the work was gone by 6 a.m. that morning. Cashman placed the order for the whole thang and Alex dropped off a kilo of crack the following afternoon.

Cashman and his clique then put the word out that they were back in power and waited for the dough to roll in.

¢   ¢   ¢

Houston Texas

Boo called April immediately after his flight touched down in Houston, advising her to come scoop him from Houston International. As Boo stood out front of the busy airport waiting on April to arrive, a tinge of worry invaded his thoughts.

He was thinking about his money and hoping that it had made it safely to its destination.

Before leaving Florida, Boo purchased a microwave from Walmart. After concealing $35,000 inside of the electronic cooking unit, he put the microwave back in its box, sealed it, then overnighted it through FedEx to Houston's Main Street Greyhound Bus Station where his girlfriend, Trice, had reserved a locker box for him online.

April pulled up in front of the airport in her pink Range.

She honked her horn twice when she spotted Boo, causing him to snap out of his cognitions.

Recognizing April as the driver of the pink SUV, Boo hopped in. During the drive to April's house the two engaged in conversation, mostly about the wild weekend they'd had in South Beach where they'd first met, before they got down to business.

"How much them thangs runnin' out here?" Boo asked.

"Whatchu lookin' for, boy or girl?"

"Girl," Boo replied.

Adding $1,500 on top of the price, she could get a kilo of coke for, April said, "Thirteen-five."

Boo couldn't believe it. "Is the shit any good?" he quizzed.

"Oh, it's good. You gonna get to test it befoe you buy it."

Nodding, Boo replied, "Aiight, if it's good I'ma jump on two of 'em."

Just then April thought about something. "Hold on, nigga. You claim you wanna buy some work, but you only got a back-pack witchu. Is the money in there?" she asked, pointing at the book bag in Boo's lap.

"Hell nawl. But it'll be here tomorrow. I need to make sure that blow right. Once that happens we gonna do business."

Boo's assertive swagger caused April's pussy to throb. She couldn't wait to get him on top of her King size bed and fuck the shit out of him.

¢ ¢ ¢

The combination of pussy, ecstacy and alcohol resulted in Boo waking up at 2 p.m. the following afternoon, dehydrated and sore.

He and April had freaked off the whole night.

"April, get up," Boo said, shaking her awake.

April got up and they both showered before getting dressed. Afterwards, April called her cousin MJ. She told him she had a pop for two bricks.

Melvin Johnson, BKA MJ, arrived thirty-one minutes later carrying a duffle bag containing two kilos of cocaine. He allowed Boo to cook an ounce from each kilo.

Satisfied with the work, Boo informed April and her cousin

that his money was in a locker at the Greyhound Bus Station on Main Street. He told them to ride to go get it. "Oh, and brang that work witchu too," Boo said to MJ as an after thought. "It's cash on delivery," he smiled.

At the Greyhound Bus Station, MJ followed Boo to his locker carrying the duffle bag containing the two kilos. Stopping in front of the miniature storage unit, Boo punched in the combination Trice had given him before he'd left. He then removed the microwave from the locker. After opening the cardboard box containing the microwave, he opened the microwave's door, revealing the bundles of cash inside.

"Yeah, looks like it's all there," MJ said, handing Boo the duffle bag of coke.

"It's all there, my nigga...you wanted twenty-seven for 'em, right?"

April had already told MJ that she'd put a $3,000 tax on the work. "Y-yeah, twenty-seven, that's right," MJ stuttered out.

"Aiight, it's thirty-one in here, so I'm finna take fo' grand out," Boo said, reaching inside the cooking unit, removing four rubber band wrapped bundles of cash.

Duffle bag strapped to his shoulder, Boo walked MJ, as he carried the microwave, to April's Range where he placed the cooking unit in his cousin's backseat, subsequent to hopping in.

April hopped out of her SUV, giving Boo a hug. "Don't be a stranger," she whispered into his ear as he palmed her fat ass.

"Shit, as long as the work stay good, and the prices the same, I'ma keep comin'," Boo declared, breaking their embrace.

"Aiight nye', I'ma hold you to that," April said, jumping back in her Range. She blew her horn twice as she was pulling off.

Boo watched the pink SUV disappear into traffic before walking back inside the bus station and purchasing an express ticket back to Jacksonville.

¢   ¢   ¢

Cashman and his crew had run through two kilos of crack in less than three days. Calling up Alex and requesting another one, Alex explained that he was out of town and wouldn't be back until the following day.

The four youths decided to hit the mall and club hop to kill time until Alex made it back.

¢   ¢   ¢

Meanwhile One Street Over

Boo arrived back in Jacksonville at six that morning. Wasting little time, him, David and Nick got right down to business converting an entire kilo into crack before twelve noon. Dirty-D was the first fiend to come knocking. He'd already stopped by Cashman's trap and seen that it was empty. He was instantly impressed with the size of the rock he scored from Boo. However, once he took a blast, he fell in love and quickly spread the word throughout Atlantic Beach that the niggas on Jackson had the best work in the hood.

¢   ¢   ¢

Ardella Road Two Days Later

Alex dropped off the new package and Cashman and company were ready for business. Strangely, no one had stopped by looking for anything the night before, causing Cashman and his peoples to have to hit the block, letting the pipers know that they were back on.

Ten minutes later they bumped into Dirty-D.

"Ay, D! What's up, my nigga? We back on and we got that fi', my nigga," Cashman advertised.

"Um…I'm scrate right nye' but when I need somethin' I'ma stop through," Dirty-D lied.

"Well, where everybody else at? Ain't nobody came through the spot since six o'clock yesterday," Jay inquired.

Taking a step back, Dirty-D said, "Yall must ain't heard about Boo 'nem yet?"

"What about 'em?" Ernest quizzed.

"Man, them niggas got them bolders fo' yo' shoulders 'round there."

"What?" Mike-Mike snapped.

Putting both palms out as if attempting to stop an attack, Dirty-D replied, "Look fellas, ain't nothin' personal out here in these screets. It's only bidness. And right nye', them niggas on Jackson done cornerd the market." Dirty-D reached in his pocket. "Look at this," he said, showing the four young niggas the dub he'd just copped from Boo.

"What's that, a fifthy?" Mike-Mike asked.

"Hell nawl, it's a dub," Dirty-D answered.

"D, that's a big ass rock for only twenty dollars. That shit can't be no good," Ernest said.

"Shittin' me! This shit a ten! Check this out," Dirty-D said, subsequent to throwing the rock to the pavement and watching it bounce twice before coming to a rest next to Cashman's foot, still intact. "This that glass! That eighty-three! What yall young niggas know 'bout that?" he joked.

"Damn," was all the four youths could say.

Breaking the pregnant silence, Dirty-D said, "Hey fellas, I would love to stay and chat, but I'm tryin' to get beamed up. So I'ma holla," he said, stepping off.

Back at the trap on Ardella, Cashman and his clique sat at the kitchen table passing a blunt, trying desperately to come up with a plan to get their clientele back.

"Got-damn-it, man! A nigga done spent all they money shoppin' and in the club, nye' we stuck wit' a brick we can't even move!" Ernest vented.

"Yeah, and as long as them niggas got that eighty-three 'round there, we ain't gonna be able to move e-muthafuckin' thang," Jay added.

"Man, I wonder where them niggas got that shit from? I mean, them niggas gotta be gettin' that shit dirt cheap to be sellin' grade-A that fuckin' big, my nigga," Cashman stated.

"Shit, it don't matter where them niggas gettin' that shit from. We can't get none. This yo' brutha trap, so we damn sho' can't have another nigga's work up in here," Jay snapped.

"Fuck, man! Damn! What the fuck we gonna do?" Mike-Mike asked, rhetorically.

"Dog, I can only think of two thangs we can do right nye', and that's it," Ernest stated, exhaling weed smoke.

"What's that?" Cashman asked.

Ernest looked Cashman in the eyes and said, "We can either lay down and be stuck wit' all that work or we can kill them niggas and get they asses out the way."

The kitchen became eerily silent after Ernest gave his opinion. They all knew that the young killer loved to resort to gunplay in any trying situation. And with the exception of Ernest, they all wanted to make sure that murder wasn't their only viable option. Because they damn sure wasn't about to lay down with all the work they'd bought.

In the days that followed, Cashman and his crew made about $1,200. Meaning they still had thirty-five ounces left to sell. Cashman and his niggas were not only furious, they were embarrassed. They felt like the niggas on Jackson were showing off and it only heightened their resolve to commit murder.

"Man, fuck this shit," Cashman spat, hopping off of his lazy boy. "We murkin' them niggas tonight!"

The others were all in agreement with Cashman, because they saw no other way to get their clientele back – other than taking a loss. There was only one thing they could do.

Eliminate the competition!

At 10 p.m. that night, the four youths dressed in all black, tying black T-shirts around the lower half of their faces. They crept up Ardella in the shadows until reaching a house directly behind Boo's trap. Each youth carried a choppa with a seventy round clip. Ernest toted his choppa in one hand and a two gallon gas can full of unleaded in the other.

Scaling a gate, they landed in the back yard of Boo's trap. The four youths sneaked to the side of the house.

Cashman peeked around the corner of the house to get a view of the front. "Damn," he said in a low whisper, turning back to face his niggas.

"What's up?" Mike-Mike asked.

"Man, it's 'bout ten smokes 'round there," Cashman answered.

"Fuck 'em, they got to go too," Ernest shot back. He went on, "I'm finna go soak the back door wit' gas and set that bitch on fi'…Jay, you need to come wit' me," Ernest said, turning to him.

Capo Cat

"Once the fi' start we gonna start bussin' into the house from the back. When yall niggas hear the first shot," Ernest said, pointing at Cashman and Mike-Mike, "Yall wet everythang out front."

Everyone shook their heads in agreement. Ernest and Jay disappeared behind the house and Cashman and Mike-Mike stayed where they were, slowly cocking their AK's, careful not to make a sound.

Moments later, gunshots resonated from in back of the house, signaling Cashman and Mike-Mike to make their move. They stepped from the side of the house, AK's blazing, cutting down everything that stood.

The men inside of the house were dumbfounded. Bullets were coming through the walls from behind the house, breaking dishes in the kitchen and shattering windows. Feeling trapped, Boo and his partners attempted to make a break through the front door, but they were stopped in their tracks. Upon opening the door, they saw and heard what looked and sounded like a severe thunderstorm taking place.

A thunderous clap accompanied by fire leaping from Cashman's AK, resembled a bolt of light striking Dirty-D as he ran from the woods. The old fiend did a front somersault after being hit high up in the back by a .762 bullet.

"What the fuck?" Boo said, slamming the door shut.

The fire on the back door had spread, causing smoke to cloud up the house. Boo led the way to the first bedroom down the hall, where the guns were kept.

¢   ¢   ¢

Cashman gave the front door of Boo's trap a violent kick after shooting its knob off. He stepped in, followed by Mike-Mike, shooting wildly in hopes of hitting any one of the fuck-niggas who'd gotten in the way of their cash.

Reaching the hallway, Cashman was in the process of turning to give Mike-Mike instructions, when out of his peripheral he saw movement down the hall.

It was David, *Boc! Boc! Boc! Boc! Boc!*, his .40 caliber barked.

Cashman dived back into the living room, pushing Mike-Mike down to the floor.

Boo and Nick had stepped out of the bedroom behind David when he started shooting at Cashman. They began bussing too. But Cashman had already moved out of the line of fire.

¢   ¢   ¢

Ernest and Jay entered the smoke filled kitchen of the run-down crack house through its burnt out back door. Easing toward the front of the dwelling, Ernest peeked around the corner just as David, followed by Boo and Nick, opened fired on Cashman.

When the shooting stopped, Cashman edged up to the wall at the top corner of the hallway. Moments later, he heard someone call out his name in a low whisper.

Subsequent to getting Cashman's attention, Ernest and Jay moved furtively to the top corner wall, opposite Cashman. Using hand gestures, Ernest instructed Cashman to shoot high on the count of three.

Stealthy advancing up the hall, Glock .40 pointed in front of them, David, Boo and Nick froze in their tracks upon witnessing Cashman's choppa appear from around the corner. The gun coughed flames like a dragon. Boo got hit in the stomach and doubled over in pain.

Seeing their leader go down, David and Nick returned fire, aiming at the corner end of the hall where the gunshots had originated. They were so caught up in their task that they didn't see Ernest roll out from the opposite corner of the hall until it was too late.

Ernest rolled from his kneeling position into the middle of the hallway, coming to rest on his stomach. Taking careful aim, he discharged thirteen shots from his AK. Both David and Nick's bodies dropped. He then got up and walked over to where their crumbled bodies lay. Ernest put one in each of their heads, making sure they were all dead.

"Got-damn, nigga!" Cashman commented to Ernest as they stood over the three corpses.

Ernest was stuck staring at his handy work.

"Ay, yall niggas come on!" Mike-Mike yelled.

The fire had spread, leaving the youths no choice but to escape out the front door.

Mike-Mike led the way. "Oh shit! Them crackas," he warned as he was about to step out onto the porch.

Two police cars were in the middle of the street, doors open, occupants out, guns drawn.

Without hesitation, the four youths opened fire on the police as if they were nothing more than some niggas in the way. They bombarded them with enough bullets to sink a battleship.

The cops might as well have only wore tee shirts, because their vests didn't shop shit.

Cashman and company cleared the gate in back of the burning house, making it back to the comforts of their trap before more police could make it to the scene. Cashman waited until the next morning to call Alex to come get them. But Alex didn't answer so he called Goldie.

"Ay, bruh, what's up wit' Alex? Why that nigga phone keep goin' to vice mail?"

"Man, the Feds got him after the club last night," Goldie answered.

"What?"

"Yeah bruh, them crackas got him," Goldie repeated. "Anyway, what's up?" he inquired, changing the subject.

"Bruh, I need you to come get us, ASAP!"

Goldie could tell that something was terribly wrong. "Man, whatchall niggas done did?"

"Bruh, just come get us. I gotta tell you in person."

As soon as Goldie arrived at the trap, the four youths hurried out the door and jumped in his car. Cashman explained to Goldie what had happened and it had him heated!

"Man, yall some dumb ass niggas!" Goldie snapped. "Yall betta hope yall get away wit' that shit, 'cause them crackas givin' niggas the death penalty for the shit yall did."

Cashman smiled. "Oh, bruh, best believe that shit ain't comin' back on us. We ain't leave a bitch standin' 'round there to say e-muthafuckin' thang," he bragged.

Goldie couldn't believe that it was his little brother sitting next to him talking about murder as if it was only a game. He realized at that moment that Cashman and his crew were too valuable to leave ducked off in a trap. He decided that he'd give them some real work.

BOOK 2WO

Revolution [change] is based upon land [money or economics]. Revolutionaries are the landless [the poor/broke] against the landlord [the rich/the system]. Revolutions are never peaceful, never loving, never nonviolent. Nor are they ever compromising. Revolutions are destructive and bloody. Revolutionaries don't compromise with the enemy; they don't even negotiate…the revolution burns everything that gets in its path…

■ Malcolm X
■ [The Chickens Come Home to Roost Speech]

Chapter 13

"Mr. Wimberly will you please approach the bench?" ordered the old, white magistrate judge.

Alex was at his detention hearing in Federal Court and the judge had called his lawyer to the bench after the government rested.

"Mr. Wimberly," the judge whispered, covering his microphone when Alex's lawyer reached the podium. "The government has some strong evidence against your client, and I hate to tell you this, but I just can't give your client a bond."

"But your honor, with all due respect, my client has never been arrested in his entire life."

The judge removed his glasses. "I understand that Mr. Wimberly, but the government's argument that your client is a threat to the community is supported by the fact that he sold two kilos of crack to an informant. ...And I've viewed one of the tapes. It was your client making the transaction. I'm sure of it."

Dejected, Marquis Wimberly ambled back over to the defense table and told Alex the bad news.

"I here by remand you to the custody of the United States Marshals," the judge stated firmly, striking his gavel.

Two U.S. Marshals escorted Alex back to the holding cells on the first floor of the courthouse. There, he learned that he wasn't going back to Duval County Jail, but was being transferred to a federal detention center in Folkston, GA.

After about an hour ride in back of a van, Alex arrived at the detention center. He was processed and taken to his pod. As soon as he put his bed roll on his bunk, he went to the phone and called his girlfriend.

Meka accepted the call before the operator was done talking. "Alex, please tell me them crackas ain't gonna give you all that time," she rattled off.

Meka was in the courtroom during Alex's detention hearing. She'd heard when the U.S. Attorney announced that Alex was charged with a two count indictment and faced ten years to life on both counts.

"Hell nawl! I ain't got no record, so how they gonna give me the time they was talkin' 'bout?"

"Bu-but that one cracka said you was," Meka explained, referring to U.S. Attorney David Miller.

"Damn, girl, you act like you don't believe a nigga or somethin'. I just told you I'ma be scrate," Alex spat.

Meka was silent for about ten seconds before saying, "Okay daddy, I believe you. When you think you gonna come home? ...And when can I come see you?" she asked in a baby voice.

"Shit, a nigga don't know when these crackas gonna let a nigga out this bitch. I go to court again next month. And I forgot to tell you, they done moved me, so you gonna have to wait until the weekend to come see a nigga."

"Where you at?"

"Folkston, GA."

"Folkston? Why they move you way out there?"

"Shit, yo' guess good as mine. This federal shit crazy, but don't sweat it though, aiight?"

"I won't, daddy."

"Okay, that's a good girl. Now I need you to hit Goldie on three way for me."

Meka did as she was told.

"What's up, my nigga?" Alex asked when Goldie answered.

"Oh shit, what up, dog?" Goldie replied, happy to hear Alex's voice.

"I'm good. You know them pussy-ass-crackas ain't give a nigga no bond."

"Yeah, Marquis told me what happened."

"It's all good though, 'cause I'ma roll wit' whatever they throw my way."

Goldie snickered. "Dog, you ain't finna do no time. Them people dead...ass wrong. Marquis filin' a motion to suppress and I know for a fact that all the evidence gonna get suppressed. Trust me," Goldie assured.

Alex understood exactly what Goldie was insinuating. That knowledge made him feel a lot better. He knew that when and if it came time, there wouldn't be a witness alive to stand against him.

"Dog, I need you to meet up wit' Meka after she visit me this weekend," Alex stated.

"Aiight, I got you, my nigga. Keep yo' head...one," Goldie said before hanging up.

Alex and Meka continued to talk until their 15 minute call had expired.

"Count time! Count time!" A male C.O. shouted, stepping into Alex's pod followed by a big breasted female C.O.

All of the inmates went to their bunks to be counted. Pod #4 was an open-bay dorm, so there were no cells to be locked in during count. Muthafuckas just posted-up beside their racks.

After count was complete, Alex sat on his bunk collecting his thoughts. Surprisedly, he was approached by another inmate. He instantly got a bad vibe.

"What up, my nigga? Don't I know you from somewhere?" the inmate asked.

"Nawl dude, I don't think so," Alex replied.

"Hmm," the inmate uttered, rubbing his chin and squinting his eyes as if trying to figure out where he knew Alex from. "I'm Sam," he finally said, extending his hand for Alex to shake.

Hesitantly, Alex reached out and accepted his hand shake. "Alex," he muttered.

"Where you from? You from Duval?" Sam inquired.

"Yeah, I'm from the Beach."

"So you a Beach nigga, huh?" Sam asked, smiling. "I'm from the Southside."

Succeeding the exchange of formalities, Alex and Sam began to chat. They conversed about everything from the hoes they'd fucked to the types of liquor they drank. It wasn't long before Sam expertly changed the subject matter of their conversation to Alex's case. He then listened intentively as Alex unwittingly gave him everything he needed.

¢ ¢ ¢

Three Days Later

"Brooks! Visitation!" A C.O. announced through the pod's door.

Alex quickly got himself together and followed the C.O. to the visiting area.

The visiting area consisted of five private booths each equipped with a monitored telephone mounted to the wall. A plexiglass divider separated the inmates from their visitors.

"What's up, baby?" Alex asked after picking up the phone in the visiting booth.

Meka was standing when he walked in, wearing some tight ass jeans and a tight shirt. She held the phone in her right hand. "Hey baby." Meka smiled.

Alex reciprocated her smile, then placed his pointer finger to his lips, gesturing for her to remain silent as she read the note he placed against the plexiglass divider.

It read: *Kendra Vaugh. Swainsboro, GA. The bitch that set me up. Tell Goldie.*

Alex sat down after placing the piece of paper back in his pocket.

Meka nodded, signaling that she got the message and sat down also.

During Alex's van ride to the Folkston Detention Center, after his first appearance/bond hearing in Federal court, the identity of the informant on his case became evident with vivid clarity. It didn't matter that he'd sold numerous kilos of crack to numerous other drug dealers, remembering the ominous feeling he'd experienced during his last transaction with Kendra Vaugh, and knowing the situation with her people was all the proof that Alex needed to finger her as the culprit.

When visiting was over, Meka went straight home and called Goldie to come over as soon as she got there. He arrived shortly after her phone call and she told him what she'd read on the note.

"Aiight, tell Alex I'm on it," Goldie said before he bounced. He called Cashman when he made it back home. "Ay, lil' bruh, I need you to come to the house ASAP."

"Gimme twenty minutes," Cashman replied, then hung up.

¢ ¢ ¢

Alex use to deal with Kendra Vaugh's husband, Victor, before he got jammed up by the Feds six months prior. They sentenced him to ten years. Three months after his arrest, Kendra stepped to Alex about buying some weight, under the guise of flipping money for her husband while he was on lock. However, the real reason that she'd stepped to Alex was because she'd agreed to cooperate with the DEA in exchange for her husband's time to be reduced.

¢ ¢ ¢

Cashman arrived a few minutes earlier than he'd promised. Goldie immediately briefed him as to what had to be done.

"Lil' bruh, I got the name of the bitch that set Alex up. I need that bitch put to sleep, ASAP," Goldie said.

Frowning, Cashman asked, "Damn bruh, a bitch set Alex up?"

"Yeah, and you got to handle this shit right or them crackas gonna fuck Alex's ass over."

"Where that bitch at?" Cashman asked, getting excited. He really fucked with Alex and was heated.

"Whoa, lil' bruh. We don't need shit to be messy, 'cause you rushin'. We makin' a killin' in the town the bitch live in."

"What town?"

"Swainsboro, GA," Goldie answered.

"Ain't that the spot you said yall had the police on the payroll? The one you said Alex found?"

Goldie nodded in the affirmative.

"Well, how in the fuck did Alex get knocked off, then?" Cashman interrogated, confused.

"Well, for one, we got the local police in our pocket. Alex got hit by the Feds. I think the Feds know them crackas up there dirty."

"Why you say that?"

"'Cause that bitch made both of the buys from Alex right

here in Jacksonville. The lawyer said the indictment came from right here," Goldie stated, pointing to the floor for emphasis.

"Ohhh, nye' I see. So you think the Feds had the broad set Alex up down here so them crackas up in Swainsboro wouldn't tip a nigga off?"

"Yep. That's why I need this shit done right. I need you and yo' niggas to leave for Swanisb—"

"What about them traps you and Alex got up there?" Cashman questioned, cutting his brother off.

"Damn, lil' nigga! I was gettin' to that," Goldie spat heatedly before continuing. "We still gonna get our money up there. That's why Mandi rollin' wit' yall. She takin' thirteen of them thangs wit' her. Yall niggas need to sell that shit and kill that bitch. I gotta make a trip to Mexico. I'ma be gone 'bout two weeks. That bitch need to be dead before I get back."

Goldie told Cashman Kendra's first and last name. "Don't fuck up, lil' nigga," he said, staring in Cashman's eyes.

¢ ¢ ¢

With Goldie's trip to Mexico being a few days away, he was busy pulling the money owed to him off the streets. John Boy had set it up for Goldie to meet his connect. He really didn't have much of a choice since Goldie had outgrown him as his supplier. So instead of holding Goldie back, John Boy decided to make him his equal. That way they could pool their money together and get a better price on the birds he was copping from Mexico.

John Boy had brokered a deal with his connect to buy five hundred kilos at $9,000 a piece – $3,000 cheaper than he'd been paying. The conncct was to front 500 more on consignment.

Coming up with $2.25 million a piece was easy for John Boy and Goldie. However, smuggling it out of the country and then smuggling a metric-ton of cocaine back was going to be a problem – a big one. But the connect, being the expert, figured the best way to make shit happen was for John Boy and Goldie to charter private jets. The connect booked the two jets through one of his numerous corporations. So with the smuggling problem solved, everything was set to go in a few days...

Chapter 14

Cashman and his crew was on US-1 enroute to Swainsboro, GA in a five vehicle convoy. Him, Mike-Mike, Ernest and Jay were all in separate cars, while Mandi, the mule, drove a mini-van loaded with thirteen kilos of cocaine and four choppas, all concealed in a hydraulic stash spot. Each vehicle displayed different state tags to throw off the state troopers.

Arriving in Swainsboro at 2:00 in the morning, Mandi led the convoy to Alex's stash house on Racetrack Street. The stash spot was a two story home with a long circular driveway that curved to its back yard. Situated in the middle of town, it was the ideal location to keep work and cash since it was in close proximity to all the hoods.

Once everyone had parked in back of the house, Mandi opened the mini-van's stash spot using a sequence of maneuvers as the combination. [She put the van in neutral, pumped the breaks twice, then cut on the air conditioner]. The entire back floor of the mini-van popped open, revealing its illegal cargo.

Cashman and his niggas promptly unloaded the bricks and choppas, placing them in the two big safes that occupied the downstairs bedroom.

"Ay, Mandi, where them hoes at?" Jay asked, holding his nuts. He was ready to fuck something.

Mandi was no stranger to the area. She'd been trafficking cocaine to Swainsboro for Alex for four months. He'd chosen her because she was white and less likely to be stopped and searched on the highway. She also had a fat ass like a sister, and loved the hell out of a black dick.

"Shiid, everybody gonna be at the Star Blazer since it's Friday," she replied, sounding black.

"Well that's where we need to be at, then," Cashman

commented.

Everyone piled into Mandi's van and she drove to the club.

¢   ¢   ¢

The Star Blazer's parking lot was thick as hell. There was a long line of patrons waiting to enter. Mandi led the way through the express VIP line, paying the group's way.

"Got-damn!" Mike-Mike exclaimed, pointing at an amazon red-bone wearing a blonde weave. She looked like the red bitch from Player's Club. She was dancing to Jim Beam's song "They For Everybody."

"What's up, Mandi?!" yelled a short stocky nigga with a mouthful of golds. He was on the opposite side of the club.

Mandi waved back before excusing herself. She walked over to the nigga, leaving Cashman and his crew behind.

"Man, I'm finna go holla at that amazon," Mike-Mike said, subsequent to stepping off.

Jay, Cashman and Ernest took a seat at a table in the corner of the club. They'd just fired up a blunt when a waitress came to their table carrying a bottle of Moet.

"We ain't order that," Cashman snapped when the waitress placed the bottle on their table.

"I know, they did," she replied, pointing at the women sitting at the bar.

Cashman looked at the two women and gave an approving head nod before motioning for the women to join them at their table.

"Man, yall can have them two hoes. I'm finna go look for Mandi fine ass," Ernest said, getting up.

"Boy, that nigga got it bad for them white hoes," Jay commented when Ernest was out of earshot.

"Damn sho' do," Cashman agreed, giving Jay dap.

"What yall dappin' each other for?" one of the women asked, standing next to her friend. The two women were now in front of Cashman and Jay's table.

Jay invited the women to a seat. "Ain't nothin'," he answered. "What's the bottle of Mo' for?"

"Oh, that's just a lil' welcome to town gift," answered the brown-skin Tara Banks look-a-like.

"How yall know we ain't from 'round here?" Cashman asked, brows raised.

The short, thick, red-bone looked at Cashman's 18 big wicked dreads and sucked her teeth. "Boy, I done lived here all my life. I ain't neva seen none of yall 'round here, except that white slut, Mandi," she said.

"Whatchall name?" Jay asked, ignoring the comment about Mandi.

The red-bone spoke first. "Jus' call me Red."

"My name Tammy," Tara Banks said.

"I'm Jay and this Cashman," Jay stated, nodding his head toward Cashman.

"Cashman? Damn, I love that name," Red declared.

Jay passed Tammy the blunt. "Whatchall gettin' in after the club?" he asked. "Or better yet, whatchall lettin' get in yall?"

"Shit," Red answered for her friend, looking at Cashman wantingly.

"Well, we might as well go get a room then," Cashman suggested, licking his lips as he stared at Red's succulent breast.

"It's whateva wit' me," Tammy said, passing Red the blunt.

Satisfied that the two women were in agreement, Jay asked, "How yall know Mandi?"

Red spoke up. "'Cause she the only white bitch that come to this club. Plus the bitch done fucked every nigga in town."

"For real?" Cashman asked.

"Hell yeah! I know three niggas that ran a train on her nasty ass. And they filmed that shit. That bitch had a dick in every hole."

"Yall from Duval?" Tammy asked.

"Nawl, we from Dade," Jay lied.

Red released a subtle sigh of relief that no one else heard.

Tammy frowned. "I thought Mandi was from Duval?"

"She is," Jay answered.

"Well how yall know her?" Tammy further inquired.

"Long story," Jay simply stated before changing the subject.

When the club was over Jay and Cashman rode with Red and Tammy to a hotel. Mandi followed in her mini-van with Mike-Mike, Ernest and the amazon. At the hotel everyone paired up with their sex partner and checked into separate rooms. Jay went with Tammy, Cashman went with Red, Mike-Mike rolled with the amazon, and Ernest shacked up with Mandi.

Cashman sat on the edge of the King size bed, inside his and Red's suite, watching lustfully as Red stood before him undressing. He couldn't wait to slide up in her. Red was fine as fuck! She stood a stout 5'6" and weighed about 140 pounds. She had a fat, stupid ass and small perky breast. She even had pretty feet.

Once Red was totally nude, Cashman reached out and gripped her waist, pulling her body close to him. The X-pill he'd popped before entering the Star Blazer caused him to want to do some freaky shit. Cashman ordered Red to place one of her feet on the bed next to him. Once her fat, bald, pussy was staring him in his face, he slid his hands down and gripped her soft butt cheeks. Looking Red in her inquisitive eyes, he gave her pouting pussy lips a hungry lick.

"Oh shit," Red moaned, grabbing Cashman's dreads.

Red's juices seemed to have an enticing effect on Cashman, because he started sucking on her pussy like a hungry baby on a nipple. Ten minutes had passed and Cashman was still feasting on Red's pussy while she did her best to stay balanced with one foot on the bed and the other on the floor.

"Please, Cashman...shit! Oh baby, let me taste that dick," Red hissed.

Cashman stopped his oral-assault on Red's pussy and laid back on the bed. Red snatched down his pants and boxers in one swift motion, releasing his rock-hard manhood. She then dropped to her knees and started sucking his dick. Red did some amazing things to Cashman's dick and balls, which caused him to cum extremely fast. "Oh shit!" he exclaimed, shooting one billion babies down Red's throat. She swallowed every one.

"Put it in me, baby. I need you to fuck my pussy," Red

begged, getting on the bed, on all fours and arching her back.

Cashman hopped off the bed and retrieved a X-pill from his pants, placing it under his thumb nail. Entering Red's hot cum-catcher from behind, he told her how good her pussy was as he began pumping her love-dungeon like a piston. After beating for about ten minutes, Cashman slipped the thumb with the X-pill under its nail into her asshole.

"Oh, Cashman! Oh, I'm cummin' on this big ass dick!" Red cried out in response to her asshole being penetrated.

Cashman continued stabbing, pulling thick globs of Red's cum from her gaping pussy-hole with each stroke.

Red had never taken ecstacy, so when the pill took effect twenty minutes later she didn't know why she suddenly felt so uninhibited. "Put your dick in my ass," she whined.

Cashman did as she wished. The thick creamy cum from Red's steaming hot pussy was all the lubrication he needed to slide up easily into her virgin anus. Cashman plowed Red's ass long and hard! He had her shaking and cumming like crazy. Finally, having held his nut as long as he could, Cashman coated Red's large intestine with his gummy man-milk. He pulled out, tireder than e-muthafucka and crashed next to Red.

The next morning Cashman woke up with Red laying naked next to him in bed. "Ay baby, get up," he said, gently shaking her.

"What time is it?" she asked in a sleepy voice.

Glancing at his watch, Cashman replied, "9:43 a.m."

Red and Cashman showered and got dressed. When Red was done fixing her hair and applying make up, she turned to Cashman and spoke with concern in her voice. "When I'ma see you again?"

"A nigga tryin' to see you tonight. What's up wit' that?" Cashman asked, taking Red's petite frame into his arms.

Red smiled, then gave Cashman a passionate kiss before breaking their embrace. She wrote her number down on a piece of paper.

Cashman put the paper in his pocket. "I'ma hit you tonight," he promised.

¢ ¢ ¢

An Hour Later

Ernest, Jay, and Mike-Mike sat in the stash spot's living room watching TV as Mandi explained to Cashman what they had to do with the thirteen kilos that Goldie had sent with them.

"First we got to take Slaughter his shit," Mandi stated.

Slaughter was a nigga who'd been getting money in Swainsbor, GA for years. He'd met Goldie at the Orange Crush in Savannah, GA a year and a half earlier and they exchanged numbers. Coincidentally, Goldie was already fucking with some niggas out of Swainsboro, GA, so when Slaughter's Atlanta plug got killed in a home invasion, and he contacted Goldie in reference to copping some work Goldie didn't have a problem serving him since the other niggas he'd been supplying in Swainsboro had nothing but good things to say about Slaughter.

"Then we got to drop Eric and Blue's shit off at they traps," Mandi furthered explained, stepping into the room where the work and guns were stored. Cashman was on her heels.

¢ ¢ ¢

Mandi navigated through the back streets of Swainsboro until she reached a section of town referred to as Red Rock. Parking in the driveway of a duplex, she honked her horn two times. Seconds later, three black males emerged from building 325 – two of which carried assault rifles. Cashman observed the unarmed man sandwiched between the two choppa toters while clutching his .40 caliber. He was the same short, stocky nigga Mandi had been talking to at the Star Blazer the night before.

"Got-damn. It's 'bout time you made it," Slaughter joked, pretending to be frustrated. He displayed a gold-tooth smile the whole while.

"I told you, you was gonna be the first stop," Mandi retorted, smiling back.

Mandi and Cashman exited the van and walked to its rear, followed by Slaughter and his goons. Just then, two more niggas stepped out of the duplex, each carrying black garbage bags.

When they reached the back of the van, Mandi simply pointed at the work on the floor board of the van's cargo area and watched as they stuffed five kilos a piece into their garbage bags, then hurriedly ambled back into the townhouse from which they came.

Mandi then removed a shoe box containing $5,000 from the back of the van and handed it to Slaughter. It was Goldie's part of the $20,000 Slaughter paid the sheriff of Emanual County every month.

After beating every case the Emanual County Police Department ever charged him with, Slaughter was stopped one night and taken to a secluded area. Sheriff West – the county sheriff arrived at the prearranged meeting spot a short while later. He got right down to business, giving Slaughter two options. Pay $20,000 per month and sell all the drugs he wanted...or die.

The choice was a no brainer.

Slaughter told Goldie about the deal he had with the sheriff's office after dealing with him for a while and began to trust him. When he did so, Goldie proposed to pay $5,000 of the $20,000 if Slaughter could arrange for the two trap houses he supplied in Swainsboro to be protected. Slaughter made it happen easily by telling the sheriff that Goldie's traps were his.

One of the dudes who'd come out carrying a garbage bag to collect the work stepped back out of the house with a duffle bag containing $200,000. The cash was what Slaughter owed for the ten kilos he'd gotten. The duffle-bag boy placed the money in the cargo area of the van and went back inside the house.

Slaughter watched his worker close the door behind himself before turning to Mandi and speaking. "What's up wit' my nigga, Alex?" he asked. He didn't know that Alex had been picked up by the Feds. Slaughter was use to Alex and Mandi delivering his work.

Hearing Alex's name mentioned reminded Cashman that he still had a lot of work to do. "He aiight," Cashman stated before Mandi could answer.

Mandi glanced at Cashman, then at Slaughter before theatrically slapping her forehead with the palm of her hand. "Damn, my bad. I ain't even introduce yall," she said. "Cashman, this is Slaughter. Slaughter, this is Goldie's brother, Cashman."

Capo Cat

Cashman pounded Slaughter's fist then asked, "Do you know a chick from 'round here name Kendra?" He started to let Slaughter know that Kendra was snitching but thought better of it. The bitch wasn't going to try and set up Slaughter or no niggas in her area. She'd hit an out of town nigga for a reason.

"It's a couple hoes name Kendra 'round here."

"The one I'm talkin' 'bout, her ole man in the Feds."

"Ohhh, you talkin' 'bout thick, red Kendra," Slaughter stated.

"Might be. You know where she stay?" Cashman asked.

"Umm...she stay on Ben Screet...614 or 615 Ben Screet," Slaughter said, thinking of the correct address.

After leaving Slaughter's spot, Cashman and Mandi dropped the remainder of the work off to Eric and Blue before returing to the stash house. Jay and Ernest were in the living room watching TV when they entered.

"Where that nigga Mike-Mike?" Cashman asked.

Mandi took the duffle bag full of money she'd gotten from Slaughter and the two Victoria Secret's bags of cash she'd received from Blue and Eric to the safe room.

"Man, that nigga went to that amazon chick's house," Ernest answered.

"Damn, that nigga got a tender dick. That bitch got him hooked already?" Cashman joked.

The three youths were still laughing when Mandi walked back into the room. "Cashman, is you ready to ride out that way or what?" she asked.

"Yeah, let's go," Cashman said before turning back to Jay and Ernest. "We'll be right back," he said.

After stopping by both addresses that Slaughter had given them and seeing that no one was home at either, Cashman decided to call it a night. He was ready to hook up with Red. Subsequent to making it back to the stash house and getting dressed, Cashman called Red's cell. She agreed to meet him back at the hotel they'd stayed in the night before.

Cashman walked into the living room where Jay, Ernest and Mandi were and spoke. "Mandi, I want you to take Jay and Ernest by them houses on Ben Street in a few hours, aiight?"

Mandi told him she'd take care of it and Cashman left for his date with Red at the hotel.

Chapter 15

Alex took Sam's pawn with his queen, trapping his king at the same time. "Check mate," he declared. He and Sam had been playing chess everyday since he'd been housed at the detention facility.

"Brooks! Attorney visit!" A C.O. opened the pod's door and announced two games later. Alex had just tricked Sam out of his knight and was going in for the kill.

¢   ¢   ¢

After retrieving his inmate ID, Alex was escorted to the Attorney/Client visiting room.

The Attorney/Client visiting room was a small room with two chairs and a table in its center. Attorney visits were the only contact visits allowed at the detention facility.

Stepping inside the legal conference room, Alex was shocked to see U.S. Attorney David Miller and two other crackas he'd seen at his detention hearing. He'd expected to see his lawyer, Marquis Wimberly. He recognized David Miller's mug immediately. *This the muthafucka who made me out to be a monster in front of the judge.* "Cracka, what the fuck you doin' here?" Alex asked, pointing at U.S. Attorney David Miller.

David Miller wore a fake smile as he sat flanked by two men who were dressed like Bo and Luke Duke off of the Dukes of Hazard. "Have a seat Mr. Brooks," he stated as if he didn't hear Alex call him a cracker.

"Cracka, I ain't got shit to say to yall. Where my muthafuckin' lawyer at?"

The Fed standing on David Miller's left spoke up. "Look Brooks. You don't have to act hard in here, okay?...By the way,

I'm Agent Ricks and this is my partner, Agent Hogan," he said, pointing his thumb at the man standing on David Miller's right. "We're DEA and we want to help you."

Alex said nothing as he stood, arms folded across his chest.

"C'mon Brooks. Have a seat. Relax," Agent Hogan encouraged, speaking up for the first time.

Alex said nothing and didn't budge.

"Okay Brooks, this is what it's gonna be, hard ass! You either work with us or go to trial, lose and get life. Because the only plea I'm offering you is life," David Miller scolded.

Smiling before grunting, Alex said nothing.

Agent Ricks matched Alex's smile, then turned to David Miller. "Isn't Mr. Brooks looking to be tried by Judge Owens?"

"Yes, that's correct," David Miller answered.

Agent Hogan started snickering. "You're fucked, Brooks. My father-in-law hates drug dealers."

After hearing that the judge handling his case was the father-in-law of one of the agents involved, Alex became nervous. However, the DEA, being masters of converting real niggas into snitches, didn't stop there. They applied more pressure.

Agent Ricks exhibited a sinister grin when he removed an 8x10 photo from the folder he was holding. He then placed it on the conference table. When Alex's eyes focused in on the images captured on the picture his legs wobbled. The shot of his girl walking out of the Salt Air Hotel with another man, who had his hand on her ass, took his breath away.

Unconsciously, Alex sat down in the chair he'd been refusing. "Aiight man, fuck it," he said after a few minutes had passed. "I got some information for yall."

The two agents and the U.S. Attorney looked at each other in disbelief. They never would have guessed that Alex would crack so easy. Unconsciously, the U.S. Attorney and the two agents moved in closer to Alex as if the biggest secret in the world was about to be revealed.

"Aiight nye', I ain't gonna repeat none of this shit I'm 'bout to tell yall," Alex explained in a hushed voice, causing all three government employees to lean in closer. "Man, yall crackas can suck my dick!" Alex spat, jumping from the table and wagging his meat. He then kicked on the door and yelled for a C.O. to come get him.

¢   ¢   ¢

When Alex made it back to his pod, he went straight to his bunk. He felt mixed emotions as he pondered Meka's betrayal. It hadn't been a whole month since he'd been locked up, and already his bitch was out fucking. Hurt and anger consumed Alex as mental images of Meka on her knees sucking another nigga's dick and calling him daddy appeared in his mind's eye. He wanted so badly to hop off of his bunk to call and confront her, but decided against it. "I'ma fix that bitch," Alex said to himself after his thoughts shifted from helplessness and self-pity to thoughts of revenge.

His first vengeful cognition was to have the nigga on the picture with Meka killed, whoever he was, but he shook the idea as quickly as it had come. "Nawl, the nigga was just bein' a man when he fucked my bitch," he surmised before another thought came. "I'ma have a nigga cut that hoe face up wit' a razor…shit! That ain't good enough. I need that bitch to suffer," he said in introspect. Then the perfect idea came to him. "Yeah, I'ma fix that bitch," he said smiling.

Alex hopped off of his bunk and called Meka. When she picked up he didn't mention anything about her infidelity. He simply carried on a conversation with her like it was all good. He'd already decided on how he was going to make her pay. But he had to control his emotions in order for his plan to work. And that's what he intended to do.

¢   ¢   ¢

After his phone call with Meka, Alex was on his way to his bunk to smoke a rip. The nigga Sam stopped him enroute. "What's   up? Tryin' to play some chess?"

Sam and Alex played five games of chess with Sam coming out victorious each time.

"Dog, you aiight?" Sam asked, feigning concern. He'd never won a game against Alex.

"Yeah, I'm good. Nigga just tired, that's all," Alex lied.

Sam, being the real slime-ball that he was, already knew about Alex's visit from the DEA. He also knew about the picture they'd showed him, because he was the one who'd suggested that they do so. "Aiight, my nigga, if you need me just holla," he said, getting up from the table.

¢   ¢   ¢

Alex showered and tried calling Meka once more before the phones were shut off for the night. There was no answer. He waited thirty minutes and tried to call three more times. There was still no answer. Angry, Alex went to his bunk and laid down. He wanted to go to sleep, but he kept thinking about Meka. Was she with the nigga on the picture right now? Was she fucking and sucking at that moment?

The questions kept popping in Alex's head, driving him mad!

"Man, I gotta get the fuck outta here," Alex thought as sweat began to form on his neck and forehead.

Fragments of conversations he'd had with Meka since he'd been locked up began to play in his head. Hidden meanings of Meka's words became evident – or at least that's what Alex thought in his mind.

Like when Meka would say, "Baby, you ain't got to call back tonight. Gon' and get some rest." That meant the nigga was coming over. Or when she'd say, "Baby, I slept so good last night when I got off the phone witchu." That meant the nigga fucked the shit out of her.

The more Alex's mind wondered, the angrier he became. "Man, I got to get the fuck outta here or I'ma have a nervous breakdown in this bitch."

"Whatchu say?" Debo asked from the top bunk.

"Oh...uh, nothing," Alex replied, embarrassed for thinking out loud. *Damn, that bitch got a nigga trippin'*, he said to himself.

Chapter 16

The Boeing BBJ traveled at a whopping speed of over 600 miles per hour, delivering Goldie safely to Jesus Diez's ranch in less than five hours. As the luxury jet made its descent, Goldie could see Jesus' enormous mansion and the four mini mansions he'd built to host guests. His estate occupied a very large expanse of acreage.

Goldie watched in amazement as a long stip of the grassy field below began parting as his jet approached. The parted field revealed a paved runway that lead into a humongous barn. Inside the barn, which was actually an air hangar equipped with air traffic control equipment, sat another aircraft. It was identical to the one Goldie had flown in on.

Jesus has spent millions to hide his secret personal airfield from Mexican and American law enforcement. "That must be John Boy's," Goldie said, referring to the other Boeing BBJ inside of the air hangar.

Stepping off his jet, Goldie was met at the bottom of the air stair by two men armed with AR-15's. A beautiful Mexican woman was also with them.

"You are Goldie, I presume?" the woman said, extending her hand.

Goldie nodded in the affirmative, taking her hand and gently shaking it.

"Welcome to my country. My name is Lonita Diez," the woman announced with a dimpled smile. "...I assume that you have your money on board the jet?" she added, getting down to business.

Thinking about the $2.25 million stashed in boxes in the cargo area of the Boeing BBJ, Goldie said, "Yeah, it's all there."

"Okay, my men will unload everything," Lonita said, getting behind the wheel of the golf cart. She patted the passenger seat, beckoning Goldie to hop in.

Arriving at Jesus' 27 bedroom English mansion, Goldie was blown away. The pristine, white castle-like estate was surrounded by eight acres of perfectly manicured land, with an adjacent 189 acres available. Entering the foyer, Goldie was even more astonished by the granite staircase and gleaming hardwood floors just beyond the cavernous vestibule.

As Goldie and Lonita journeyed through the great room into the kitchen, Goldie counted at least five men holding AR-15's, scattered about the mansion. When they stepped out onto the sundeck, Goldie observed John Boy lounging in a deck chair next to an Olympic size swimming pool. He was accompanied by an old Mexican man who also lounged in a deck chair.

"So this how you do it, huh?" Goldie said, smiling.

Hearing Goldie's voice, John Boy jumped up. "Oh, shit! What's up, my nigga?!" he asked, happy to see his young partner. "I see yo' ass finally made it."

"Shiid, nigga you know a nigga ain't finna miss out on this move," Goldie commented, smiling.

Just then, Jesus stood up from his chair. "Hello, my friend. John Boy told me good things about you," he said, extending his hand.

Goldie satisfied the gesture while inconspicuously checking out Jesus' attire. It was a mixture of old west meets modern day drug dealer. Jesus donned a cowboy hat, a polyester shirt with an orange ostrich skin collar, and heavily starched Wranglers. He wore a solid gold rope chain around his neck with an AK-47 medallion. It complimented his gold Rolex watch and gold rim sunglasses. His orange ostrich skin boots were made from the same ostrich that the collar of his shirt was made from.

"John Boy told me good things 'bout you too," Goldie replied after the hand shake.

"Good, good," Jesus responded, giving Goldie a penetrating stare. He paused for a few seconds, staring into Goldie's eyes before saying, "I'm going to be honest with you. I don't do much business with blacks because I don't trust them. I've been dealing with John Boy for about five years and he has earned my trust. When John Boy asked me to meet with you I had my reservations; however, I honor his judgement, so here we are," Jesus professed, outstretching his arm before carrying on. "Now, with that being said, I'm going to explain how we will conduct all future business. You two are purchasing one half ton of cocaine and receiving an additional half ton on consignment. This is a lot of blow; enough to get you and your entire family killed. And this goes without saying, if you are caught with it, you take your life sentence and don't mention my name. There will only be one transaction per month. Both of you know the price, so if you ever need to increase supply I will know by how much money you send aboard the jet. I will only need to see you two once every six months. Now, are there any questions you may have about what I just said? Ask them now or wait for our next meeting six months from now."

Goldie raised his hand as if he was a student in class. Jesus acknowledged him with a head nod, signaling for him to speak. "What if the work bad?" Goldie asked.

Jesus gave Goldie a tight smile. "I never had bad coke. But if for some strange reason I do, send it back and I will exchange it."

"You gonna keep matchin' what we buy?" John Boy quizzed.

"Of course. It's easier that way…Anything else?" Jesus asked after a few seconds passed with no one talking. "Well, I guess that concludes the business. Now let's celebrate," he said smiling.

¢ ¢ ¢

Two hours after the meeting at Jesus' ranch, Jesus, Lonita, John Boy and Goldie rode in an armored stretched Hummer, sipping champagne. They were in the center of a motorcade consisting of four other Hummers, all of which were armored and equipped with bullet proof windows, gun portals and run-flat-tires. There were two Hummers in front of them leading the way through the dust filled streets of Culiacan. They were occupied by eight heavily armed men. Behind them were two more Hummers occupied with an equal amount of heavily armed men.

Reaching their destination, which was Club Cho Cha – the most exclusive strip club in the city, Jesus' 18 man security detail exited their Hummers armed with Cuernos de Chivos [which means goat horns in English]. The Mexican gangsters referred to the AK-47 by this name because its seventy round clip curled like a goat's horns.

The security detail formed a perimeter before Jesus, Lonita, John Boy and Goldie exited the stretched Hummer. Inside the establishment, Jesus and his entourage were seated in a plush VIP area, encased in plexiglass and furnished with a long sectional couch, crystal end tables and a full bar. It had an excellent view of the stage, where two buck-naked Mexican women with big titties and flat asses were putting on a show. One of the women was on the floor on all fours as the other one *fucked-the-shit out* of her from the back with a big ass dildo.

"Got-damn, my nigga. You see that shit?" Goldie asked John Boy, who watched in stunned silence as the two foot dildo disappeared into the Mexican woman's pussy.

"H-hell, yeah. Man, that hoe ruined!"

Jesus looked over at Goldie and smiled. "You can have them both if you like."

Catching a disapproving look from Lonita before answering, Goldie replied, "Nawl man, I'm scrate."

A few hours later they left the club and went to a casino. Jesus and John Boy went straight to the poker tables and Lonita and Goldie opted for Black Jack.

Before placing any bets, Goldie and Lonita decided to watch a few hands first. A couple minutes of silence passed before Lonita spoke. "You made a good decision by not taking my father up on his offer back at the club."

Goldie was confused. "What you talkin' 'bout?" he asked.

"I'm talking about when he offered you the two women. He was testing you."

"What kinda test was that? Shiid, niggas fuck hoes."

"I can understand that, but it's a weakness that my father shuns."

"What about you?" Goldie asked with a raised brow.

"What do you mean, *what about me?*"

"I'm talkin' 'bout that look you had on yo' face when yo' daddy asked a nigga did he wanna fuck them two hoes. What was that all about?"

"Goldie, I'm going to be honest with you. ...I'm attracted to you," Lonita said, dropping her head so that Goldie couldn't look into her scandalous eyes.

Shock registered on Goldie's face. "Oh, so this another one of yo' daddy's test?" he asked in disbelief.

Lonita feigned offense. "Goldie, my attraction is genuine. Do you think that my father would use his only child in such a manner?"

Shrugging his shoulders, Goldie stated, "Shiid, I don't know. You tell me."

"Do you have low self-esteem or something?" Lonita asked, stabbing at Goldie's vanity.

"Hell nawl," Goldie replied.

"Well why wouldn't you believe that I'm interested in you?"

"Look, Lonita. I done been 'round. And I done fucked wit' some bad bitches in my time. But most of 'em wanted to fuck wit' a nigga 'cause I got that cash. But witchu, what could a nigga like me give you that you ain't got?"

"Goldie, it's not about money or status with me. And to be honest, I only want a small piece of you," Lonita said, glancing at Goldie's crotch.

Goldie peeped the play and stated, "How would yo' daddy feel if he knew his lil' girl was gettin' pounded by this black dick?" he said, grabbing his meat.

"First I want to say that I'm glad that you understand what I mean by *wanting a small piece of you*. Or should I say *big* from the looks of it. What I do is my business and what my father doesn't know can't hurt him."

Goldie was blown by Lonita's answer, but at the same time decided he'd take her up on her offer. He glanced back at her once more, taking in her looks.

Lonita was 4'11" and weighed about 130 pounds. She was thick in all the right places. Her ass wasn't as appled out as a sister's, but she made up for it with how wide it was. Her face was blemish free. Long black hair and hazel eyes completed her.

Yeah, I'ma gon' and give her some of this Mandingo and have her ass fucked up, Goldie thought to himself before signaling the Black Jack dealer to deal him in.

¢　¢　¢

Ten hands and $3,000 in the red, Goldie decided to cash in his chips. He looked to his left and spotted Lonita at the Black Jack table with four cards down in front of her. She was deep in thought. Lonita raised her cards slightly and Goldie read her hand. Her four cards added up to eighteen.

"Tell 'em to hit you again," Goldie whispered into Lonita's ear.

Lonita nodded at the dealer and was hit with a three of hearts. She won $25,000.

"Look like you the lucky one tonight," Goldie replied as Lonita was picking up her chips.

"The night's not over yet. You can still get lucky," Lonita stated in a sultry voice. "Let's go find my father and John Boy," she added, switching her wide hips and ass as she walked away.

They found Jesus and John Boy at the casino's bar, both drunk out of their minds. They were leaning shoulder to shoulder to keep each other from falling off of their stools.

"Father, I think it's time we leave," Lonita scolded him in an irritated voice. She hated when her father drank – which was very-very often.

Jesus looked at his daughter and dropped his head. He could tell by her tone of voice that she was too angry to argue with. "Okay, okay...c'mon buddy, let's get out of here," he slurred, patting John Boy on his back.

Lonita reached in her purse and pressed a button on a small electronic device that alerted the security detail that they were about to exit the casino.

The security detail was waiting at the entrance of the casino when Jesus and John Boy stumbled out of the doors followed by Lonita and Goldie. As the group moved enroute to their vehicles, all hell broke loose.

The first series of shots came from somewhere in the East of the parking lot followed by more from the West. Eight members of Jesus' security detail went down immediately after being hit by .50 caliber rounds.

Goldie didn't know what was happening as gunfire, which sounded more like TNT exploding, resonated in rapid succession.

On instinct, he pushed Lonita to the ground, next to a F350. And in the same motion he reached down, retrieving an AK-47 from the dead fingers of one of the fallen security team. He came up bussing back at the muzzle flashes in the East.

John Boy was laying next to Jesus on the pavement. "What the fuck goin' on?" he asked Jesus, who was laughing hysterically.

Boom! was the deafening sound that echoed in the night air as a vehicle about fifty yards away was struck by a rocket propelled grenade. Glass and debris scattered all over the parking lot.

What the fuck was that? Goldie thought, but was too busy firing to dwell on the question.

"Man, we gotta get outta here!" John Boy shouted over the heavy gunfire.

The Hummers were about thirty yards away. The vehicles in the parking lot offered some cover against gunfire, but was useless against the rocket propelled grenades.

Boom! Another RPG exploded, this time hitting a truck about sixty yards away.

"Fuck this shit! Ay, yall run for the Hummers!" Goldie barked before picking Lonita up from the pavement, throwing her over his shoulder.

Goldie led the way to the Hummer while simultaneously firing to the East of the casino parking lot to keep their attackers from getting a clear shot. Jesus and John Boy followed the remaining members of the security detail as they brought up the rear, firing toward the West.

Making it to the Hummers safely, they all piled in. What was left of the motorcade then sped out of the casino parking lot.

¢   ¢   ¢

Back at the ranch, John Boy, Jesus, Lonita and Goldie were seated in the great room recovering from the ambush. Jesus spoke, "Those bastards did a better job of trying to kill me this time than the last," he declared with a hint of humor in his voice. He then broke out into an uncontrollable laughing fit.

Goldie was speechless. *This muthafuckin' wet-back gotta be crazy to think shit funny. Them muthafuckas was shootin' rocket launchers at our asses*, he thought to himself.

John Boy and Goldie weren't strangers to gun play and murking niggas, but the Mexicans took shit to another level.

"Man, who the fuck that was tryin' to kill us?" Goldie asked, seriously frustrated.

"That, my friend, was the Commission," Jesus answered, still thinking shit was funny.

"Okay, and?" Goldie snapped.

"They are our rivals. They want us dead so that they can take over our distribution routes. We've been at war with them for three years. Lazorito Cort—"

"Hold the fuck up," Goldie interrupted Lonita. "Yall been beefin' wit' them muthafuckas for three years and they ain't dead yet?"

Feeling disrespected by Goldie's insinuation of his imcompetence, Jesus' demeanor changed. "I've been trying my damnedest to kill that sonofabitch! But he's as slippery as a wet moccasin. To tell the truth, the closest I've come to killing the bastard is when I had the church that his youngest son, Marco, was getting married in blown up during his wedding. One-hundred-twelve people were killed and not one of them was Lazorito Cortez! He wasn't even at the wedding," Jesus finished, shaking his head.

Got-damn! Goldie thought to himself. *This muthafucka blew up a church full of people to kill one muthafucka?* Goldie remained silent for a few more seconds while contemplating how vicious Jesus was before saying, "Well whatchu gonna do 'bout that muthafucka?" he asked.

Jesus shrugged his shoulders. Looking Goldie in his eyes he said, "Kill the bastard before he kills me."

Once everyone said their peace, Jesus went to bed. Lonita offered to take John Boy and Goldie to their guest houses. The three climbed in one of the many golf carts that they used on the ranch and rode off.

John Boy was the first to be dropped off. However, when Lonita arrived at the guest house that Goldie was to stay in, she suggested giving him the grand tour of the residence.

Goldie followed close behind Lonita as she climbed the spiral staircase just beyond the foyer. She opened the door to the master suite, allowing Goldie to step inside before closing and locking the door behind him.

Wasting little time, Lonita turned and pushed Goldie onto the California King size bed in the center of the room. She began to undress before Goldie's back hit the mattress. Once Lonita was totally nude, she climbed in bed next to Goldie and began to rub his hardened member through his jeans. Shock registered on her face when she felt Goldie's entire length. *There was no way Goldie's dick could be so big,* Lonita thought, rubbing it again to make sure that what she felt was real. Still unsure, she asked, "Goldie, is that all you?" She didn't wait for an answer. She quickly unzipped his pants and pulled them down to see for herself. "Oh, my, god!" Lonita said when Goldie's dick popped out of his pants. "Your dick is so fucking big!...and black!"

Lonita had never seen a black dick up close. She'd seen a few in a couple of pornos, but it was nothing like the real thing. Goldie, on the other hand, was at a loss for words. Lonita sounded so corny commenting on his dick the way she did.

"I'm going to suck the blood out of this black cock," Lonita said after grabbing Goldie's pussy-plunger. Lonita then stuffed as much meat into her mouth as she possibly could.

At first Goldie was afraid Lonita was going to bite his meat off. Then he felt her soft tonsils massaging the head of his dick. Lonita began to jiggle Goldie's balls, causing him to squirm. The feeling got so good to Goldie that he sat up on his elbows, admiring what Lonita was doing to him. Goldie's toes curled in view of what she was making him feel.

Lonita's head bobbed rapidly as if she were trying to suck the life out of Goldie. Knowing that Goldie was staring as she handled her business, Lonita locked eyes with him and continued to suck his dick with sheer passion. She was totally zoned out. In between sucks she began to speak. "Ummm…you taste so rich…ummm. I want to…feel this…ummm…dick in my stomach….uummm."

Lonita was sucking Goldie's dick like she was possessed.

"Oh shit, I'm 'bout to cum," Goldie warned moments later.

Lonita immediately stopped sucking and squeezed the shaft of Goldie's swollen manhood. The pressure stopped him from cumming. Seeing that Goldie wasn't about to cum anymore, Lonita straddled his dick. She was so wet and horny that she took Goldie's nine inches with ease. "I'm going to glaze this dick," she hissed as she slowly began to ride Goldie's pole. She leaned forward and stuck her tongue in Goldie's ear, whispering, "Beat this pussy, Poppi."

No further encouragement was needed.

Goldie gripped both of Lonita's butt cheeks, spreading them apart as she leaned forward, allowing him to feast on her nipples. He raised her up slightly and commenced to throw dick up in her.

"Oh Poppi, fuck me!" Lonita squealed.

Goldie fucked her while laying on his back for a few more minutes, then rolled her over and got on top. "Buss that pussy open," he demanded.

Lonita did as she was told, extending and spreading her legs as wide as she could, placing both big toes on the head board.

Goldie dived right in and began pounding.

"Damn, I love this fucking black cock! Fuck!" Lonita said through clenched teeth. Goldie hammered her love-dungeon relentlessly.

Goldie was punishing her ass! He was stroking so hard that his dick missed the pussy on the down stroke and entered Lonita's ass. He felt a hot liquid shower his crouch and stomach area.

"Oh my god! Oh my god!" Lonita repeated as she came.

Goldie had stopped stroking, thinking that he'd hurt her. But he was wrong.

"Don't stop Poppi," Lonita begged, putting Goldie's fuck-rod back into her thirsty *asshole*. Goldie began stroking again. "Cum in it, you big dick nig— sonaofabitch!"

Balls deep in Lonita's big asshole, Goldie went ballistic.

He rabbit fucked Lonita in her ass until the nut he'd been holding back exploded out of his dick with the force of a category five hurricane. "Fuck!" he cried out during his release. He was so tired that he crashed next to Lonita, both drenched in sweat.

Chapter 17

"Ay, Marquis, what's poppin'?" Alex asked his lawyer as he stepped into the attorney/client visiting room.

The lawyer was rummaging through some papers in his briefcase. Without looking up, he answered, "Just came here to go over some things with you. How are you holding up in here?" he asked, still digging in his briefcase.

"Other than bein' in here wit' this case over my head, I'm good, I guess."

"Good, good," Marquis Wimberly said, finally finding the papers he'd been searching for. He looked up. "Alex, we are set for trial two and a half months from now and I just got notice that the government has added a witness to your case." Alex sat up in his chair, back straight. "Alex, we have a problem," Marquis stated, grimly.

"Anotha witness? Where they got anotha witness from?" Alex asked, annoyed by all of the bad news he'd been getting.

"From what I gather, this new witness was locked up with you and said that you talked to him about your case."

"I ain't talked to nobody 'bout my case. Man, them crackas lyin'."

"Do you know a guy by the name of Sammie Williams?" Marquis asked.

"Yeah, I know him. That's my dog. Why you askin' 'bout him for?"

"Your dog? You guys kill me," Mr. Wimberly said, shaking his head in disbelief. "Your 'dog' is the new witness that the government just added."

Alex didn't know what to say. All of him and Sammie's conversations played back in his mind. Sammie had conveniently been moved to Baker County Jail two days prior. *Fuck!* Alex thought.

"Alex, I'm going to need to know what this new witness can say about you."

"Whatchu mean, *what he can say*?" Alex asked with an attitude.

"Look, it's obvious that you've said something to this individual that the government finds useful. Now, I need to know what was said so that I can prepare a defense."

"Man, how them crackas gonna use a felon as a witness, anyway?" Alex inquired, not understanding the logic behind the government's procurement of criminals.

Mr. Wimberly smiled. "Alex, we're talking about the Federal Government, here. They will do anything to get a conviction. Now tell me what Mr. Williams can get on the stand and say about your case."

Alex thought for a moment, then explained that he'd told Sammie about large amounts of drugs he'd sold, cars he owned, places he'd been – the whole nine. When Alex finally finished talking, his lawyer sat stone-faced, staring at him like he was crazy.

"What?!" Alex stated angrily.

"Got-damn-it, Alex! You've really fucked up my case! I told your ass not to talk to anybody! About anything! Now can you see why?!"

Alex tuned the angry lawyer out as he continued to rant-and-rave about Sammie and Alex opening his mouth to the rat. It had really fucked up his case. *Okay*, Alex thought, *First Meka, nye' this fuck-ass-nigga, Sammie. Man I'ma fuck ova' both them bitches when I catch 'em.*

Alex's thoughts were interrupted when his lawyer stood and began placing papers back into his briefcase.

"Hopefully the private investigator will find enough dirt on Mr. Williams to discredit his testimony." The lawyer finished.

At the conclusion of the attorney visit, Alex was returned to his pod. He was mentally exhausted. He climbed into his bunk and just as he was about to close his eyes, he heard the pod's door open and a C.O. announce mail call. His name was the third one called.

Alex walked downstairs and retrieved his mail. It was from

Meka. Returning to his bunk, he read the letter she'd wrote to him and was heated! *Stank ass bitch! Talkin' 'bout she keepin' it tight for a nigga,* he snorted to himself. He had to control the urge to hop off of his bunk to call and curse Meka's ass out. *I can't believe this bitch!* He said in introspect, tearing up her letter.

His negative cognitions were halted when he heard another C.O. step into the pod and shout, "Pill line!"

A smile spread across Alex's face at the thought of getting some pussy later that night.

The officer that had announced pill call was Cocena Tubbs, or Ms. Tubbs as the staff at the detention center and most inmates called her. Alex had started fucking her a week after arriving at the institution.

Cocena wasn't a dime by a long shot. In fact, Alex wouldn't have given her ass the time of day had he bumped into her on the streets. She had a pretty face, big titties, tone legs and clear skin. But she was chubby and had a flat, wide ass. The only thing that kept Alex fucking with her was her pussy. She had that good, for real!

Alex jumped off of his bunk and stood at the top tier's railing. Cocena spotted him and blushed. Alex had her spellbound. She'd never so much as gotten a traffic ticket, yet here she was fucking with an incarcerated drug kingpin and smuggling weed into the jail for him.

Alex also had Cocena smuggling letters that contained incriminating material out of the detention facility to be mailed to Goldie. Cocena opened one of the letters and read it. She then realized just how serious Alex was in the streets.

In the letter Cocena had nosed into, Alex was trying to confirm whether a female witness against him was dead. At first Cocena wanted to confront Alex and go off on him for involving her in a murder conspiracy. But after thinking about the situation she decided that the woman, whoever she was, probably deserved what she had coming. Being around criminals all day had caused Cocena's outlook on life to change dramatically. Instead of reporting Alex to the proper authorities, she said to *herself,* "Fuck that hoe. Bitch shouldn't be tellin' on niggas, anyway."

The letters that Cocena smuggled out of the jail for Alex

were never mailed directly to Goldie. Instead, they were mailed to a P.O. Box in Jacksonville that was rented under an assumed name.

Once Cocena sashayed out of Alex's pod, he got busy writing Goldie about his new problem – Sammie jumping on his case.

¢   ¢   ¢

Later that night, Cocena entered Alex's pod again. This time she came to get some cleaning supplies out of the mop closet for the night orderlies to do their nightly cleaning. Upon hearing the pod's door open, Alex's bunkie, Debo, looked over the concrete divider and saw Cocena coming up the stairs. Jumping off of his bunk, he went downstairs, passing Cocena on the way, to chill with his partner Big Al on the bottom tier.

Alex had already given him the heads-up that Cocena would be coming through.

Walking to the supply closet, Cocena passed Alex's bunk. It was situated in one of the only two blind spots in the pod. Cutting her eyes, she was instantly disappointed. Alex laid in his bunk covered with his blanket from head to toe.

Damn! I wanted me some of that dick! Cocena thought, forcefully turning the knob on the supply closet's door.

Moments later, while in the supply closet, Cocena was bending over to pick up a spray bottle. She suddenly felt a presence. Then something hard and blunt poked her on her ass. She looked back over her shoulder just as Alex closed the supply room's door behind him.

"Oh, Alex, that's what I'm talking about, baby," Cocena moaned as Alex embraced her from behind, kissing and sucking on the back of her exposed neck.

Cocena reached back and began to gently massage Alex's dick through his Dickies.

"You love this dick, baby?" Alex whispered hotly into Cocena's ear.

"Umm humm, daddy," she purred.

"Well suck it like you love it, then," Alex challenged.

Cocena turned and dropped to her knees, pulling down

Alex's pants and boxers as she went down. She inserted his rigid swipe into her mouth and went to work with no hands. "Ummm, this dick taste like candy," she commented while unbuttoning her shirt, exposing big D-cup sized breast. She wore a black lace bra.

Cocena stopped sucking just long enough to place Alex's throbbing cock between her large breast, pressing them together. Afterwards, Alex began to stroke his enlarged member upwards, letting it slide between Cocena's big-ass-titties into her tantalizing mouth. The friction had him on the verge of cumming. So he stroked faster. He humped Cocena's face as if her mouth was a big-fat-coochie.

"Ah, shit!" Alex grunted after busting a leg-buckling nut into the back of Cocena's throat.

Cocena continued to slurp and slob on Alex's sensitive dick head until he fell to his knees, overwhelmed by the euphoric sensation.

"Oh no you don't, nigga!" Cocena scolded him quietly as Alex was on his knees trying to catch his breath. "I need me some of that dick."

Cocena hurriedly pulled down her pants. She left one leg in, in case of an emergency. After aggressively pushing Alex back until he was laying on the floor of the cramped supply closet, she happily straddled his raw, cum laddened dick. She began to rock back and forth, causing her big, long titties to jiggle in Alex's face.

"Turn around and ride it," Alex whispered.

Cocena did what was asked of her, turning around and riding Alex reverse *cowgirl* as he massaged her swollen clit. "Oh, shit baby," she gushed quietly.

Alex watched as her butt cheeks contracted. Cocena knew that Alex was enjoying the view, so she decided to spice things up a bit. Using one of her hands, she opened her butt cheeks. With her free hand she stuck one of her fingers into Alex's mouth, letting him suck on it to get it wet. She then inserted it into her ass and finger-fucked herself while simultaneously bouncing on Alex's thick love-muscle.

Unable to control the building orgasm in his loins, Alex gripped a handful of Cocena's hair and released thunderous nut into her gaping cum-bank.

Capo Cat

Feeling Alex's cum discharge into her pussy, Cocena had an orgasm so strong it felt like an outer body experience. Spent from the ride, she collapsed forward, still in reverse *cowgirl* position.

"Ms. Tubbs?" A voice came over Cocena's walkie talkie as it crackled to life.

"Oh shit!" Cocena muttered, quickly retrieving her radio out of her pant pocket. "Yes, this is Ms. Tubbs."

"Ms. Tubbs, what is your location?" Cocena's supervisor, Sergeant Smith asked.

"Umm, I-I'm in pod 4," she stammered.

"Okay, I'm going to need you to watch the cameras while I go up front to take a call."

"Ten-four," Cocena replied before looking over at Alex. "Baby, I got to go," she said, then hastily got herself together. "Do you need anything?" she asked as an after thought.

Alex took an envelope out of the back pocket of his Dickies. "Mail this off tomorrow," he said, handing Cocena the envelope.

Cocena placed the letter into her pocket and gave Alex a peck on the lips. "I'll see you tomorrow, baby," she promised, then left to watch the cameras.

Cocena felt as if she was floating on air. Alex had the best dick in her book, hands down. She began to daydream about having his baby. All the while her pussy was leaking both his and her juices into her thong as she sat at the control desk watching the cameras. *Ooooh*, she thought. *I love that man.*

Chapter 18

"Jacksonville, twenty-seven miles," Cashman read aloud as he and Red passed a sign at the Georgia, Florida State line.

He and Red had been spending a lot of time together, so when Cashman received a call from Kismet that morning, asking him to come to Jacksonville immediately, he brought Red along with him.

Before leaving Swainsboro, Cashman instructed Mike-Mike and Jay to break into both houses on Ben Street to see what they could find out concerning Kendra Vaugh's whereabouts.

Five minutes after entering Jacksonville City limits, Cashman and Red passed the Krystals off of US-1, close to Edgewood. The same place that Alex was arrested after making his final sell to Kendra Vaugh. Ironically, homicide detectives were out canvassing the parking lot for shell casings. The chalk out line of a body was evidence that a murder had occurred there.

Red viewed it as a bad omen and said a silent prayer.

After reaching Goldie's house, Cashman parked, then he and Red walked to the door. He rang the door bell. Moments later, Kismet answered and invited them in.

Kismet led Cashman and Red into the living room where she offered Red a seat. "Cashman, I need to talk to you in private," Kismet stated.

"Okay, let me introduce yall first. Red, this my brutha's ole lady, Kismet. Kismet, Red."

¢   ¢   ¢

Kismet led Cashman into the game room. She closed the door behind him after he entered.

"What's up," Cashman asked.

Kismet shook her head and sighed. "That damn Alex has ran his mouth to some nigga he in jail with and now the Feds using the nigga as a witness."

"Hold up! So you sayin' the Feds gonna use a jailhouse snitch?" Cashman asked, astonished.

Kismet shook her head. "Exactly."

Cashman looked puzzled. "How the fuck? Damn, the Feds petty like that?"

Kismet massaged her temples. "I talked to Alex's lawyer yesterday. He said the Feds will do just about anything to win a case."

"Fuck! If it ain't one thang it's anotha."

"Yeah, tell me about it," Kismet agreed. "I didn't want to bother your brutha with this mess since he's out of the country on business...so I called you."

Cashman began pacing the floor. "Nawl, you did the right thang," he commented.

He was already under a lot of pressure because of the Kendra Vaugh situation. Now he'd encountered a whole new problem on Alex's behalf. "Fuck! Fuck! Fuck!" Cashman barked. "Did the Feds let the nigga who jump on Alex's case out of jail?" he asked as he continued to pace.

"No, they transferred him to some other jail...Ba-Baker County Jail."

"Baker County!? Did you say Baker County?" Cashman asked excitedly.

"Yeah, Baker County," Kismet uttered, wondering why Cashman was so happy all of a sudden.

Cashman took his phone out of his pocket and punched in some numbers. "Kiesha...This Cashman. Yeah, J'ville Cashman...Damn, we'll talk 'bout that later...Ay, I'm finna shoot down there...Oh, gimme 'bout forty-five minutes...Aiight." Cashman ended his call with a smile.

"Boy, I know you ain't trying to get some ass in a time like this?" Kismet questioned.

"Hell nawl! That hoe work at Baker County Jail and I'ma use her to get to that new witness against Alex."

"Oh…"

Kismet pulled Alex's letter out of her pocket and handed it to Cashman. He read it and stored all of the pertinent information from it in his head. He gave the letter back to Kismet and they returned to the living room. Red stood up and grabbed her purse as soon as she saw Cashman.

"Nawl, chill baby," Cashman said as he motioned with his hands for Red to sit back down. "Red, somethin' important just came up. I'ma need you to stay here wit' Kismet while I go handle it."

"How long you gonna be gone?" Red asked.

"Shit, 'bout two days."

Red frowned. She didn't like the idea of being dropped off way out of town with a complete stranger. But it seemed she had no other choice. She reluctantly agreed to stay with a head nod.

Cashman dug into his pocket and extracted a large wad of one-hundred dollar bills. He counted off ten notes and handed them to Red.

"What's this for?" she asked.

"Oh, that's a lil' spendin' money in case yall go shoppin' or somethin'."

Red smiled, then gave Cashman a peck on his lips. "Thank you, daddy," she said, feeling a lot better about the situation.

Cashman returned her intimate gesture before heading for the door. "I'll call you later," he said before walking out of the house and jumping into his rental. He high-tailed it to Kiesha's house.

¢ ¢ ¢

Cashman arrived in Sanderson, Florida ten minutes earlier than he'd expected. He pulled into Kiesha's driveway, blew his horn, then hopped out of his rental. Kiesha saw him out of her front door before he could take two steps. "Heey baby," she squealed as she ran into Cashman's outstretched arms.

She gave him a kiss and a hug. Kiesha was older than Cashman. Ten years older to be exact. But that didn't change the way she felt about him. Besides, Cashman had her convinced that she was only five years his senior.

Although Kiesha hadn't seen Cashman in a while and they'd only had sex twice, Cashman made it his business to stay in touch with her. And she was happy with that. They'd originally met at Jim's Place – a Jacksonville night club. Cashman was there with Alex and Goldie, compliments of Tony Pascal Sr. – a local club promoter.

¢   ¢   ¢

It was a Wednesday night at Jim's Place. Happy hour was in full effect. All of the professional women and ballers were in the house. Kiesha was there with two of her friends when she caught Cashman's eye. He was staring at her from his stool by the bar. To Kiesha, the way Cashman was gawking her, seemed as if he was famished and she resembled a hearty meal. However, the real reason that Cashman was ogling her was because he could tell that she was an out of towner.

Kiesha and her friend's hair styles were nice, but played. They wore tight-ass body suits with their employee name tags too, while others had come to the club straight from work, so they wore their work clothes. Kiesha and her girls were another story. They had actually gotten off from work, went home and changed into the most provocative shit in their closet, then pinned their employee name tags back on and hit the club.

"Now how country is that?" Cashman thought. "Do these hoes want everybody to know they got a job? ...Fuck it," Cashman said to Alex before taking another sip of Henny.

A short while later, Cashman spotted Kiesha again. This time she was on the dance floor. Jim Beam's song "Love Handles" was blaring out of the club speakers and it seemed that Kiesha had the floor to herself. The nigga who she'd originally went to the dance floor with just stood back and watched her work all that ass in admiration. She had a forty-eight.

Kiesha loved all of the attention she was getting. When she caught Cashman watching her this time – with his mouth agape – she winked at him and licked her luscious lips seductively. Cashman felt his dick jump and waved her over to him. Kiesha gave him a one-million dollar smile and continued dancing.

Once Jim Beam's song was over, Kiesha walked to the bar where Cashman, Alex and Goldie were seated. She stopped and stood in front of Cashman. "What's up cutie?"

"Shiid, what's up witchu?" Cashman shot back, lusting at her voluptuous figure.

"Nothin', just here with my girls having a little fun after work, that's all."

Cashman was loving her accent. "Where you from? I can tell yo' ass ain't from 'round here."

"Sanderson," she answered. She noticed the perplexed expression on Cashman's face then added, "It's about forty-five minutes away from here...Boy, I'm tellin' you all my business. What's yo' name?" she quizzed after catching herself.

Cashman was so intrigued by Kiesha's accent that introducing himself had completely slipped his mind. "Cashman."

"Okay, I'm Kiesha."

They shook hands.

"Well, Kiesha, whatchu doin' after the club? It's a long drive back to Sanderson from here."

"Shiid, I don't give a damn! I'm going home. I got to work tomorrow."

Cashman knew from reading her name tag that she was a correctional officer at the Baker County Jail. "Shiid, I wanna go home witchu. Let me take you home."

"Go home with me?...You ain't even got a mustache yet. How old are you, anyway?" Kiesha asked, amused.

"Gurl, I'm twenty-one," Cashman lied.

Kiesha shifted her weight, placing her hands on her hips. "Boy! You still a baby. I'm twenty-seven years old. What I look like takin' a baby home with me?" she asked in her country twang.

Cashman smirked. "I may be young, but I got grown man pockets."

Kiesha's eyes bulged at the sight of the fat knot of bills Cashman flashed as he spoke. *Damn, this young nigga scrapped!* She thought.

Cashman, sensing that Kiesha was considering his proposal, grabbed her by the waist. He pulled her close. "What's it gonna be?"

Kiesha was bending to the pressure. And being the materialistic bitch that she was, she asked, "What kind of car you drive?"

When Cashman told her the white convertible 600 Benz out front, it was a wrap! No further game was needed.

"Umm, let me go holla at my girls. I-I'll be right back," she said before stalking off.

Cashman had rode to the club with Goldie, in Goldie's 600. But he knew that his big brother would let him borrow the car if he needed it. Besides, Alex had drove his Lex, so Goldie could just catch a ride home with him.

Cashman turned and tapped Goldie on his shoulder. "Bruh, I need to use the Benz until tomorrow. That hoe I was just talkin' to leavin' wit' me and I told her yo' six hundred was mine."

Goldie laughed. "Got-damn, ole flodgin' ass nigga. Man, you ain't gotta lie to them stank hoes. Anyway, I thought you wanted me to drop that work off for the trap I'm lettin' you open up on Ardella tomorrow?"

"Shiid, I still do! I'ma be back befo' twelve tomorrow afternoon," Cashman assured his brother.

Goldie handed him the keys to the Benz. He really didn't want to sell Cashman the work the following day. Goldie silently hoped that Cashman stayed gone all day the next day, so he'd have an excuse not to let him open up the trap on Ardella. Then he could work on stopping him from selling drugs altogether.

Kiesha returned to the bar with her two friends. "This is who I'm leaving with," she said, pointing at Cashman. "If I turn up dead he's my killer," she joked.

The two women assessed and sized Cashman up, then quickly focused their attention on Alex and Goldie.

Kiesha huffed. "Damn, yall some thirsty ass hoes. I'm trying to show yall who I'm leaving the club with and you two bitches are over here sweating his friends!" she scolded in a humorous manner.

"Oh, girl, I'm sorry. I'm Deya," one of Kiesha's friends stated while extending her hand to Cashman.

"Cashman," he replied loud enough for both women to hear

him over the music.

"I'm Vedra," Kiesha's other friend stated.

Cashman gave her a simple *what's up nod*, then introduced the ladies to his group. "This is my big brutha, Goldie," he said while touching Goldie's shoulder. "And this is our good friend Alex." He pointed out with his thumb.

Both groups exchanged pleasantries. Afterwards, Cashman dapped Goldie and told him he was about to bounce.

"Aiight lil bruh, be safe," Goldie said.

"I will," Cashman replied before throwing his arm around Kiesha's neck and walking her out to the parking lot.

When they reached the Benz, Cashman opened the passenger door for her, then hopped in the driver's seat.

"How we get to Sanderson?" Cashman asked after putting the key in the ignition.

"Take I-10 to 301," she instructed.

Cashman sped out of the club parking lot headed for the highway. When he jumped on I-10 he stomped the gas pedal. Kiesha was literally pinned to the seat as the Benz reached speeds of 150 mph and better. At first she wanted to tell Cashman to slow down, but she didn't want to come off as green. Then she started to get excited as she watched Cashman expertly handle the V12 engine.

Damn, this nigga crazy! He got this pussy wet already, Kiesha thought, spying Cashman out of her peripheral.

They made it to Kiesha's house in record breaking time. They weren't even in Kiesha's bedroom yet before they were both buck-naked. When they did make it there, Cashman pushed Kiesha on her bed, inserted his dick into her wet cum-box and fucked the cowboy shit out of her. He beat Kiesha's pussy so long and hard that her voice became hoarse from screaming.

"Please baby, let it breathe!" she cried out.

But Cashman kept pounding that ass. It wasn't until he'd bussed three nuts that he finally complied with her pleas. Later, when Cashman was sure that Kiesha was asleep, he stealthly crept up out of her house and headed back to Jacksonville. But not before leaving his cell number and five hundred dollars on her night stand.

Shit, I gotta get home, Cashman thought. *If I ain't there by the time Goldie decide to drop that work off, I can kiss my trap dreams goodbye.*

¢   ¢   ¢

After a long embrace, Cashman followed Kiesha into her house.

"What brings your ass to Sanderson, negro?" Kiesha asked in an accusatory tone.

They were seated in her living room. It still looked the same.

"Damn, a nigga can't just miss you and want to see you?" Cashman asked, feigning offense.

"Nigga please," Kiesha stated dismissively. "I haven't seen your ass since the last time you wanted some pussy...Nigga, something's up."

Kiesha may have come from a small town, but she wasn't slow.

Cashman grinned. "Aiight, you got me. I got a proposition for you."

"Look, I ain't trafficking no dope, I ain't lettin' you keep no dope in here, and I'm not fuckin' your friends," Kiesha said and folded her arms across her chest. With one eyebrow raised she stared at Cashman, insinuating that she was listening.

"Kiesha, I need yo' hel--" Cashman's phone vibrated, stopping him mid sentence. "Hold on," he said, holding up his pointer finger. "Let me take this call," Cashman said excusing himself. He walked into Kiesha's kitchen to talk in private.

"Hello?"

Just then, Cashman's line beeped. It was Kismet. He didn't answer her call.

"Yeah, Jay, what's good?"

"Man! You ain't gonna believe this shit. Dog, we went in one of them houses on Ben Street and found out some bullshit."

Cashman's heartbeat quickened. He knew something was terribly wrong. "Shit man, whatchall found out?" he eagerly asked. Jay exhaled loudly. "My nigga, that hoe you fuckin' wit' is poison."

"What hoe? Nigga, whatchu talkin' 'bout?"

"That bitch Red, man. Man, that hoe the po'lice. That's the bitch that set Alex up."

"What!? Man, stop playin'," Cashman said, hoping Jay didn't hear his voice crack.

"My nigga, I shit you not...Man, we ain't even have to break in the other house, 'cause as soon as we went in the first one, the first thang I saw was a big ass oil paintin' of Red and some dude. So now I'm fucked up. I can't believe this shit. I'm thankin' maybe the hoe on the paintin' ain't Red. So I look 'round some mo' and find a ole high school ID. I look at the picture and now I'm sho' it's Red on it. Then I read the name, Kendra Cole. By this time Mike-Mike done found the hoe marriage certificate, letters from her husband in prison, mentionin' Alex in 'em. Shit, he even found a subpoena for her to appear in Federal court in the Middle District of Florida on Alex's trial date."

To say that Cashman was crushed was the understatement of the century. "Got-damn, man," he mumbled almost inaudibly.

"Ay, you aiight?" Jay asked, concerned for his friend.

"Ye-yeah," Cashman stuttered.

"Good, 'cause we gotta plug this hole, ASAP!...Man, ain't no tellin' what that hoe done told the Feds 'bout us!"

Cashman agreed. "Dog, I need you and Mike-Mike back in Jacksonville today. Hit me as soon as yall get in town."

"Aiight," Jay said, hanging up.

Cashman returned Kismet's call.

"Hello?" she answered the phone.

"Ay Kismet, what's goin' on?" Cashman dead panned.

"Boy, what's wrong with you?" Kismet asked, concerned. She could hear the despair in Cashman's voice.

"Oh, I-I'll tell you in a minute. What up though?"

"Well, I just talked to Al—"

Cashman cut her off. "Is Red 'round you?"

"Hell no! I don't talk around people I don't know."

"Oh, okay...whatchu was sayin'?"

"I was saying that I talked to Alex's lawyer today and he told me that the Feds are seeking a superceding indictment against him for tax evasion tomorrow. He said that the indictment will be based partly on Sammie Williams' testimony to the Grand Jury."

"Wha-what the hell kinda indictment they tryna get again?" Cashman asked. To him that shit sounded like a super indictment that a nigga couldn't beat.

Kismet answered his question. "A superceding indictment is an add on to an indictment that a person already has. It's another count with more penalties."

"Oh," Cashman said feeling a little bit better. "So that nigga Sammie Williams gotta go to court in Jacksonville tomorrow?"

"Yeah, that's where they're having the Grand Jury at," Kismet answered then continued. "It's suppose to be secret, but Marquis found out about it."

A mischievous smile spread across Cashman's face as he began to entertain murderous thoughts. He'd developed a plan just that quick.

"Cashman!" Kismet called into the phone for the third time.

"...huh? Oh, my bad," Cashman replied, coming out of his thoughts.

"What had you so down earlier? You sounded like you lost your best friend."

Cashman took a deep breath. "Man, this shit crazy."

"What Cashman? Tell me."

"Man...man, Red a snitch."

"What!? Red? You talking about your girlfriend, Red? The same bitch you left over here?" Kismet asked incredulously.

"Yeah, that one who set our boy up."

"Well, why in the hell is she at my house, then? And why are you still with her? Do your brother know about this?!"

"Nawl, Kismet. I just found this shit out right befo' I called you."

"Oh, okay. Well, what are you going to do?"

"Shit, it's only one thang I can do," Cashman answered sadly.

"Well don't worry about it, I'll handle it."

"What?" Cashman barked, confused.

"I said I'll handle it!" Kismet barked back.

"But Kis—"

"Look nigga, you handle that other thing and let me handle this!"

Kismet hung up in Cashman's face. Cashman stood staring at the phone in his hand, wondering what had come over her.

What the fuck she mean she gonna handle it? He pondered.

When Cashman walked back into Kiesha's living room she was still seated in the same spot he'd left her.

"Who was that, yo' bitch," Kiesha snapped.

Cashman ignored her question. "Like I was 'bout to say, I gotta proposition for you."

"What kinda proposition? I ain't wit' no bullshit, Cashman."

"Bit— ...it ain't no bullshit. It's simple for real. I just need some information. I'ma pay you ten grand for it."

"Ten grand?!" she bellowed. *Damn, I wonder what I could know worth ten G's?* she pondered. "Shiid, nigga, whatchu need to know?" she asked impatiently.

"Aiight, it's a inmate at the jail you work at finna testify against a friend of mine in court tomorrow. I need to know how and when he'll leave from there."

"Shit, that's all? 'Cause I can get his momma address if you need it."

Cashman laughed. "Yeah, that's it."

"What's the inmate's name?"

"Sammie, Sammie Williams."

"Oh, hell nawl! I know him. He just got there right?"

"Yeah, I thank so."

"Damn, that nigga snitchin'?" Kiesha asked, wondering how a thugged out looking nigga like Sammie could be a snitch.

"Look Kiesha, can you find out what I need to know or what?"

"Yeah, I gotcha, damn. Let me run up here to the jail and find out tomorrow's movements. I'll be right back. You just stay here and make *yo'self* at home."

¢ ¢ ¢

Kiesha entered Baker County Jail under the guise of being in the area, and deciding to drop in to check her schedule for the week. She knew that she couldn't ask any of her coworkers for any information pertaining to Sammie. If she did and something happened her name would be the first one implicated. So, with that fact in mind, Kiesha snuck into the captain's office looking for the following day's intinerary.

Snooping around Captain Bullard's office, Kiesha found out what she was searching for in one of the file cabinets. She scanned over it.

Sammie Williams...Pick up for court 7:30 a.m....U.S. Marshals Service.

Kiesha quickly and quietly exited the office.

¢   ¢   ¢

"There they go right there!" Jay said, pointing at the Crown Vic driven by the block-head U.S. Marshal. It had pulled out of the sally port of the Baker County Jail, headed to the courthouse.

It was 7:45 a.m. and the marshals were right on time. Jay, Mike-Mike and Cashman were parked across the street from the jail in a stolen Astro van – watching! Jay and Mike-Mike each had an AK-47 in their laps as they sat in the back of the van.

"Look at that bitch-ass-nigga...That nigga look like he ready to tell somethin'," Mike-Mike stated. He was referring to Sammie, who sat in the back seat of the Crown Vic.

The two U.S. Marshals sat up front.

Kiesha had told Cashman what time the marshals would be to the jail to pick Sammie up. She had also told him which route the marshals usually took to transport inmates to the Federal Courthouse in Jacksonville. She gave Cashman the information before he stabbed her nine times and left her body on her kitchen floor. Cashman set her house on fire so there would be no evidence of his ever being there.

"Okay, here we go," Cashman said as he pulled out into traffic behind the Crown Vic. He waited for a few cars to get directly behind the marshals before he began to follow them.

Now, trailing by three cars, Cashman spied the Crown Vic make a left turn onto 301.

Muthafuckas fallin' right into the trap, he thought to himself as he followed the marshals, trailing them at a short distance out of the Macclenny City limits.

"Yall niggas get ready," Cashman commanded.

Both Jay and Mike-Mike cocked their AK's. "Clak! Clak! Clak! Clak!"

The plan was simple enough. They were to follow the marshals out of the city limits then pull up along side of them and open fire. Since most of 301 was rural farmland and it was a two way road most of the route, all they needed was for no other cars to be insight. Then they could handle their business. The fact that it was early in the morning was a big plus since traffic was so sparse at that time of day.

Fifteen minutes later, the Astro van was directly behind the Crown Vic. The last car between them had just turned off. Cashman glanced into the rearview and saw that no other cars were behind them. They were about two miles away from the getaway car they'd stashed earlier. Nothing but farmland surrounded them on both sides of the road.

"This is the perfect time," Cashman said as he made his move.

Stomping on the gas, the Astro van jerked forward. Once the van was a car length away from the marshal's bumper, Cashman swiched lanes as if they were about to pass the Crown Vic. The clueless marshal in the driver's seat looked over just in time to see the van's side door slide back, exposing two menacing black teens aiming AK's at him.

"Mother of God," were the last words the block-head U.S. Marshal uttered before the young niggas opened fire.

Mr. Block-head U.S. Marshal shook like he was in the electric chair as the bullets tore through his flesh. He took ten rounds instantly. The passenger took three to the chest and one in his side. Sammie got hit five times in his upper body as Jay spread the wealth to the back seat of the out of control vehicle.

The Crown Vic veered off of the road and crashed into a tree. It exploded on contact. After witnessing the Crown Vic burst into flames in the rearview, Cashman stopped the van and backed up to the burning vehicle. Once he was close enough to it, Jay jumped out to make sure there were no survivors. There were none. However, Jay let off twenty more rounds into the burning, twisted metal to make sure.

"Let's go!" Cashman yelled.

Jay jumped back into the van. Cashman drove about two miles down 301 then turned off onto a dirt road. He stopped next to an 87 Chevy Caprice. He, Jay and Mike-Mike hopped out of the van and doused it with gasoline. They set it ablaze. Once the van started to incinerate, Jay and Mike-Mike threw their AKs into the flaming Astro van. With that taken care of, they all jumped in the Chevy and shagged-ass back to Jacksonville.

Chapter 19

"Order!" the authoritative voice resonated throughout the conference room of the U.S. Attorney's Office.

A meeting was being held between the top representatives of various law enforcement agencies. The subject matter was the formation of a joint task force.

"I need for you all to be quiet and have a seat…We really need to come up with a reprisal in response to the tragic event that occurred today. Please!" Paul Barker bellowed.

He was the U.S. Attorney for the entire Middle Disrict of Florida. He'd just left a press conference with the mayor, in which he'd been unable to give him any anwers or suspects to name. He was pissed!

There was still a small amount of chatter inside of the conference room so the U.S. Attorney added, "Please give me your attention!"

Reluctantly, everyone in the room got quiet and took a seat.

"Thank you ladies and gentleman," replied Paul Barker after everybody finally complied with his request. "As you all know, two U.S. Marshals and a Federal informant were gunned down earlier today in cold blood. It is my understanding that they were on their way to a Grand Jury in which the informant was to give testimony against a man by the name of …" He paused as he searched through his notes. "Alex Brooks," he said after he'd found the name. "…we have reason to believe that Mr. Brooks is somehow involved in this horrific crime. So, without further ado, I'm going to introduce you all to Assistant U.S. Attorney David Miller. He's prosecuting Mr. Brooks on a drug case and has more indepth knowledge of what we're up against."

David Miller stood and shook Paul Barker's hand. "Thank you," he replied to Paul Barker and to the various representatives of the other law enforcement agencies.

The conference room was packed. All sixteen chairs around the conference table were occupied. There was also law enforcement personnel standing around the room.

David Miller cleared his throat. "As you all have heard, my name is AUSA David Miller and I'm prosecuting Mr. Brooks on a distribution case...First, I want to say this...I understand how you all must feel about the loss of two good men in the line of duty. Trust me, we are going to make those responsible pay for their deaths!"

Everyone in the room started clapping. David Miller raised his hands after a few moments to silence the room. Once the room was quiet again, Chief U.S. Marshal, Dan Baily, raised his hand.

"Yes, Mr. Baily," David Miller replied after reading Dan Baily's name tag.

"Where is this Alex Brooks, slime-ball, now?"

David Miller glanced around the room. "Right now he is, and has been for some time now, detained at the Federal Detention Center in Folkston, GA. I ma—"

"Let me get this straight," said Hank Fields from the Florida Department of Law Enforcement (FDLE), cutting in. "This guy is in jail and has the juice to have two U.S. Marshals and a Federal informant hit from his cell?"

The Assistant U.S. Attorney smiled. "Ladies and gentleman, we're dealing with a drug organization unlike any we've ever seen the likes of before in this state."

He walked around the conference table to the slide projector. On cue, Special Agent Ricks turned off the lights. Jesus Diez, standing impeccably dressed on the deck of a 200 ft yacht appeared on the projector screen.

"This is Jesus Diez," David Miller said while pointing at the photo of the Mexican drug lord. "He's very rich, very powerful, and very dangerous. Mr. Diez imports tons of cocaine into this country annually and is this guy's supplier..."

David Miller clicked the remote control in his hand and the screen changed. A picture of John Boy standing in the front of a coffee shop talking on his cell phone replaced Jesus' photo.

"This is John Watts, AKA John Boy, AKA Johnny Ghost,"

David Miller stated. "He's a native of Jacksonville, but has since relocated. Before he moved away however, he was the target of a DEA investigation. But the investigation unit lost track of him after he moved out of Florida. Earlier this year he resurfaced in an investigation being conducted by the DEA in the Washington, DC area. Now, I've spoken to the Special Agent in charge of the DC office and he informed me that Mr. Watts is distributing hundreds of kilos per month in the tri-state area. This guy is very smart as well as dangerous."

The screen changed again and a picture of Goldie hopping out of a Porsche 911 appeared.

"Now this guy," David Miller said while pointing at the photo of Goldie, "is Lucifer in the flesh. I'm sure you local guys have heard of Sultan Jackson, AKA Goldie!"

Heads were nodding all around the conference room.

David Miller continued. "This guy is so dangerous the DEA up in DC wants to find a way to band him from ever setting foot in their town again! They said that he visited Mr. Watts up in DC a few months back and stayed for about three months. They said before he left there were about ninety drug related murders commited. We've linked Mr. Jackson to at least ten murders here in Jacksonville. This guy's an 18 year old lost soul that puts no value on life, period! For you guys who aren't local, Mr. Jackson is the largest drug dealer in northeast Florida. Not only does he supply 50% of the cocaine entering into Jacksonville and her surrounding counties, he distributes to other sourthern cities outside of Florida as well."

"Excuse me," interrupted Adam Bowen, special agent in charge of the Tampa branch I.R.S. "Did you say that Sultan Jackson was only eighteen?"

"Yes, that's correct," answered David Miller.

"Well tell me something," Adam Bowen stated. "How does an eighteen year old kid control 50% of the drug market in a city the size of Jacksonville?"

David Miller smirked. "Our psychologist said that it's likely that Mr. Jackson has a very high I.Q. He said it's somewhere in the 150 range."

"Shit! The fucking kid's a got-damn genius!" Adam Brown

exclaimed.

"Yes, a mind is a terrible thing to waste," snorted David Miller before clicking the remote again, causing the picture on the screen to change.

Alex's picture replaced Goldie's.

"Finally, we come to Alex Brooks," Assistant U.S. Attorney David Miller said, pointing to the picture of Alex walking out of a night club with two half naked blonds. "Mr. Brooks was detained without bail on a charge of distribution of 2,000 grams of cocaine base. He's a few years older than Mr. Jackson, yet they are very close friends. We've tried to get Mr. Brooks to cooperate with us, but he has elected to go to trial instead. His trial date is two months from now..."

David Miller walked back in front of the room. "As you all can see, this organization could indeed carry out an atrocity like the one that transpired today and think nothing of it. That's why I'm going to need all of your help to bring them down. Our joint efforts will avenge our fallen friends!"

The whole room erupted in applause.

David Miller looked around the conference room at all of the law enforcement personnel and noticed that agent Ricks was no longer present. "Thank you," he replied once more before taking a seat.

U.S. Attorney Paul Barker stood up. "I want you to all participate in a joint task force I'm forming for an operation dubbed White Gold, we wi—"

Assistant U.S. Attorney David Miller tuned Paul Barker out after seeing Agent Ricks come back into the conference room looking distraught. The agent hurriedly approached him.

"We have a problem," Agent Ricks whispered into David Miller's ear. The Assistant U.S. Attorney quickly stood and led Agent Ricks into the hallway. "What's the problem?" he asked anxiously.

"We can't seem to reach Kendra Vaugh. I've been calling her since we found out about the marshals and Sammie's murder and she hasn't called back. I even sent a pair of agents to her house. They said that they knocked on her door and when no one answered they went around back." Agent Ricks dropped his head.

"David, the agents said that someone had forcefully entered Kendra's house and ramshacked it."

David Miller felt like vomiting. "Shit! Shit! Shit!" he spat before storming back into the conference room.

"Are you alright?" Paul Barker asked after he watched David Miller storm in, hastily retrieve his briefcase, then head back for the door.

David Miller froze in his tracks at the door. He turned on his heels and addressed the room full of law enforcement personal. "I-I'm sorry, you will all have to excuse me. The only witness I have left against Alex Brooks in missing."

A chorus of murmurs could be heard around the room.

"That's terrible," Paul Barker replied. "Please, you're excused."

"Thank you," David Miller said before stalking out of the conference.

Chapter 20

"Nigga! Did you see how I made that cracka head explode?!" Jay excitedly asked.

He, Cashman and Mike-Mike were chilling in Cashman's bedroom.

"Nigga, that was my work! I'm the one who knocked the taco meat outta that cracka head!" Mike-Mike snapped.

Jay's face scrunched up. "Nigga, whatchu mean yo' work?! Man, I was the first nigga to pull the trigga, ole scead-ass-nigga!"

Cashman threw his hands up. "Man, will yall two niggas shut-the-fuck up! Whatcha want my momma to hear yall?"

"Nawl, man, my bad, dog," Jay said apologetically.

"Yeah, my bad," Mike-Mike added. "This nigga just had me hot, talkin' 'bout he done checked the cracka."

"I did, nigga!" Jay retorted.

Cashman's phone rang, silencing the room. He glanced at the number. It was Kismet. "What's up, sis?" he asked.

"I need you to come take out the trash for me. It's too heavy."

"The trash? Oh…okay," he said, realizing what she meant by her request.

Cashman fell silent.

"Cashman!" Kismet called into the phone.

"Huh?... oh yeah," he muttered, snapping out of his remembrance of Red. "I'ma send Jay and Mike-Mike to handle that."

"Okay, tell them to hurry up, alright. And Cashman?"

"Yeah," he answered.

"She chose this for herself."

Cashman hung the phone up in Kismet's face. "Man, I need yall two to go over to Goldie's house."

"For what?" Jay asked.

"Kismet said she done took care of the Red situation," Cashman said, voice cracking at the end.

"What?! Nigga, I thought you was bullshittin' 'bout Kismet takin' care of Red," Mike-Mike said.

Cashman's facial expression sent a signal to both teens that he no longer wanted to discuss the issue any further.

"Aiight, dog, don't worry. We'll take care of it," Jay affirmed.

Jay and Mike-Mike were about to walk out of Cashman's room when he stopped them.

"Make sho' yall dump her body somewhere it can easily be found. She at least deserves a decent burial," Cashman solemnly admonished.

Jay and Mike-Mike agreed with head nods.

¢ ¢ ¢

Kismet and Red had stayed up late the night before drinking champagne and engaging in girl talk. Naturally, the more they talked, the more Kismet dreaded the fact that she'd commited herself to killing Red. However, four glasses of White Zinfadel later – Red's being spiked with Ambien – Kismet started to feel her inhibition abate. Red was on her fifth glass and could barely keep her eyes open. The alcohol and powerful sleeping pills had taken effect.

"Gurl I'm so damn sleepy," Red slurred.

"Let me help you to bed," Kismet volunteered.

Red thanked her new friend. She knew that she could never have made it to the guest bedroom on her own. As soon as they reached the bed, Red collapsed face first onto its softness. Seconds later, she fell into a coma-like slumber. She couldn't hear nor feel a thing. Even during her transition into eternal life…

¢ ¢ ¢

When Jay and Mike-Mike arrived at Goldie's house, Kismet let them in. She led them to the guest bedroom. There, Red's corpse lay bound by its ankles and wrists to the bed. Once Red had fallen to sleep the night before, Kismet tied her to the bed using head wraps. She didn't want to make a mess, so she placed a small trash bag over Red's head and suffocated her to death.

"Damn, she bluer than e-muthafucka!" Jay spat, referring to Red's skin complexion.

"Could yall just hurry up and get her out of here!" Kismet barked.

Jay and Mike-Mike took the plastic bag off of Red's face. They untied her from the bed and rolled her body up into a sheet. Mike-Mike asked Kismet for the keys to Goldie's six hundred. He had to move it out of the garage to make room for the Caprice. There was no way they could carry a body wrapped in a sheet out of Goldie's house in broad day light.

Mike-Mike moved the six hundred out of the garage and parked it in front of Goldie's house. He backed the Caprice up into its place. When Mike-Mike got back inside the house, Jay was coming down the hallway carrying Red's corpse on his shoulder.

"Damn, my nigga! Why don't you take yo' finger out yo' ass and help a nigga wit' this body!" Jay snapped before dropping the corpse to the floor.

Red's body landed with a thud. Mike-Mike grabbed her ankles and Jay seized her under her armpits. Mike-Mike could tell that rigor mortis had started to set in because Red's legs were stiff. They carried the corpse through the kitchen, into the garage, placing it into the Caprice's open trunk. Jay went back into the house and told Kismet to close the garage because they were about to leave. He then jumped back into the Caprice and drove off with Mike-Mike to dispose of Red's body.

Chapter 21

"Mr. Brooks, I have some good news for you," Alex's lawyer, Marquis Wimberly stated after Alex took a seat across from him in the Attorney/Client conference room. "I'm filing a motion to dismiss your case after I leave here today. The government no longer has any witnesses to testify against you."

Alex was puzzled. "Mr. Wimberly, you must got my case mixed up wit' somebody elses. I got two witnesses against me. I done seen the news reports about Sammie and them two marshals gettin' murked, but what about Kendra Vaugh? She still a witness, ain't she?"

The lawyer looked baffled. "Mr. Brooks, you mean to tell me that you don't know?"

"Know what?"

"Mrs. Vaugh, the other witness against you was found dead on the east side last night. Someone made an anonymous call to police and gave the address to an abandoned house where a female body could be found."

"Man, is you sho'?"

"Positive," the lawyer answered. *Damn, I wonder who else Mrs. Vaugh could've crossed? I just knew that Alex was behind her death,* Mr. Wimberly thought to himself.

The lawyer stood up and placed the motion to dismiss and a few other papers back into his briefcase. "Well, Mr. Brooks, I'm about to head on down to District Court and file this motion. Without any witnesses, the government will have no other alternative but to drop both counts in your indictment. You should be out of here within a week."

"Bet that up!" Alex smiled before standing to shake his lawyer's hand.

"You're welcome," the lawyer retorted.

Alex was about to walk out of the Attorney/Client conference room when he heard Marquis Wimberly call his name. He turned and faced the lawyer.

"For god's sake, Alex, stay out of trouble," the lawyer stated to the young relict.

Alex smiled, then walked out of the door.

When Alex got back to his pod he went straight to his bunk. He had to get his thoughts together. "How the fuck did Kendra Vaugh end up dead, in Jacksonville?" he wondered. *Did Goldie 'nem get her?* "And this bitch Cocena talkin' 'bout she pregnant and shit! She only two weeks late…how the fuck she just know her baby mine! Damn, am I the only nigga hittin' that pussy? Shit, I must be the only fool hittin' raw. Fuck!"

Alex's thoughts shifted to the shit he was going to do to Meka when he got out. A devilish grin played across his face. If Meka knew what Alex had in store for her she'd leave the country. She had died a thousand times in Alex's mind. Now she was about to finally feel some backlash from her unchastened behavior.

There were times during Alex's brief incarceration that he thought he'd never be able to get revenge on Meka. Times when the darkness obscured the light at the end of the tunnel. When it seemed that the got-damn deck was stacked too fucking high! Those days were over. He wasn't about to go to prison for god-knows-how-long. He was going to be released as soon as his motion to dismiss was granted.

Shit, I should go call that dirty bitch right nye'. Yeah, that's what I'ma do. I gotta let that hoe know I'm 'bout to get out. I don't wanna get out unannounced and surprise the hoe and catch her wit' a nigga. Hell nawl! Shit will fuck my whole plan up, Alex thought to himself.

Alex hopped off his bunk and called Meka. After she accepted the call he told her that he'd be getting out within a week.

"For real, baby?! I knew you was gonna beat that shit!" Meka exclaimed.

But her tone betrayed her words. Meka had fucked up and counted Alex out. Listening to her slut-friends, she had fucked around on a good nigga.

"Gurl, do you, 'cause that nigga gonna be gone for a long time!" Meka's so-called friends would say. "Chile boo, them Feds got a 97% conviction rate. That poe-ass-nigga ain't gonna beat them people."

What Meka's ass should have considered was the other 3%...but she didn't. Alex and Meka began to talk about all the things they were going to do once Alex was released. The time flew by and before they knew it their fifteen minute call was over...

Alex hung up the phone. He was about to go back to his bunk when he saw Cocena. She was staring at him through the plexiglass on the pod's door as she stood in the hallway. She was waiting on the control booth to pop the door to the pod across from Alex's. The two locked eyes.

"I'll see you later," Cocena silently mouth right before the door she was waiting for opened.

That night Alex tossed and turned in his bunk. Sweat was pouring down his face profusely. "You like to fuck, huh bitch?! You like this big dick, huh bitch?! I'm gonna fuck you like you fucked me!" Alex spat to Meka. She was sprawled out on her stomach while he stood on her back. He was viciously stabbing her in the rectum with a broom stick.

"Alex!" a soft voice called while shaking him.

He quickly sat up in his bunk. He looked delirious. "Oh, shit. It was just a dream," he whispered, focusing in on his surroundings.

"Damn, baby. Who was you dreaming about?" Cocena asked. She was ogling Alex's hard dick as it pressed against his blanket.

Alex ignored her question. "Baby, I got some good news," he said after regaining his bearings. "Them crackas gotta let me go. I'll be out this bitch in less than a week."

"For real? That's wonderful," Cocena said sarcastically.

"Damn, what's wrong witchu?"

"Nothing," Cocena pouted.

"C'mon, Cocena. Tell a nigga what's on yo' mind."

"Alex, I've taken two pregnancy tests and they both came back positive."

"And?"

"What the hell do you mean, 'and'?"

"Nawl, I'm just sayin'…Gurl, you know if the baby mine I'ma take care of it."

"I've already told you it's yours. Before you, I hadn't had sex in three months. You're the only person I've been having sex with."

"Okay, the baby mine. That still ain't good enough reason to look all down and heartbroken. Gurl I'm gettin' out. You should be happy…what? You want a nigga to stay locked up forever?"

Cocena didn't answer because that's exactly what she wanted. She wanted to be the only woman Alex sexed.

"Gurl! You crazy!" Alex exclaimed. Cocena's silence confirmed his suspicion.

"Alex, be real…You know damn well that when you touch those streets you're going to forget about me."

"No, I won't. I was gonna get you a apartment in Jacksonville since you pregnant and shit."

"Well, what about your girl? I'm sure she ain't going to approve of none of this."

Cocena didn't know about Meka's betrayal. And Alex kept it that way.

Alex grabbed Cocena's hand, placing it on his hard cock. "Don't worry 'bout her, worry about yo' self."

Cocena sighed. "Okay, daddy."

Alex smiled. He loved it when she called him daddy. He pulled back his blanket, exposing his enlarged member.

"Damn, daddy. I've been craving your cum all day," Cocena said prior to enthusiastically inserting Alex's fuck-pole into her wonderous mouth.

Alex lay back on his bunk, watching with great pleasure as Cocena's head bobbed. "Shit, I need this dick suckin' bitch close by. She definitely gettin' relocated to Jacksonville," he contemplated internally.

Chapter 22

Goldie, John Boy, Lonita and Jesus rode quietly on a four seater golf cart. They were enroute to the landing strip on Jesus' ranch. Hours earlier, the Boeing Business Jets had arrived and were promptly loaded with cocaine.

Jesus had it all figured out. Once Goldie's jet left his ranch in Mexico, it would make a pit stop at a secret landing strip outside of Gulf Port, Mississippi. There, the cocaine would be unloaded off of the jet, then reloaded into two separate tractor trailers. The tractor trailers would be driven to a secret warehouse located in Jacksonville, FL. Once in Jacksonville, the cocaine would be unloaded then reloaded into Uhauls to be placed in mini storages throughout the city.

John Boy's would do something similar. His jet would make its pit stop at a secret landing strip on the outskirts of Dayton, Ohio. The cocaine on board would be unloaded then reloaded into two separate tractor trailers. The tractor trailers would then transport the cocaine to another secret warehouse located in Detroit, Michigan. There, it would once again be unloaded then reloaded into Uhauls to be placed into mini storages throughout the city.

Jesus had financed secret airplane landing strips and warehouses all over the United States. There was practically no place in the country that his illicit product couldn't reach.

After saying his goodbyes to everyone, John Boy boarded his jet first since it was in front of Goldie's on the landing strip. Goldie gave his friend a mock salute as the door to his Business Jet closed. Moments later, John Boy was airborne, on his way to Ohio, then back to Michigan.

Goldie walked to his jet, followed by Lonita and Jesus. Before boarding he turned to Jesus and shook his hand. "It's been a pleasure doin' bidness witcha."

"Likewise," Jesus retorted.

Goldie faced Lonita. "Take care of the ole man, will ya," he joked before giving her a hug.

"I'll call you tonight," Lonita whispered into his ear during their quick embrace.

Goldie gave a slight head nod to let her know that he'd heard her. He then boarded his jet.

Once he was seated, the co-pilot approached, handing him an envelope. He then returned to the cockpit without so much as uttering a word. Goldie opened the envelope just as the jet sped up the runway.

Dear Goldie,

Hey baby! I want you to know that I had a great time with you. I put an extra one hundred kilos on board your jet. It's from my private stash. I want $8,000 a piece for them. Take as long as you need to pay me back. But be sure to pay my father back promptly. Well, I hope you have a safe trip, baby. Please stay in touch...

Your lover, Lonita Diez

Shit! How could I not stay in touch witchu? Goldie said to himself before kicking back. He had a smile on his face.

The pit stop at the landing strip outside of Gulf Port was brief. The ten man crew Jesus had on standby unloaded the cocaine in no time. After the last kilo was removed, the jet was back in the air once again, enroute to Jacksonville. About an hour later it touched down at Jacksonville International Airport. There was a short taxi to a private jet hangar, where Kismet and Cashman waited in Goldie's white 600. Goldie had called Kismet from the satellite phone on board the jet after taking off from the landing strip outside of Gulf Port. He told her what time he'd be landing in Jacksonville and for her to meet him at hangar 17.

As soon as Goldie reached the bottom of the airstair Kismet rushed into his arms. He had to fight the urge to pick her up. Kismet was now five months pregnant and her stomach had grown since he'd last seen her. Once Kismet released Goldie from her embrace, Cashman gave him a manly hug.

"What's up, lil' bruh?" Goldie said.

"Shit."

"Good. Help me get my luggage."

The two brothers loaded the luggage into the trunk of the Benz. Kismet sat patiently in the driver's seat waiting on them to finish.

"Ay bruh, did you get to take care of that bitch Kendra Vaugh?" Goldie asked as soon as they got into the car.

"Yeah. Kendra got handled."

"Good work, lil' bruh. Alex should be straight nye'. Them crackas ain't got a witness no mo'."

Cashman sighed. He didn't want to take credit for something he didn't do. Although he didn't lie to Goldie, his vague answer had insinuated that he'd killed Kendra Vaugh. "Yeah, big bruh. That nigga gonna be straight. But...ummm...I ain't really handle the Kendra Vaugh situation."

"What? Nigga, whatchu mean you ain't handle Kendra Vaugh? You just said you did!"

"Nawl..I-I mean, she did get handled. I just ain't personally take care of her."

"Man, cut the bullshit and let me know what the fuck you talkin' 'bout."

"Bruh, Kismet killed that bitch."

Kismet quickly cut her eye at Goldie as she drove.

"Kismet did what?!" Goldie bellowed, facing Kismet.

"Baby, don't be mad at me. I really didn't have a choice," Kismet nervously explained.

"Noooo, Kismet! Baby, what did you do?" Goldie asked, voice filled with sorrow.

"I'm sorry, Goldie."

Cashman breathed loudly. "Look bruh, it ain't her fault," Cashman said before telling Goldie everything that had happened in his absence. He told him how he, Mike-Mike and Jay had killed Sammie Williams and the two U.S. Marshals after Sammie had become a witness against Alex. He told him how he'd met Kendra Vaugh by chance at a night club in Swainsboro, GA and had fallen in love. He didn't leave out a thing.

Goldie sat reserved ensuing Cashman's summation while

mulling things over. "Damn, I can't believe Kismet had it in her to murk a bitch. Shit, I know she still stressin' over her daddy gettin' killed and her momma been on her ass about bein' pregnant, but damn...I wonder how she killed the bitch anyway?" Goldie glanced at Cashman's reflection in the rearview mirror. *And this nigga,* Goldie thought while shaking his head, *and his trigga happy friends is off the meat rack. I mean, damn. Did they have to kill the two U.S. Marshals too? Shit!...oh well, ain't nothin' a nigga can do 'bout it nye'*, Goldie concluded, ending his internal debate. "Shit, I can't be mad at yall. Yall did whatchall thought yall had to do," he said out loud, breaking the solemn silence in the car. "So when that nigga Alex gettin' out?" Goldie quizzed.

"I don't know exactly. His lawyer said any day now," Kismet replied.

"That's good, 'cause a nigga finna step they game up out here," Goldie declared, rubbing his hands together.

Kismet parked the car in Goldie's driveway. She then went into the house while Cashman and Goldie stayed behind to retrieve Goldie's luggage.

"Bruh, you say you gonna step yo' game up, huh?"

"Am I?!...Shiid, I got damn near a ton of raw on the way to the city that I got for the low, low. Cashman, big bruh 'bout to do it real big. That lil' shit that Seph and Chino runnin' through here, bruh, I'ma show them they ain't the only muthafuckas that's *street raised.*"

During Goldie's month long trip to Mexico, all he did was fuck Lonita – on the down low – and plot. He had devised a plan to leave the drug business and go completely legit within five years. Goldie knew that he couldn't deal drugs forever. And on the level he was playing he'd get a life sentence for sure if he got jammed up by the Feds. He wanted to be a father to his son. And to do that he had to be alive – and free.

Cashman and Goldie took the luggage inside. Once there, Cashman asked to borrow Goldie's car so he could go handle some business.

"Go head," Goldie said, tossing him the keys off of the kitchen table.

Cashman caught the keys and left.

¢ ¢ ¢

"Kismet, what made you, of all people, kill that girl?" Goldie asked as he lay naked next to her in bed. They'd just finished making love thirty minutes prior.

"I don't know. I really didn't know what else to do. You were out of the country. Cashman was trying to handle the other thing. Alex's trial date was coming up...Goldie, I know how close you and Alex are. I guess....I did it for you," Kismet stuttered sincerely.

Goldie smiled. "Thank you, sweetheart. And trust me, I ain't mad atchu. I guess what I really wanna know is how you feelin'? You know, after killin' somebody..."

Kismet sat up. "To be honest, I don't feel anything. Kendra couldn't put up a fight. And I never saw her face as she died."

Goldie wanted to know how Kismet had killed Kendra, but he thought it would be in bad taste to ask her. The two young lovers didn't speak while they both pondered the conversation they'd just had. Moments later, Kismet laid her head on Goldie's chest. It wasn't long after that they were sound asleep.

Goldie's phone rung as it lay on the night stand, waking him up. He looked at the screen. The area code displayed was on it. Goldie smiled. The code meant that all of his cocaine had arrived and was safely tucked away in mini storages throughout the city. Since it was 7:30 a.m. he went ahead and got up. He had a very busy day in front of him.

Goldie's first order of business was the purchase of three vehicles: two Lamborghinis and a Dodge Viper. He got dressed, stuffed $1,450,000 from his stash into a duffle bag, then drove to World Imports. Jerry hooked the paper work up in less than an hour. Goldie instructed him to have the Viper delivered to his mom's house, and the two Lambos to his.

Next Goldie went to meet up with Katrina Freeman and Kimberly Dawson of K&K Real Estate. After seeing the castle that Jesus called a home, he wanted to move. Jesus' house made Goldie's look like a hovel. Goldie decided to give Cashman his old home and he and Kismet would move into a new one.

When Goldie left K&K Real Estate he'd spent $1,000,000 as a down payment on a $10,000,0000 59 ft beach mansion. The home was purchased through a holdings company that Katrina Freeman – one half of K&K Real Estate – had set up for him. Like Jesus Diez, Goldie would use the corporate shield to his advantage.

Goldie arrived at Curly's Jewelry twenty minutes later. He was looking for an engagement ring for Kismet. Goldie entered the establishment and was met at the center display case by none other than Curly himself.

"Hey, what's up, Goldie?" Curly exclaimed with a friendly smile. He knew that whenever Goldie patronized his business that a lot of money was going to be spent.

"You, my man," Goldie shot back.

"Whatchu need today, my friend?"

"I'm lookin' for a engagement ring."

Curly chuckled. "Ah, so Kismet has finally locked you down, huh?"

Goldie had purchased hundreds of thousands of dollars worth of jewelry from Curly over the years. Curly had only met Kismet once, but he knew that she was Goldie's special lady.

"What price range are you looking for?" Curly asked, feeling stupid after the words had slipped from his mouth.

Goldie shot him a sinister stare. "I ain't got no price range."

"I-I know. I'm sorry," Curly quickly stammered. "I have just the ring for you. I'll be right back."

Curly excused himself and went to the back of his store. He returned five minutes later carrying a small velvet jewelry bag. Curly placed the jewelry bag on the display case and pulled out a jewelry box containing the largest, clearest, diamond Goldie had ever seen.

"Got-damn! That's a fuckin' rock!" Goldie commented.

"Yes, my friend. This is a five karate flawless diamond. It doesn't belong to me, but it's for sale."

"I want it," Goldie expeditiously replied.

Most of the diamonds that Curly sold were smuggled into the country or sold to him by international crime figures. Curly, a jewelry designer, moonlighted as a fence for a few of Interpol's most wanted criminals.

"Three hundred thousand," Curly said, stating his price for the stone.

"Two-hundred stacks! Not a got-damn penny mo'!" Goldie reciprocated.

"Two-seventy-five!" Curly shot back.

"I'll give you a quarter and that's it!"

"Sold!" Curly said with a tight smirk.

The two men relaxed their respective game faces. Price wars were par for the course everytime Goldie shopped at Curly's.

Goldie gave Curly his address. "I want it on a white-gold band, delivered to me by 9 p.m.," he said over his shoulder, heading for the door.

"Ay, Goldie!" Curly called.

Goldie turned around.

"Make sure you have al-"

Goldie cut him off. "I know. I know. All large bills."

Curly smiled and gave Goldie the thumbs up. He watched him back pedal a few steps, turn on his heels, then walk out of the store.

¢   ¢   ¢

At 9 p.m. sharp Curly delivered the engagement ring to Goldie's house. Goldie took possession of the ring and handed Curly a briefcase containing $250,000. Kismet was upstairs getting dressed while the two men conducted business. Goldie had made 10 o'clock reservations for them at Ruth's Chris.

Kismet had been sleeping most of the day. So she was surprised to see the two Lamborghinis parked in Goldie's three car garage.

"When did you get these?" Kismet asked, pointing at the blue Lamborghini.

Goldie opened the black Lamborghini's passenger door. "Oh, I got 'em today. The blue one is Alex's. I got Cashman a Viper."

"Dayum! Buy me something," Kismet joked, taking a seat in the Lambo.

Goldie closed the passenger door, hopped in the driver's

seat and flushed it to Ruth's Chris. Upon arrival, the maitre'd escorted them to their reserved table. It was located in the far back corner of the restaurant. A smooth jazz melody played in the background. It was skillfully composed by a live band. The vibe was ultra-soothing.

"This is so romantic," Kismet said as Goldie pulled a chair out for her. She sat down. "I love this place."

Goldie had just sat down when a waitress appeared at their table. "Thank you," he replied after the waitress handed them their menus. "Let us look over these for a minute befo' we order. But I'll take a double shot of Scotch straight up and a Ceasars Salad for right nye'."

Kismet stared at Goldie strangely, but spoke to the waitress. "I'd like an apple juice and a Ceasars Salad."

"Coming right up," the waitress remarked before sauntering off.

Once the waitress was out of earshot, Kismet spoke. "Scotch? Negro, when did you start drinking Scotch? What happened to Henny or Remy?"

Goldie reached across the table and grabbed Kismet's hand. "Baby, when I said I'm steppin' my game up, I wasn't just talkin'. A lot of shit finna change. We was hood rich befo' my trip to Mexico. I been a millionare. But nye' we Silver Spoons rich. That mean we gotta start livin' different. I'm 'bout to open a few businesses and make some power moves in the streets. When I'm done we gonna be set for life."

The waitress returned with their salads and beverages. She asked them were they ready to order. Goldie winked and told her to come back in fifteen minutes.

Goldie took a sip of his Scotch, then turned back to Kismet. "Baby, I know I ain't been the best boyfriend in the world. But startin' right nye'. I'ma try."

Goldie stood up and grabbed Kismet's left hand. Just then the lights in the restaurant got dim. The band changed their tune to the instrumental of "For the Love of You" by the Isley Brothers. "Kismet, you my everythang and I wanna spend the rest of my life witchu."

Kismet looked around baffled. She could hear Goldie's

voice booming out of the restaurant's P.A. system. When she finally returned her gaze to Goldie, he was on one knee looking up into her eyes. He pulled a jewelry box from his pocket and opened it. Kismet started hyperventilating. Goldie placed the ring on Kismet's finger. Tears coursed her pretty face as she stared at the huge diamond.

Kismet was so entranced she didn't realize that all of the restaurant's patrons were watching them.

"Will you marry me?" Goldie asked, voice clearly audible over the P.A. system.

The band stopped playing. Anticipation filled the atmosphere.

"Yes! Oh god, yes!" Kismet sobbed, hugging Goldie tightly around the neck.

Everyone in the restaurant started clapping and cheering. They gave the couple a standing ovation. It wasn't until all the commotion had died down that Kismet and Goldie ordered their meals. They ate quietly, then left the restaurant in the midst of more applause and well wishes from the patrons and staff.

Driving down JTB, Goldie passed the exit to his house and contined east.

Kismet looked over at him. "Where are we going?" she asked. She was anxious to get back to the house so they could consummate their new engagement.

"It's a surprise. Just relax and enjoy the ride."

Twenty minutes later they were on A1A riding along the Ocean Highway. Large beach houses and luxurious estates could be seen in the distance. Goldie flipped on his blinker and turned onto a private road. He stopped at an iron gate with an electronic key pad posted in front of it. He typed in a numeric code and the gate opened. He drove through and around a curve, stopping in front of a mansion that looked like a small version of the White House.

"Who-who's house is this?" Kismet asked, awed by its beauty.

Goldie reached into his pocket and pulled out a set of keys. He dangled them in Kismet's face.

"Oh my god! Goldie, is this yours?" she asked, pointing at

the house.

Goldie shook his head. "No, it's ours."

Kismet thought that she'd heard wrong. "What?!"

"It's ours," Goldie repeated.

Kismet was flabbergasted! There wasn't a word invented that could express her feelings. She honestly thought that she would never be completely happy again after her father's death. She almost felt guilty when she thought about what her life would be like if her father was alive. Kismet had everything. A baby on the way, a fiancé and a new mansion. What more could a girl ask for?

Chapter 23

Goldie killed the Lamborghini's engine and got out. He was about to walk around and open Kismet's door but he was too late. She'd exited the car right behind him. They walked hand and hand into the house. Stepping into the foyer was like stepping into a dream. Kismet was overwhelmed by what she saw.

The floor was made of marble, imported exclusively from Italy. An 18x18 foot crystal chandelier hung from the center of the sixty foot vaulted ceiling. There was a spiral staircase with porcelain steps and 18kt gold railing. The place looked like Heaven.

Goldie gave Kismet the grand tour of the mansion. There were ten bedrooms, five full baths and a guest house. Not to mention the luxuriant amenities, like the indoor swimming pool, the shooting range and the golf course. Goldie told Kismet that he was giving her a $250,000 furniture allowance. She could start having things delivered as soon as the next day. Kismet couldn't be happier.

They christened the mansion with a quicky on the island in the kitchen.

¢   ¢   ¢

The following day, Goldie was startled awake at 11 a.m. by his phone ringing. "Hello?" he answered. He was laying in bed with Kismet at his old house. They rode back after making love in the mansion.

"What up, my nigga? Yo' boy out!"

"Who this? Alex?" Goldie asked excitedly.

"Yeah, nigga! Who else? Them crackas just let a nigga out. I'm in the detention center parkin' lot. Come get me!"

The hour long drive to Folkston, GA only took Goldie forty minutes to complete.

"Got-damn! What the fuck is that?" Alex asked himself when the blue Lamborghini rocketed into the detention center's parking lot.

The inmates on the rec-yard stopped what they were doing to view the exotic vehicle. Alex was trying to see who was driving the Lambo, but the pitch-black auto tint made it impossible.

Vroom! Vroom! Vroom! Vroom! Goldie toyed with Alex after putting the Lamborghini in neutral. He put it in park, threw the door up and hopped out. "What up, ole scead-ass-nigga?"

"Ohh, shit! This you?!" Alex asked, referring to the Lamborghini.

"Nawl, man, this you," Goldie answered, tossing him the keys.

Alex was speechless for a moment. "...man, what kinda car is this?"

Goldie smiled. "A fast one," he said, getting into the passenger seat.

Alex fishtailed the Lambo out of the detention center's parking lot. During the drive back to Jacksonville he and Goldie engaged each other in conversation. Alex told Goldie about what he'd been through mentally and emotionally with respect to Meka and Cocena. He also pulled his coat to how dirty the Feds were playing. Goldie, on the other hand, talked about all the cocaine he had stashed in mini storages, his plan to expand his drug clientele and his goal of opening a few businesses.

Alex was undoubtedly interested. He was dying to get his beak wet. Especially when Goldie promised him one-hundred kilos at $12.5 a piece. All he asked for was a little time to get his house straight before getting his hands dirty again.

When they made it to Goldie's house Alex followed him inside. He needed to use the phone. Alex called Meka.

"What's up, Ma?" Alex asked when she answered.

"Alex?! When you got out, babe?" she exclaimed, recognizing his voice.

"A lil' ova' a hour ago."

"Nigga, you been out a hour? Why you playin' wit' me?

When you comin' home?" she asked in mock anger.

"Gimme 'bout thirty minutes."

Alex hung up the phone with Meka and told Goldie he'd hit him later. He hopped in his Lambo and drove to his cousin Harold's trap. Harold was inside playing a video game when Alex pulled up. The low rumble of the powerful V12 engine brought him to the door. A gold-tooth smile appeared on Harold's face when he saw Alex climb out of the Lamborghini.

"Got-damn, cuz. What the hell is that you drivin'? And when you got out? …man, you ain't escape did you?"

"Hell nawl, I ain't escape! And that's a Lamberdini," Alex said, mispronouncing Lamborghini.

"Oh…well, why you got that hot muthafucka in front of my trap? Nigga, what you want? I gotta hurry and get yo' hot ass from 'round here. Cuz, I love ya and I'm glad to see ya, but that shit you drivin' look like some year 2050 shit! And it don't belong in front no drug-trap."

"Damn, ole fearful-ass-nigga! I won't be long. Let me get a ounce of 'dro and ten fat ass dubs of hard."

Harold led Alex inside of the trap and gave him what he requested. He wanted to question him about the crack but thought better of it.

"Aiight, cuz I'll holla," Alex said, dapping Harold before stepping out of the door.

"Aiight then, cuz…Ay, cuz?"

Alex looked back.

"Man, please don't drive that car 'round her no mo'."

¢   ¢   ¢

Alex arrived at his two story townhouse twenty minutes after leaving Harold's trap. He crossed his threshold and instantly felt out of place. Alex felt like his space had been violated. Like he was visiting some place other than his home. He closed and locked the door behind him. Still the weird feeling remained. He felt like he was in the wrong place and that his door was wide open.

Meka heard Alex's entrance and quickly finished beautifying herself in the bathroom mirror. She stepped into the

Capo Cat

living room wearing her birthday suit and a pair of six inch heels.

Got damn this bitch bad. Alex thought.

"Heeyy, babe! You missed me?" Meka asked, rushing into Alex's arms and giving him a hug and kiss.

Alex was pissed that Meka had the audacity to kiss him in the mouth, knowing damn well she'd been sucking the next man's dick. Nevertheless, Alex concealed his disdain and played along with Meka's game.

"Gurl, you know I missed this," Alex replied, palming a handful of ass.

Meka grabbed his hand and led him into their bedroom. She laid back on the bed, spread her legs and started to slowly finger-fuck herself. Alex's dick filled with blood instantly.

"What are you waiting for, daddy?" Meka moaned.

Alex's primal instinct overpowered his anger and better judgement. He didn't even think about Meka's betrayal before quickly undressing and jumping buck-naked between her thick thighs. After a grueling half-hour fuck-fest, Alex and Meka laid intertwined, each in their own thoughts.

Shiid, I know my pussy good. Look at 'im, sleep already... That tired ass nigga Marley better not pop his ass up over here, Meka thought.

I hope this bitch don't thank she gettin' away wit' nothin'. That pussy damn sho' been tampered wit'! Alex thought before dozing off.

He woke up hours later and climbed out of bed. His movements woke Meka up out of her slumber.

"Where you goin' babe?" Meka asked.

"Nowhere. I'm 'bout to roll a blunt and take a hot bath."

"Uumm, that sounds real good, babe. Call me when the water ready and the blunt's in the air."

"Shiid, gurl, I'm finna take my bath dolo! It's been a minute since I been able to do that!"

Meka was salty, but she understood or at least she thought she did. There were no tubs in jail.

Alex put on his pants and walked to the hall closet to get some underclothes and his bath robe. He grabbed everything he needed then went to the bathroom, closing and locking the door behind him. Alex cut the water on and set its temperature. Reaching into his pocket, he pulled out an ounce of 'dro, two blunts and the bag of crack. Alex split both blunts and filled one with straight 'dro. The remaining blunt was filled with 'dro and sprinkled with one crushed up dub of hard white. Alex took the laced blunt to Meka and lit it for her before returning to the bathroom, locking the door and taking his bath.

Twenty-five minutes later, Alex felt refreshed. He dried off, put on his underclothes and robe, then went back into the bedroom with Meka. The room smelled like burnt plastic mixed with weed.

"Gurl, is you aiight?" Alex asked Meka, who was staring at him blankly.

Meka tried to respond but her mouth was numb.

"Ay gurl, why you lookin' at a nigga like that?" Alex asked, knowing the answer.

Meka's eyes were wide open. She kept involuntarily moving her jawbone from side to side. "Boy, where you get that weed?" she finally slurred.

"Why? You like it?" Alex asked, trying desperately to suppress his laughter.

"Hell yeah! That shit some fi'! I heard bells rangin' and shit when I hit it," Meka commented, almost incoherently.

¢ ¢ ¢

Three weeks after Alex was released, Meka had unwittingly smoked about four ounces of crack. She was slowly but surely starting to resemble the crept keeper. She had lost twenty pounds and counting. All she wanted to do was smoke what she assumed was fire-weed and get fucked by Alex. She'd go days without eating.

If Meka wouldn't have been so high all of the time, she would have noticed that Alex had started to dog her out. She thought that he was being extra freaky when he'd violently fuck her in the ass while calling her every kind of bitch under the sun. When he finished he'd cum in her face. Whenever Meka would suck his dick, he'd fuck her in the mouth real hard and reckless until she'd throw up. Then he'd wipe the green and yellow bile off of his dick onto her face and hair.

One night while fucking, Meka copped an attitude. The crack-laced weed she'd been smoking wan't getting her as high as it first had. She was miserable. She wanted to hear the bells again.

"Alex, I'm tired of you fuckin' me in my ass!" Meka complained as Alex was pounding the bottom out of her large intestine.

"Fiend bitch! I ain't tryna fuck you in yo' nasty ass twat!"

Meka was shocked. Alex had never talked to her like that before – or at least she'd never comprehended him doing so through her crack induced reality.

"Fiend? Fuck-nigga, who you callin' a bitch?"

Alex had been drinking all day and his sharp words – although his true feelings – had slipped out.

"Nigga, my pussy ain't nasty!"

Meka was looking back at Alex with a menacing scowl on her face as he relentlessly slid his enlarged love-muscle in and out of her ass. Upon seeing that Alex was ignoring her, while callously humping sparks out of her butt-hole, Meka climbed off of the bed and got in his face. "Nigga, yo' momma a bitch," she spat, enraged.

Alex didn't like the idea of Meka disrespecting his mother so he mushed her face. "Gone, bitch, befo' I beat cho' ass!"

Meka had had enough of being called a bitch. She attacked Alex like a rabid cat, scratching and clawing. Alex, feeling the sting from the wounds he sustained, reflexively hit Meka with a hard left hook, putting her on her ass. He caught a glimpse of his reflection in the wall mirror and noticed his face was bleeding.

"Bitch! I'ma kill you!" he yelled before grabbing a handful of her weave. Alex then drew back to punch her in the face.

Meka sat on the floor in tears. "Alex! Please! Don't!" she pleaded, covering her head with her arms just as Alex's fist was inches away from contact.

Alex froze.

"Baby, why are you doin' me like this?" Meka asked, sounding innocent.

"You know why, bitch!" Alex snarled, releasing her weave.

Meka still tried to play dumb, so Alex told her about the

picture that the Feds had shown him. He added a few lies for good measures. When he was finished talking Meka just stared at him in horror.

"Alex, I'm so –"

Alex cut her off by placing his palm in her face. "Ay, bitch, ain't no need to say sorry. Just gon' and get yo' shit and get the fuck out!"

"But – but Alex, I ain't got nowhere to go," she pleaded.

Alex rolled his eyes. "Go to that nigga, bitch! I don't give a fuck! But you gettin' yo' stank ass outta here!"

Meka sucked her teeth. "You know what, Alex? Fuck you! I was tired of yo' lil' dick ass, anyway!"

Meka knew she'd fucked up with a good nigga and she was hurt. Surprisingly, she had the audacity to subconsciously blame Alex for her whorish ways. She wanted him to feel her pain, and she was doing a good job at it, because Alex was pissed! Meka's comment about his dick had him heated. He really wanted to beat the shit out of her, but chose to expose what she'd been smoking instead.

"Oh, I got a lil' dick, huh?"

"Hell yeah! You got a lil' dick – bitch! I don't even know why I fucked witcho do-boy-ass, anyway?"

"Do-boy? Bitch, I ain't nann nigga do-boy!"

Meka smirked. She knew she'd struck a nerve so she mined a little deeper. "Goldie young ass yo' daddy, nigga ... you fuckin', son-son!"

Instead of the response that Meka was expecting, Alex did something totally different. He fell into a hysterical laughing fit. Meka was bewildered. So much so that her head involuntarily turned sideways like a curious dog.

"Nigga, what's so fuckin' funny?" she asked, having had enough of Alex's laughing.

"You, bitch!" he curtly replied.

He was no longer laughing.

"Okay Mr. Belvedere, I'll be yo' bitch," Meka replied with her hands on her hips. "But fuck-nigga, when I leave here I'ma be wit' that same nigga you seen on the picture, hoe."

"Well, I hope that nigga can support yo' habit!"

"Nigga, I ain't got no habit!"

"Bitch, you a got-damn crackhead!"

Now it was Meka's turn to have a laughing fit. "Yeah," she said cracking up. "You might be right. I think I do got a habit. A habit of spendin' yo' money, sucka!"

"What about all the weed you been smokin'?" Alex smirked.

"What about it? Weed come from the Earth!"

"Trifflin' ass bitch! I was puttin' crack in yo' shit. You a fiend, hoe! Oh, you quiet now, huh? Well I got a present fo' yo' ass befo' you go!"

Alex stalked over to the closet and dug around on the shelf. He retrieved a brown paper bag that had Diet Alert written on it and a bag of crack. He tossed Meka the paper bag, all the while holding in his laughter. Meka caught the bag and looked inside.

"What's this?" she asked, confused.

She had pulled out a glass pipe.

"It's what you smoke these on," Alex spat, tossing her the bag of crack that Harold had delivered earlier.

Meka felt her stomach bubble and farted as soon as the bag of hard white touched her palms.

"Oh, and don't forget this," Alex added, tossing her a lighter.

Chapter 24

Six Months Earlier
Unmarked police cars swarmed a run down row-house on the corner of Highland Avenue. A hour earlier, rookie Officer Steve Mullin arrived at the residence in reference to a complaint filed by Duke Power Company – Spartanburg, South Carolina's electric authority. Someone had been tampering with the house's meter box. For the past six months the meter man had been recording the same exact amount of usage.

When Officer Mullin set foot on the property he heard loud music emitting from inside of the house. After banging on the front door and getting no answer, he decided to walk around back. As he passed an open window on his way, the smell of marijuana invaded his nostrils. He looked inside to satisfy his curious nature.

Sherod Miller, AKA Chop was inside of his stash house smoking some killer 'dro while laboriously re-rocking multiple kilos of cocaine. Oblivious to Officer Mullin's prying eyes, he continued on with the task before him. He'd already broken down one kilo and mixed it with Bolivia. What Officer Mullin witnessed however, when he peeked into the window was Chop pouring the cocaine and cut mixture out of a brown paper bag onto a sheet of plastic. The clueless drug dealer used a dust pan to shift the illicit mixture around while simultaneously misting it with acetone from a small spray bottle.

Officer Mullin ran back to his cruiser and radioed into headquarters. "Patch me in to Detective Alexander, narcotics division," he said to the operator.

Moments later, the detective's voice could be heard over the radio. "Yes, this is Detective Alexander, how may I help you?"

"Detective, my name is Officer Steve Mullin and I stopped

by a residence in reference to a complaint filed by Duke Power Co..."

He went on to explain what he'd witnessed and how his routine investigation led up to such a large discovery.

¢   ¢   ¢

An Hour Later
Boom! The front door of the house flew off its hinges.

"What the fuck was that?" Chop asked himself after hearing his front door being kicked in.

He ran into the next room and grabbed his AR-15 just as the police came through the door.

"Police! Drop your weapon, now!" an officer demanded, aiming his Glock .40 at Chop's baldhead.

Chop did what he was told. He was forcefully handcuffed and taken down to the station. The police left him in the interrogation room alone for almost an hour before anyone came to question him. Finally, Detective Alexander stepped in carrying a large box. "Mr. Miller, you're in a lot of trouble, man."

Chop smiled arrogantly, but said nothing as Alexander began to remove the box's contents. He placed them on the conference table. Five large ziplock bags of cocaine, two kilo's still in their original wrapper, three beakers and a triple beam scale.

"We turned your Desert Eagle and the AR-15 over to ballistics for them to have a look at," the detective informed.

Chop still wore an unwavering smile. He knew there was no way in hell that the cops could have gotten a search warrant for his stash house. He never sold any drugs out of it. "Ay man, yall might as well let me go. Yall ain't got nothin' on me. Where was yall search warrant? That wasn't my house...Shiid, I was just visitin'."

"Oooh, so that's why you have that stupid fucking smirk on your face. You think you have an illegal search and seizure defense. Ha, I guess you're not familiar with Pendicski versus Maine? ...Look pal, we've got you by the balls. We had every got-damn right in the world to come into that house and drag your black ass out," Alexander said, standing up and pointing in Chop's face.

He gave the bewildered drug dealer a brief summary of the events that led up to his arrest. By the time Alexander had finished talking, Chop wanted to kick his own ass.

Damn! Why I had to try and beat Duke Power? Them crackas ain't playin' 'bout they money, Chop thought in introspect.

He'd switched the stash house's electric meter with a rigged one that he'd bought from a crackhead.

A commotion outside of the door startled Chop out of self-admonishment. Then two white dudes barged into the interrogation room dressed like the *Men in Black*. They showed Chop their badges. "DEA," they both said in unison, ignoring Alexander's angry glare.

"Got-damn-it! Who the fuck let you two numb-nuts in here?" the detective barked.

He was tired of his narcotics team doing all of the grunt work while the DEA took the credit.

"Alexander, please…I mean, do we have to go through the same song and dance everytime we meet up?" Agent Taylor asked. He exhaled. "Now, you know the routine, get out and give us thirty minutes with this guy!" he commanded.

The detective reluctantly stood up and stalked out, leaving Chop alone with the two DEA agents.

Taylor took a seat. "Hello, Mr. Miller, my name is Special Agent Harry Taylor and this is my partner Mike Shoemaker," he said, nodding towards the other man. "We heard an officer requesting back up over our scanner, after he'd witnessed a man mixing a large quantity of cocaine at one of our target addresses. …Miller, we've been watching you. We've been watching you for quite some time."

Although the room was cold, sweat started to form on Chop's forehead. He didn't know that the Feds were on his ass. The thought of it made him nauseous.

Agent Taylor continued. "I'm going to be frank with you, Miller. We don't want you. We want Lil Hezy and Brown-eyed Ron. We know they're your suppliers and we need you to make a few buys from them for us. If you do that, we'll forget any of this ever happened," he said, motioning to all of the contraband on the table.

"C'mon, man. Don't make me do that. I got a wife and kid... Man, them dudes don't play," Chop pleaded.

Agent Shoemaker was pissed! He wanted to dive across the table and bitch-slap Chop's pussy-ass. He'd bet Taylor $50 that it would take him at least 48 hours to flip the big, black, ugly drug dealer. And here this dumb gorilla-looking nigger was about to tell everything he knew in less than 48 seconds. Chop's statement alone proved a conspiracy existed between him and the two men in question, signifying that Taylor had already *wiggled the head in*. Agent Shoemaker gazed at Chop, disgusted, knowing that within the next two minutes his partner would *have his entire dick up his ass*.

Taylor smiled on the inside. "Hey guy, I'm not the one who told you to sell dope. And I surely never told you to carry guns. I mean, you had a fucking AR-15 in your possession, not to mention the Desert Eagle. Man, you're looking at no less than 15 years for this one."

Chop felt faint. The time Taylor had mentioned undoubtedly knocked all of the fight out of him. All he wanted to do then was to go home to his wife and daughter and never touch drugs again. "Man, I want to help my se--. I-I mean, yall, but them dudes ain't no joke. I know for a fact they 'bout they bizness. If I fuck them niggas up, me and my family dead."

Agent Taylor nodded. "Oh, you don't have to worry about that, they'll be old men if they ever see the streets again."

Dropping his head, Chop pondered the fifteen years he was facing. He added it to his twelve year old daughter's age. "Twenty-seven...Damn! She'll be married wit' children by then. Shit I'll be fifthy," he thought before looking back up at the two detectives. "Okay, man, fuck it...I'll do it. I don't wanna go to jail."

BOOK 3HREE

...do you recall the Coca-Cola jingle: "I'd love to buy the world a coke..." [Well], the bottom line is: *they'd love to sell the world a Coke*...What does it mean?...It means that the U.S. capitalists have taken a turn, a right turn. And it's affecting the economic structure of the entire world. We're in a brand-new game.

...a new economic arrangement has taken hold, one that exists irrespective of language, custom, ideology, flags, and most of all, territory...

They need to develop new marketplaces...The U.S. capitalists are threatened by a limitation of marketplaces. They not only need to sell the world a Coke, they're moving to do it...It's a play-or-pay proposition [roll or get rolled over]: *They will buy a Coke...*

■ Huey P. Newton
■ [From A Taste of Power by Elaine Brown]

Chapter 25

A single tear escaped Cashman's eye as Kendra Vaugh's casket was lowered into the ground. All of the mourners present wondered who the young man dressed in the black Armani suit was as he purposefully walked back to his black on black Dodge Viper. Victor Vaugh, who was also present at the gravesite, pondered Cashman's identity, as well did the two U.S. Marshals that escorted him back to an awaiting van.

Cashman sped out of the cemetery feeling a pain unlike he'd ever felt before. Red was his first true love and she was dead. As Cashman merged onto I-95, he applied pressure to the gas pedal. He was listening to Jim Beam's "Real Nigga Radio Mixtape" zoned out to the song "Butterlies." His destination was home. Cashman was oblivious to his surroundings as he drove. He couldn't see the road, nor feel how fast he was driving. The only thing that his senses could interpret was the beat of the music as he reflected back on his life and the choices he'd made. His heart felt like there was an empty void inside of it. Like something vital to his survival was missing. Yet, Cashman drove on as he pondered the future of his existence.

Hours later, Cashman arrived home. It had only been a week since Goldie had given him his old house and moved. Cashman dropped his car keys on the living room table and looked around his new home. *Is it all worth it?* He asked himself after taking in the view.

Although Cashman had been in the game a short while, it seemed to him like an eternity. He'd sold more cocaine than the average drug dealer could sell in their entire criminal careers. He'd killed more people than most soldiers did during times of war. But what was it all for? What did the future hold for him? He went to bed that night with his mind in turmoil.

The next morning Cashman was awakened by loud banging on his front door. He looked at his alarm clock.

It read 7:23 a.m.

Cashman reached under his pillow, grabbed his Glock .40 and cocked it.

Clack! Clack! The powerful gun sounded.

"Who is it?" he asked, reaching his front door.

"Cashman, open the doe', man!" A familiar voice commanded.

Cashman opened the door and stepped back as Goldie ambled in followed closely by Alex. He could tell by their facial expressions that something was wrong. Cashman closed his door and turned to face Goldie as he paced. "What up, bruh?" he asked.

Goldie stopped pacing, looked up at Cashman and shook his head. "The Feds hit Brown-eyed Ron 'em from Savannah last night. Mandi say twenty-three niggas got picked up wit 'em."

"They got Hezy too?" Cashman asked.

"Most likely. Mandi said the paper only had Brown-eyed Ron's name listed, you know him and Lil Hezy always together," Goldie answered.

"Damn," Cashman stated somberly while shaking his head. "We was s'posed to go to the Kentucky Derby this year."

Alex had a look on his face like he'd drank a cup of sour milk. "The Kentucky Derby?! Nigga!" Alex exclaimed in a high-pitched, shrill voice. "Did you just hear what Goldie said?"

Cashman looked puzzled. "Yeah, I heard him. He said the Feds hit Brown-eyed Ron 'em. ...shit, them crackas hittin' niggas everyday, what the fuck?" he said, shrugging his shoulders.

Alex couldn't believe his ears. *Is Cashman really this clueless?* He wondered.

He didn't know if Cashman was disguising his fear with his nonchalant attitude or was he just naïve when it came to the Feds.

Goldie spoke up. "Lil bruh, the Feds be investigatin' niggas befo' they come get 'em. Mandi said them crackas watched them niggas for six months. Just thank lil bruh," Goldie said, tapping his pointer finger against his temple, "how many times you done served Brown-eyed Ron or Hezy in the past few months?"

Cashman's mouth dropped open. "Aww, shit!"

"Nye' you see what a nigga talkin' 'bout?" Alex asked.

Cashman shook his head, "Yeah, man, damn! This shit is serious!"

"Lil bruh, go get dressed. We gotta meet Brown-eyed Ron's wife after she come from court. She talked to Kismet this mornin' and told her what time its over. By the time we get to Savannah she'll be outta there."

Cashman went up stairs and came back down twenty minutes later, dressed and ready to go. Goldie was using the house phone. Cashman looked on curiously as his big brother questioned the person on the line and shook his head in the negative after each reply.

"Well, call me when you leave the doctor," Goldie said before hanging up.

"Who that, Kismet?" Cashman asked.

Goldie sucked his teeth. "Nawl, that was Lonita tellin' me her period late."

Alex jumped from his seat. "Lonita?...You talkin' 'bout Jesus daughter, Lonita?"

Goldie sighed. "Yeah, man, that Lonita. Boy, a nigga done fucked up! Man, Kismet gonna kill me."

"Kismet?...well, yeah, she done bodied a bitch. But you need to be worried 'bout Jesus! Didn't you say he ain't like niggas?" Cashman questioned.

"Got-damn! Jesus gonna be mad as shit when he find out he finna have a half-nigga grandbaby," Alex added jokingly.

Goldie bussed out laughing as he imagined Jesus holding his black grandchild.

¢   ¢   ¢

The trio reached Savannah in less than three hours. Goldie noticed that he was down to a quarter of a tank of gas and stopped at a gas station on Abercorn to fill up. Alex went inside to pay. Goldie pumped the gas. The tank was almost full when out of nowhere a black Crown Vic with dark tinted windows and government plates pulled up to the pump next to Goldie's. Moments later, two white men exited the vehicle.

"Sultan Jackson," one of the men replied as they approached.

Alex was walking out of the store, looking down at the lottery ticket he was scratching off when he walked up behind the two officers. "Goldie, if a nigga win thi-. What the fuck?" he muttered, looking up, recognizing two DEA agents.

The agents heard Alex's startled remark and quickly turned to face him. "Oh, Mr. Brooks!" they replied in unison.

Goldie closed his gas tank. "Man, who the fuck is yall two crackas?" he spat, pointing at the two agents.

Special Agent Ricks ignored Goldie's question as he turned around to face him. "Isn't it ironic that we run into you boys all the way up in Savannah, GA? I guess yall came to check on Brown-eyed Ron and his crews? Don't worry, you guys will be joining them shortly. And that goes for you too, Cashman," Ricks said, pointing at Cashman as he sat in the backseat of Goldie's Porsche.

Agent Hogan spoke. "Mr. Brooks, you got away the last time. But don't think for one fucking minute that the U.S. Government would allow criminals to murder its own and get away with it!"

Alex got into Hogan's face. "Cracka, I see I'ma have to put my lawyer on yall asses. What the fuck yall followin' us for?"

Agent Hogan released a hearty laugh. "We're not following you all. We just left the Federal courthouse seeing about your crime partners, Brown-eyed Ron and Lil Hezy. We know that you guys were supplying them," Hogan divulged, then continued. "We've been working jointly with the DEA up here, so it's only a matter of time before someone starts talking. Then guess what?" he asked, but didn't give anyone a chance to answer. "We come pick yall asses up," he spat before turning on his heels and walking back to the Crown Vic.

"Now, yall folks have a nice day," Agent Ricks added with a smirk.

He stalked off to join his partner.

Goldie and Alex jumped back in the Porsche with Cashman after watching the two DEA agents drive off. Everyone in the car was silent as they made their way to meet Precious – Brown-eyed

Ron's wife – at their East Savannah home. Fifteen minutes later they pulled into the driveway of a two-story frame house that looked out of place in the neighborhood surrounding it. Precious had been expecting Goldie and was at the door when the trio reached the porch.

"Them crackas tryna give my baby life!" Precious cried into Goldie's shoulder as soon as he stepped into the foyer.

Goldie held the devastated woman close until they all reached the living room. He sat down with her on the couch. "Don't worry 'bout the boo-games them crackas playin', Precious. Them crackas can't give Ron life. That nigga ain't even got a record," he stated dismissively.

Precious shook her head in the negative. "No, Goldie. The judge said he facin' a mandatory life sentence. They-they chargin' him as a king pin," she said, bursting with more sobs and tears.

Goldie was baffled. "Brown-eyed Ron ain't no king pin," he said.

What Goldie didn't understand was that Brown-eyed Ron had been charged under the 848 Statute. Federal law states that anyone who supplies over five people in a conspiracy is considered a kingpin. It doesn't matter if the person indicted under the 848 king pin statute only buys one ounce at a time. If he or she sales drugs to five different street level dealers, they're considered king pins, even though they're street level dealers themselves.

Precious reached into her pocket and retrieved a folded piece of notebook paper. "Ron told me to give you this," she said, handing Goldie the note.

Goldie took it and began to read.

What's up, my dude? I guess you know what it is. Them folks want a nigga to scream on yall, but you know a nigga don't rock like that. But I'm going to tell you this, them folks did their homework, so be safe. All I ask is that you look after my people for me. Because I might never see the streets again. It's twenty-five of us on this case besides me and Lil Hezy, so we got like twenty-three potential witnesses against us. Me and Hezy told them lil' niggas to testify against us and go home. I know that shit sound crazy, but most of them lil' scary niggas gon' tell anyway. Yall ain't got shit to worry about, me and Hezy the only ones that know about yall. Anyway, like I was saying, they got me and Hezy down bad. We sold an informant about six keys over the last four months. The nigga name Sherod Miller, but they call him Chop. Me and Hezy sold to that fuck-nigga, so we gonna gone and lay down.

It's been real, Ron

Goldie's eyes had watered up after reading Brown-eyed Ron's letter. He liked Brown-eyed Ron a lot and hated that he was in such a fucked up situation. However, Goldie's grief wasn't the result of him losing a friend that he was emotionally attached to [to the system]. No, his grief was out of the respect and admiration he now held for Lil Hezy and Brown-eyed Ron [for nobly considering sacrificing their liberty for him as well as others, when they could have easily taken the path of least resistance like so many others]. He was feeling guilty.

Goldie turned his attention back to Precious. "Look, I want you to visit Ron and tell him I'm gonna get him and Lil Hezy the best lawyer money can buy. Tell that nigga anybody who snitch, they family members dead! Tell that nigga I said not to give none of them niggas the okay to snitch on him. After you visit him and tell him what I done told you, I want you to brang the kids wit' you to Jacksonville and stay for a while."

Chapter 26

Meka left the townhouse that she had shared with Alex. Her whole world was complete turmoil. She had nothing more than the clothes on her back. Alex had even stripped her of her car keys before kicking her out. She wandered around aimlessly, on foot, for hours pondering her plight. She felt suicidal. She began to question God about her life and what she had to live for.

During Meka's three year relationship with Alex, his jealous ways had caused her to become isolated from her family. So she had no place to go and very few people to turn to. The only friend she had besides the superficial sack chasers that convinced her to step out on Alex was Kismet. But she was too ashamed to tell her what she had done.

It wasn't long before Meka found herself on a park bench with the pipe and lighter that Alex had given her in one hand and the bag of crack in the other. Common sense told her to drop the pipe and crack and walk away. But the pain held her where she was. The weight of her situation had thrown her into a depression induced, hypnotic state. Before Meka became aware of what she was doing, she'd placed a piece of crack on her pipe and had taken a blast. Seconds later, she heard the bells again and all of her problems disappeared.

¢   ¢   ¢

Across the street in an unmarked car sat Ricks and his partner.

"Ricks, I don't know if my eyes are playing tricks on me or if these binoculars aren't worth a damn, but it looks to me like Alex's girl is smoking crack."

Agent Ricks snatched the night-vision spy-glasses from out of his partner's hands. "Got-damn-it, you're right! ...Oh shit, she has a bag full of crack, too!"

A smile spread across Hogan's thin lips. "Let's bust her ass. Maybe we can get her to roll over on Alex and the rest of those sociopaths. It's obvious she's been kicked out. I guess that picture came in handy after all."

The two DEA agents had been watching Alex's house every since he was released from jail. When they saw a dishelved Meka leave, walking on foot, they decided to tail her. Operation White-Gold was in full effect and Hogan and Ricks, as well as the other members of the Joint Task Force, were gathering as much evidence as they could to present to the Grand Jury.

Both Agents quietly exited the unmarked. It was 3:30 a.m. when they crossed the empty street, stealthy besieging Meka as she blissfully inhaled another numbing blast of crack vapors, her world further filled with turmoil.

"Freeze!" Agent Ricks barked, gun drawn.

Taken by complete surprise, Meka choked on the smoke in her lungs and started coughing. "Who... what's goin' on?" she asked after catching her breath.

Hogan stepped up. "You're under arrest for possession of crack co-"

Meka struck out running. It took the two agents a few seconds to comprehend what had happened before giving chase. Meka was headed straight towards the woods on the other side of the park. She was a lot faster than the out of shape men, so she held a sizable lead on them.

"Damn-it, I'm going to fix this bitch!" Hogan huffed, out of breath.

He pulled out his taser and fired while maintaining full stride. Two metal prongs entered Meka's back, followed by an electric charge that immobilized her immediately. She fell to the ground, striking her head on a brick, knocking her out cold. Meka woke up hours later handcuffed to a hospital bed with bandages wrapped around her head. She had suffered a mild concussion and needed six stitches to close the gash she'd sustained from her fall.

The first person Meka saw when her eyes blinked open was Agent Ricks. She heard a toilet flush, looked to her left and saw Agent Hogan stepping out of the restroom, drying his hands with a paper towel.

"Where am I?" Meka asked.

"You're at Memorial Hospital. You were tasered a few hours ago, fell and hit your head," Ricks informed.

"Why was yall fuckin' wit' me? Yall ain't have to taser me."

"You better be glad I didn't shoot your ass...running from me, hell," Hogan replied, assuming the role of the bad cop.

"Hey, be nice to the lady. She's going through enough stuff as it is without having to deal with your attitude!" Ricks scolded, playing the good cop role perfectly. He placed his hand on top of Meka's. "My name is Agent Ricks. I'm with the DEA and that's my partner Agent Hogan," he said, pointing at the other man. Ricks continued, "Meka, I'm here to help you. My partner found your bag of crack and he wants to charge you federally. Now, if he does that, you're looking at a minimum of five years in federal prison. I can help you, but you've got to tell me where you got the drugs from."

Meka's eyes became slits. She was infuriated! *Who the fuck do this pink-dick muthafucka thank he fuckin' wit'?* She asked herself.

She was mad at Alex for kicking her out and getting her hooked on crack, but she wasn't about to turn him over to the white man. "Cracka, yall got a bitch fucked up! What? Don't look stupid. Yall know yall gave me them rocks for some of this pussy. So how yall crackas gon' taser me, beat my ass, and still be threatenin' a bitch?"

Hogan's face turned fire red. "Why, you lying black bitch!" he spat before lunging at her.

Ricks grabbed his partner's hand just before he made contact. "She's not worth it," he replied, pulling him back and forcefully pushing him out of the room.

After calming Hogan down and convincing him to take a walk, Ricks walked back into Meka's room. He tried once more to persuade her to cooperate. Meka vehemently declined, then cursed him out like a dog.

Ricks threw his hands up in mock surrender. "Okay then, have it your way. Just be ready to go to jail as soon as the doctor releases you," he said before leaving Meka's room.

¢   ¢   ¢

Later that evening, Meka was visited by a doctor. He stepped in carrying her chart. After checking her vitals, the doctor took a seat in one of the chairs next to her bed. "Hello, Ms. Davis, my name is Dr. Duenaus," he said while leafing through the papers clamped to his clip board. "Okay…here we are. Alright, I got your lab results back about twenty minutes ago and I have some very bad news," he said in his thick foreign twang.

Meka sat up in bed. Her heartbeat quickened in anticipation.

Dr. Duenaus cleared his throat. "Ms. Davis, I'm sorry to have to tell you this, but you're HIV positive."

Meka saw her life flash before her eyes. She began to hyperventilate while trying desperately to free her wrist from the handcuffs.

"Oh my god! Please, Ms. Davis, calm down," Dr. Duenaus pleaded upon seeing how violently the bed shook as Meka fought to deliver herself from bondage.

Her wrist had started bleeding. Dr. Duenaus had seen enough. He pressed his panic button and three nurses rushed in. "I need twenty cc's of Triaval Stat!" he demanded.

Two of the nurses stayed and held Meka down while the third one scurried out of the room. She returned four minutes later with a needle and shot Meka up with the powerful sedative that Dr. Duenaus had requested. Moments later, Meka was sound asleep…

¢   ¢   ¢

Meanwhile, at the SunTrust building in Downtown Jacksonville, the devil and his assistants held Meka's fate.

"But David, with all do respect, you really need to make this happen. This could be the break we've been waiting for," Agent Hogan explained.

He and Ricks were inside of Assistant U.S. Attorney David Miller's office trying desperately to convince him to indict Meka.

They both knew that it was a good chance that Meka would never talk, but she had called them crackers and they wanted revenge.

David Miller leaned back in his swivel chair, behind his large desk, rubbing his chin. "Guys, I'm sorry, but I just can't do it. I mean, it was only seven grams of crack and you guys said you seen the girl smoking the stuff. She doesn't even have a criminal record. Not to mention her unwillingness to cooperate with you guys in the first place. I don't think an indictment against her will change her position. I truly believe it's a waste of time going after her."

Both agents were pissed, but they kept their anger under wraps.

"Okay, what's up with Ann Jacobs? Did you hear anything from her?" Ricks asked the Assistant U.S. Attorney, switching the subject.

Ann Jacobs was prosecuting Brown-eyed Ron and Lil Hezy's case. She worked for the U.S. Attorney's Office in the Southern District of Georgia.

"As a matter of fact, I have. She said that Brown-eyed Ron had started talking and that most of the other guys on the case have signed a no cooperation plea. She said that Lil Hezy's trial date is already set."

"Does Lil Hezy know that Brown-eyed Ron is cooperating?" Hogan asked.

"Nobody does, outside of law enforcement. And we need to keep it that way," David Miller answered. "Now what's up on yall's end? How's the investigation going?"

"Things are going smoothly. We have tails on Goldie, Alex, and Cashman...Hell, we're basically following everybody associated with these guys," Ricks informed.

David Miller stood up, hinting that their little conference was over. "Okay guys, that's very good, keep me posted. Also, don't forget about the task force meeting we're having on the 26th of this month. That's two days before the Grand Jury starts to convene."

The two agents left the U.S. Attorney's office and decided to ride by Cashman's house before heading back to the hospital. As they entered Cashman's subdivision, he drove past them in his

Dodge Viper, going in the opposite direction, followed by Agent Tara Tate and her partner, Dallas Henry. To the casual observer, the DEA agents looked like a husband and wife out for an evening drive. But in reality, they were members of the joint task force dubbed Operation White-Gold.

Agent Ricks hit Tara Tate on her radio. "Tara, this is Ricks. I just passed you and Dallas coming in, what's going on?"

"Well, as you can see, we're following Cashman. But about an hour ago Goldie stopped by his house and exited his car carrying a duffle bag. He stayed inside for a little under thirty minutes, then left empty handed."

"Did you see Cashman leave with the duffle bag?" Ricks anxiously inquired.

"No, we didn't. He had his car parked in his garage."

"That's okay, stay on him and give me an hourly update," Ricks replied, ending the conversation.

¢ ¢ ¢

Meka woke up seemingly normal an hour after her psychotic episode. When Dr. Duenaus learned of her miraculous improvement, he walked back to her room, accompanied by the hospital's chaplain. After explaining to her the effects that HIV has on the human body and divulging treatment options, Dr. Duenaus gave the Chaplain the floor. Chaplain Fry spoke to Meka about her spirit and the hereafter for almost twenty minutes before praying with her.

Dr. Duenaus paid close attention to their interaction. Satisfied with Meka's behavior, he signed her release papers.

¢ ¢ ¢

Nurse Williams advised Ricks and Hogan that Dr. Duenaus had okay'd Meka's release. Ricks thanked the nurse for the information then asked her to have Meka dressed as soon as possible in order for them to take her to jail. Nurse Williams picked up her phone and delegated the task to one of the hospital's CNA's.

Twenty minutes later, the two DEA agents were escorting a handcuffed, chapfallen Meka to their unmarked Crown Victoria.

The ride to the jail was pretty much uneventful, for Meka totally ignored every question fired at her by Hogan and Ricks. Upon arrival at the Duval County Jail, Meka was booked, processed and assigned a dorm.

¢   ¢   ¢

Meanwhile in Another Part of the City
Cashman whipped his Dodge Viper into the mini storage facility off of Southside Boulevard, stopping in front of Unit 3117. Inside was a black Ford 350 Dually with black tinted windows. Cashman pulled the big truck out then backed his Dodge Viper into its place. After securing his storage unit, Cashman hopped back into the Dually carrying the duffle bag that Goldie had given him.

Cashman drove to the gas station adjacent to the storage facility to gas up before his trip. He went inside, gave the store keeper $60 for his fuel and went back out to pump his diesel. He was oblivious to the watchful eyes of the lady and man that occupied the white Maxima parked next to the tire pump.

After filling up, Cashman jumped back onto Southside BLVD and made a left turn onto Beach. Within thirty minutes he was on I-95 headed to Swainsboro, GA.

¢   ¢   ¢

"Ricks, come in," Agent Tate's voice could be heard as it came over the radio.

Ricks was driving the unmarked while Hogan rode shotgun. They had just pulled out of a Dunkin Doughnuts drive-thru.

Ricks picked up his walkie-talkie. "This is Ricks, come in, Tara," he said, recognizing her voice.

"Ricks, I think Cashman's about to make a move," she urgently stated.

She went on to remind him about the duffle bag that Goldie had taken into Cashman's house. She informed him of the vehicle switch up at the storage facility, and the fact that they had just passed the Florida/Georgia state line.

"Well, did you see Cashman at anytime with the duffle bag?" Ricks asked.

"No sir, I didn't. We couldn't follow him into the storage facility without our cover being blown. But right now we're on I-95 headed north and I think I should pull him over."

"Tara, baby, you don't get paid to think, honey, so forget about pulling him over. As a matter of fact, get that thought out of your mind, right now. Do you know what his lawyer would do to your case if you stopped Cashman and found drugs inside of his vehicle?" Ricks asked, but answered himself. "He would destroy it. The kid has good license. Anyway, he's not going to cooperate against his brother. Our objective here is to prove that a conspiracy exists and to tie as many of these scum-bags as possible to it. Now just keep following him and update me every hour."

"Ten-four," Agent Tate said before placing her radio into her lap and turning on the cruise control.

¢   ¢   ¢

Duval County Jail
"Cindy Lewis, Tammy Car, Shameka Davis, get ready for court!" The C.O. shouted through the open door of the dorm.

Meka jumped out of her slumber when she heard her name being called. Her sudden movement caused her cellmate to wake up. Meka surveyed the cramped confines of the cell and suddenly remembered where she was and the events that had placed her there.

"Gurl, is you alright?" Meka's celly asked, noticing the bewildered expression on her face.

They hadn't had a chance to introduce themselves to one another because it was after lockdown when Meka arrived in the cell. Her bunkie had been asleep and Meka was drowsy off of the medication she was given for her head wound. Meka had fallen asleep as soon as her back touched her bunk.

Meka focused in on the strange woman and nodded. "Yeah, I'm cool. They just called my name for somethin'," she muttered.

"You just came in last night, right?"

Meka nodded yes.

"Well, you gotta go to court today. …what you did, anyway? Hold on, don't even answer that. My name is Sabrina…Sabrina Bouknight, but people call me Kabuki," Meka's celly said, extending her hand.

"I'm Shameka Davis, but you can just call me Meka."

The two women shook hands.

"Nye' what you did? 'Cause I can pretty much tell you what yo' bond gonna be?" Kabuki stated.

"I got caught wit' some rocks, but the Feds wanna charge me."

"Damn, you better hope they don't. Them crackas ain't playin' 'bout that crack. Shiid, if the Feds don't come get you for court, bond out and hide," Kabuki advised. She continued. "Simple possession charges don't carry a big bond."

Meka looked shook. "What about you? What you did?"

"Oh, I'm in here for organized fraud, but I'm good. The feds can't give me no more than thirty months."

"Thirty months?" Meka thought. "Damn, that's a lot of time," she said.

Meka was taken to her arraignment on the first floor of the Duval County Jail. Lucky for her, the Feds hadn't touched her case and Judge Moore granted her a $5,000 bail. She only had to pay a bondsman ten percent of that to be released. When Meka made it back to her dorm, everyone was up, so the common area was occupied by a sea of dishevled and dirty looking women. It had a rancid odor, like rotten fish, ass and garbage combined.

She walked straight to her cell. She glanced at her bunkmate, Kabuki, who was using the phone. Meka needed solitude. She needed to get her thoughts together so that she could come up with a plan to get out of the hell-hole she'd fallen in. She didn't even have the $500 to pay her bail. Alex had taken her last penny.

Wishing she had started her a bank account a long time ago, Meka thought of Kismet. Although Kismet had advised her to save for a rainy day, Meka knew that Kismet would come pay her bond. She was just ashamed of her appearance. Meka's unwitten crack habit had shed twenty pounds off of her thick frame.

Meka laid on her bunk for about thirty minutes before a light bulb cut on inside her head. "Oh shit, I'ma call Alex. I know he'll at least get a bitch outta jail… I'm still gonna fix his ass, but I need him right now."

At Alex's Townhouse
"Oh, this dick is so good! Oh, baby, beat this fat pussy. That's right, feed your baby…cum in this pussy."

The phone rang, interrupting Alex's session.

"No! No, don't answer that!" Cocena panted breathless as Alex pounded her cum-soaked pussy from the back.

Alex ignored her and reached for the phone. "Hello?"

"You have a collect call from, 'Meka' at the Duval County Jai-"

Alex pressed one. *I wonder what the fuck she did?* he asked himself.

As soon as the call was connected, Meka began begging Alex to bond her out of jail. She told him what she was charged with and her bond amount. She also told him she had something very important to tell him concerning life and death. Alex agreed to bond Meka out before their call ended. He called Freeman's bail bonds afterwards. He gave Chris all of Meka's information subsequent to telling him that he'd be there within the hour with her bond money.

¢   ¢   ¢

Cashman arrived in Swainsboro, Georgia three and a half hours after gassing up in Jacksonville. Parking in the back of the stash house, he pondered the mission before him and felt a little bit apprehensive. Goldie wanted him and Mandi to deliver ten kilos of cocaine to Cleveland, Tennessee and hang out with the buyer, James Wooden aka Big Woo, for about two weeks to see how he conducted his business.

Big Woo had asked Goldie to match his purchases and Goldie was considering his quarry. He'd been dealing with the Tennessee drug dealer for about 18 months. Goldie told Big Woo that he was sending his brother to inspect his operation before making a decision.

Cashman used his key, and stepping inside of the stash house, surprising Mandi and Ernest as they fucked on the living room couch.

"Got-damn, yall couldn't make it to the room?" Cashman quizzed.

He walked upstairs without uttering another word and took a nap.

Cashman woke up two hours later and went back downstairs. There, Mandi and Ernest sat fully clothed watching *Juice* on the big screen. After sitting down on the loveseat across from them, Cashman advised Mandi of the trip Goldie wanted them to take. He then asked them both how business was going in the small town.

"Shit, everythang good. We was 'bout to call Goldie for some moe' of them thangs, 'cause Slaughter 'bout out," Mandi answered.

"Yeah, and the trap work 'bout gone too. We got 'bout four birds left," Ernest interjected.

Cashman stood up. "Okay Ernest, call Goldie now and place the order. And Mandi, gon' and pack yo' shit. We gonna hit the road first thang in the mornin'."

Cashman went outside and transferred the duffle bag of cocaine from out of the Dually into the hydraulic stash spot in the mini-van. Unbeknownst to him, Agent Tara Tate and Dallas Henry were parked across the street, oblivious to what he was doing in the backyard.

¢   ¢   ¢

Back in Jacksonville

"Damn, I hope this nigga done paid my bail. It's been 'bout seven hours since I talked to Alex's ass!" Meka complained aloud.

It was after lock-down and all of the inmates were secured in their assigned cells. Kabuki was on the verge of screaming because Meka was aggravating the hell out of her. She couldn't even get into the book she was reading. Her cousin had ordered her *Boo Baby* by PLEX. She was a big fan of BADLAND

Publishing, but Meka's whining ass was killing her concentration.

Shit, this geekin' bitch betta be glad them crackas gave her ass a bond. Shit, if I had one I woulda been gone, Kabuki thought to herself.

¢ ¢ ¢

An hour later Meka was told to pack up. It took about forty-five minutes for her to be processed out. Alex was waiting in his Lamborghini when she exited the jail. Hopping into the exotic whip, Meka jumped straight into Alex's shit as soon as her door was closed.

"Bitch! You gave me that shit! You gave me AIDS, muthafucka!" she screamed as she clawed and scratched Alex's face.

They were still in the jail house parking lot. Meka's accusation had caused Alex's heart beat to increase. He wanted to hit her back, but his brain had locked up and couldn't send the correct signal to his hands. Alex grabbed the deranged woman by her wrist and tried to calm her.

"Girl, what you talkin' 'bout?"

He was squeezing Meka's wrist while searching her eyes, praying that he'd heard wrong.

"Bitch, you ain't deaf! Yo' dirty-dick-ass gave me AIDS!"

Fear seized Alex. "Hoe, I ain't got no AIDS! You got that shit from that green-ass-nigga you was fuckin' behind my back."

"No bitch! You got it from that bitch Sha-Sha's sick ass and gave it to me, bitch! You think I ain't know you was fuckin' that broke-down-ass hoe?"

She fucked Alex up with that one. He had heard the same exact shit about Sha-Sha.

"Aiight, look, we gotta keep this shit a secret. ...who else you done told?" Alex quizzed.

Meka's frown said it all. Shifting into drive, Alex pulled out of the Duval County Jail's parking lot. His thoughts were in disarray. As he drove he could faintly hear Meka's voice as she bitched about going home to bathe and change clothes. Little did she know that Cocena was at Alex's townhouse, so her going there was out of the question. Alex was taking her to a hotel. When they pulled up at the Best Western, Alex noticed his phone lighting up. It was Cocena calling from his house.

Oh shit, Cocena! Damn, she might have that shit too, if I got it...Aw'man, the baby, Alex said to himself.

¢ ¢ ¢

Back in Georgia

"Ricks, let me radio you back," Agent Tate urgently said into her walkie-talkie.

"Why? What's going on?" Ricks shot back.

"Cashman has switched cars and is on the move again," she answered.

Tara Tate and her partner Dallas Henry were parked down the street from the stash house. Through her binoculars, Agent Tate spied Cashman seated on the passenger side of the mini-van as it pulled out of the driveway. Mandi was driving. The two agents began to follow as soon as the mini-van reached the end of the block. They had no idea that they're destination was Cleveland, Tennessee.

Chapter 27

Jimmy Cam took the last $1,000 stack out of his duffle bag, placing it in a safe he kept at his grandmother's house. As the leader of his own Blood set, he sat on top of a $200,000 a month drug empire.

Stepping out into the hallway, Jimmy bumped into the very person he was trying to avoid.

"Boy, why you ain't been answerin' my calls? I been callin' yo' big-head ass for two days," Jimmy's sister, Teresa complained.

Jimmy and his sister were really close. Their mother and father were killed in a car accident when they were kids. However, as of late, Teresa had been getting on Jimmy's nerves with her carefree spending habits. She'd been tricking Jimmy's money off on young pussy, like she was a nigga or something.

"Gurl, I know what you was callin' 'bout. Didn't I just give yo' ass five grand last week?"

"Nigga, that was last week! I need three stacks today. Shit, you won't let a bitch get they own money. So what I'm 'pose to do? You gon' let a bitch get they own money, gon' and give me a few bricks and let me grind for mine...ain't no pressure."

Teresa was use to blowing cash. Before losing trial and serving three years in a women's Federal prison in Tallahassee, Florida for facilitating a cell phone during a drug crime, she was running through no less than three kilos a week.

Jimmy had made a promise to himself to never let his sister get her hands dirty after her release from prison. "Damn sis, gon' and get it outta that shoe box under my bed," he relented.

Terese smiled and gave Jimmy a kiss on the cheek before making a beeline for his bedroom.

"Ay!" Jimmy called after her prior to knocking on his grandmother's bedroom door. "Make sure you only get three grand, nye'."

"Come in," Ma Cam said, hearing her grandson's knock.

"Hey, Ma. You okay?" Jimmy asked, entering Ma Cam's bedroom.

"Yeah, son, I'm okay. These ole bones ain't let Mamma down yet."

"Okay, good. Ma, I paid the last mortgage payment earlier today. This yo' house, nye'."

Ma Cam smiled. "Jimmy, you're such a good boy. Mamma don't know what she would do if something happened to you. When you gonna go to church wit' me again?"

Ma Cam loved her grandson with all of her heart. Jimmy was the spitting image of his father. Every since Jimmy, Jr. was born, Ma Cam took a special interest in him. When he was a kid she used to take him with her to church and just about every where else she went.

"I don't know, Ma. But it'll be soon," he smiled.

"Son, you need to come to church. I know what you out there doing in them streets. And if I know, God knows. He's been showin' you mercy, son. And by His grace you still here. Baby, why don't you stay in tonight and we can have Bible study and I'll bake you some chocolate chip cookies like I use to?"

"Maybe tomorrow, Ma. I got a lotta thangs to do tonight."

Ma Cam sighed. "Fine, but let's at least pray before you go."

And that's what they did. They held hands, bowed and prayed. Ma Cam prayed for the deliverance of her grandson from Satan's clutches, and for him to be forgiven for his sins. Jimmy also prayed for forgiveness, as he did every night before falling asleep. He also prayed for his grandmother's continued health. He prayed for his sister. Lastly, he prayed that if and when the shit jumped off and niggas finally punched his clock, he prayed that he'd be reunited with his parents up in Heaven.

Jimmy hugged and kissed his grandmother after prayer and told her he had to go. Walking out of her bedroom, he saw Teresa coming down the hallway.

"Jimmy, I needed five-grand instead of the three I asked for," Teresa explained.

Jimmy grinned while shaking his head. "Aiight sis, but you gotta slow down witcho spendin' in the future," he preached before turning and leaving Teresa in the hall wondering if he'd bumped his head.

Teresa knew that she could get anything she wanted from her brother, but he'd bitch first. However, this time he only smiled and gave her some advice. *Nigga must be goin' to get some pussy,* she mused. She heard Jimmy open and close the front door behind himself.

When he stepped out into the cool night air, he took a deep breath before descending the porch steps. An eerie feeling washed over him when he reached the bottom. Glancing at the time on his Rolex, something told Jimmy to go back inside and call it a night, but duty called. He had to re-rock two kilos and cook a half-kilo for his traps.

Making it to his car, Jimmy heard a gunshot and was knocked to the pavement by a violent force. He heard footsteps fast approaching as he lay sprawled out on his stomach, on the cold asphalt. He turned over just as three masked men stood over him, aiming pistols in his face. One of the men said something, but Jimmy couldn't hear him because he sounded so far away. Jimmy began to pray before seeing the muzzle flash that ended his life.

¢   ¢   ¢

Teresa heard the gunshots and stormed out of the house as the killers sped off in the black sedan. Spotting her brother laying next to his BMW, she rushed over to him. Tears began clouding Teresa's vision upon observing the bullet hole in Jimmy's forehead. "Oh my God!" Teresa heard her grandmother scream. She looked back just as Ma Cam collapsed behind her, clutching her heart.

¢   ¢   ¢

Arriving at the hospital in the back of an ambulance, Teresa watched in tears as the medical techs did everything in their power to revive Ma Cam. But she was gone. She'd suffered a massive heart attack and was pronounced dead twenty-three minutes after her grandson.

Homicide detectives appeared at the hospital shortly thereafter. They questioned Teresa before allowing her to go to the morgue to pick up her grandmother and brother's property. Teresa caught a cab home.

Alone in her bedroom, Teresa sat on her bed next to two large brown paper bags, containing her dead relatives' belongings. Crying, Teresa began the painstaking process of going through her brother's stuff first. Jimmy's Presidential Rolex with the diamond bezel caught Teresa's attention immediately. She was kind of out of it when she'd discovered Jimmy's body, but for some reason she subconsciously thought that some niggas had robbed and killed her brother. Granted, finding Jimmy's Rolex, his Cuban link and a large sum of cash inside of the bag completely shattered that theory.

Jimmy's phone was also in the bag. Teresa strolled through his incoming call log. She wrote down the numbers of his most recent calls, then returned the last call he received, because it was repeatedly on the list.

"Hello?" Fat Boy said, answering his phone.

"Morris, is this you?" Teresa asked, recognizing his voice.

"Yeah, who this callin' from my dog phone?"

"This Tee. ...Morris, some niggas done killed my brutha."

Morris, aka Fat Boy, was Jimmy's best-friend. They'd been inseparable since elementary school.

"What?!" Fat Boy exclaimed.

"Jimmy gone, Morris. Some niggas killed him," Teresa stated somberly.

"Oh, hell nawl! Not my nigga! Who the fuck did that shit? Where you at?"

Fat Boy was firing off questions so fast Teresa couldn't answer them.

"Morris, just come to my grandma's house. I'll be here."

It took Fat Boy less than fifteen minutes to get there. Teresa saw the despair and gloom in her brother's best-friend's eyes the moment she invited him in. Leading Morris to her bedroom, Teresa offered him a seat on her bed before showing him Jimmy's property and explaining her theory as to why he'd been murdered.

"I think it was a hit," Teresa divulged, picking up some of Jimmy's cash with one hand and his Rolex with the other. "It wasn't no robbery 'cause he still had all this on him," she said, referring to the watch and the money. "I just don't see why a nigga would kill Jimmy. He played fair wit' everybody. Did you tell anybody else about Jimmy?" Teresa asked.

"Nawl, I came straight here. I ain't say shit to nobody."

"Good, 'cause we gonna have a meetin' over here tomorrow. Tell all the homies to be here by 12 p.m. and not a minute later," Teresa instructed.

Teresa was a naturally aggressive leader, just like her brother. So Fat Boy accepted her command as if Jimmy had spoken.

"Where Ma Cam at? How she takin' this bullshit?" Fat Boy asked, noticing he hadn't seen the friendly old lady who he loved like a mother.

"She gone, too. She, she died of a heart attack when she saw Jimmy layin' in the street."

Fat Boy dropped his head and cried. He'd lost his best-friend and a woman he loved like a mother, all in one night. He felt a pang of guilt knowing that he'd pressured Jimmy to prepare the work for the following day, when it was really his job to do so. Had he not been chasing ass, Jimmy and Ma Cam would still be alive. Snapping out of his reverie, Fat Boy stood and gave Teresa a hug, promising to return with all the homies the following day.

¢   ¢   ¢

Sleep didn't come easy for Teresa that night. And when she finally did drift off, she was startled awake by the phone ringing.

"Hello?" she answered in a groggy voice.

"Hey, Goldie Locks, it's me. You aight?"

"Hell nawl, I ain't aiight. ...Hold on, you sound like you know somethin'. What's up?"

"Yeah, I know what happened and I'm sorry."

Capo Cat

"Okay, what happened then, since you know so much?"

"Look baby, I know what happened to Jimmy, and I know who was behind that shit."

The caller had Teresa's undivided attention when he admitted to knowing who was behind her brother's murder.

"Aiight, who did it, then?" Teresa quizzed, suppressing the eagerness in her voice.

"Big Woo," the caller said before hanging up.

Chapter 28

"Ay man, let me get a ounce of 'dro?" the passenger of the '96 SS Impala asked Lil K-Mac as he stood in front of Big Woo's Gault Street, one-stop shop.

Lil K-Mac turned to his lieutenant, conveying the order with a hand signal.

"Circle 'round, we got that!" Fat Tank shouted from his chair on the porch.

The black SS sped off and turned the corner. Fat Tank yelled to Body Wash – who was inside of the trap – telling him to have an ounce of 'dro ready.

Fat Tank had been running Big Woo's Gault Street spot for going on two years. Since he weighed about 400 pounds and stood a stout 5'5", conventional work was out of the question for him. He could hardly move. However, he ran Big Woo's trap with an iron fist.

Body Wash stepped out of the house and passed Fat Tank the ounce of 'dro he'd requested. Tank, in turn, beckoned Lil K-Mac [the bomb man] to grab the sack.

"Damn, I told them niggas to spin' the block, not drive across town," Fat Tank said, watching as a blue Grand Prix turned the corner.

...Niggas/they comin' to getcha/Betta watch yo' back/Nigga's... was the song by the New Orleans rapper BG, emitting from inside of the car. Its back windows eased down in seemingly slow motion.

Lil K-Mac gawked at the red bandana tied around the barrel of the SKS before its handler squeezed the trigger. The force of the bullet slamming into Lil K-Mac's chest lifted him off of his feet and sent him crashing into the grill of Body Wash's box Chevy.

Tank caught a slug to his shoulder, spinning him out of his chair.

The Grand Prix then sped off, leaving the air thick with the smell of gun powder.

¢   ¢   ¢

James Wooden, aka Big Woo or Woo for short, was a Gangsta Disciple out of Cleveland, Tennessee. He ran his set and was Cleveland, Tennessee's number one weight supplier – since Jimmy Cam had been killed. Jimmy had held the number one spot for ten years.

"Man, I can't understand why them muthafuckin' slobs shot up my got-damn spot," Big Woo said to the other two men in the room.

He was in his den with his cousin from East St. Louis, Maine, and his right hand man Wayne. He was trying to figure out what provoked the Bloods to hit his Gault Street trap. And more importantly, who told them to since Jimmy Cam was dead.

As Big Woo continued to whine about his trap being hit up, Wayne thought that it was amazing how Woo had convinced himself that he was the victim. It had only been two days since Jimmy Cam had been murdered and shit had quickly taken a turn for the worst for the gang leader.

Big Woo had asked Goldie to front him more work and had even offered to allow one of Goldie's people to stay in Tennessee with him for a couple of weeks to inspect his operation. Big Woo offered to do this to appease Goldie's apprehension. He also did it thinking that after killing Jimmy Cam, shit would be sweet and he'd be able to take over the Blood's turf with ease.

Consequently, Big Woo had depended on no one finding out that the GD's were behind Jimmy Cam's death, thus giving them an advantage and making it easy for them to strike the Blood's with a blow that they'd never recover from. But he'd miscalculated, because the Bloods knew exactly who killed Jimmy and he was under attack. And to make matters worst, Cashman was to arrive within the hour.

"Shit, we gotta keep this shit wit' the Bloods contained until Goldie's lil' brutha leaves. A nigga can't be gettin' shot at and shit wit' the connect's brutha 'round," Big Woo stated.

Unbeknownst to Big Woo, the Bloods had all met up the day before at Teresa's grandmother's house. During their meeting, Teresa was voted the new shot-caller by an unanimous decision. And true to the saying, *hell has no fury like a woman scorn*, Teresa immediately ordered three teens she'd randomly picked from the assembly of Bloods, to shoot up one of Big Woo's traps.

"Woo, man, come on, you know you had Jimmy killed. Whatchu thought was gonna happen?" Wayne asked.

"Shit, I know that, you know that, and Maine know that, but how the fuck the Bloods know? Why they shoot my shit up, of all people?" Big Woo questioned.

"Man, we don't even know if it was the Bloods. Yeah, the nigga dropped a red flag, but shit, we don't know for sho'," Maine interjected.

Wayne and Big Woo looked over at Maine like he was crazy.

Big Woo was about to respond when his phone rang. "Hello?"

"Hey, this Mandi. We made it."

"Aiight, meet me where you met me at last time. I'ma be there in about fifteen minutes. Yall can follow me out to my house. Yall can stay wit' me while yall up here," Big Woo offered.

After the call, Big Woo informed Wayne and Maine that he had to go and that he'd get up with them later. They all left Big Woo's house, oblivious to the black SS Impala parked two houses down.

¢   ¢   ¢

Agent Tara Tate and her partner Dallas Henry sat in their Maxima across from the Friendly Inn's parking lot, watching as Cashman and Mandi stood outside of their mini-van talking to Big Woo. Agent Henry snapped picture after picture as the trio engaged in conversation. A short while later, the agents were shadowing the mini-van once again as it followed the Corvette driven by Big Woo.

Agent Tate looked over at her partner. "That big guy must be buying from our guys. This case is getting bigger and bigger everyday," she commented, shaking her head.

"It sure is. I'm going to contact the field office here in the morning and have these pictures developed. Hopefully we can have the big guy in the Corvette identified."

The two agents watched as they drove past. They had to circle the block to avoid having their cover blown.

¢   ¢   ¢

Big Woo noticed his porch light was off as he climbed out of his car, tucking his pistol in his waist. *Damn, I coulda sworn I left that muthafuckin' light on,* he thought, walking back toward the mini-van.

Mandi had just closed the driver's side door when her heart damn near leaped from her chest. Frozen in place by the intense fear, Mandi stared unblinkingly at two dark figures as they rose from the bushes in front of Big Woo's house.

As Big Woo approached Mandi, he watched her eyes bulge out and her face contort into a mask of pure terror. Instinctively, he glanced behind him, ducked and dove between the bumper and fender of the mini-van and Corvette. A barrage of gunfire began to report as he rolled.

Mandi yelped after catching a slug to her stomach and throat.

Meanwhile, Cashman, hearing the first volley of shots being squeezed off, began to feverishly manipulate the radio knob, AC switch and emergency brake release to open the dashboard stash box. Finally, the dash opened up, allowing him to retrieve his Desert Eagle. The windshield shattered the instant he clutched the large handgun.

The gunmen made their escape when the black Impala skidded to a stop at the end of Woo's driveway. Big Woo popped up and fired ten rounds at the dark figures as they fled to their car, but missed. Seconds later, the powerful LT1 motor rocketed the Impala down the street.

Agents Tate and Henry had turned back onto Big Woo's street just as the black Impala flew past them. Their police scanner was buzzing with dispatch asking for all available units to respond to a call about multiple shots being fired in a residential area. Passing by Big Woo's house once again, the agents spied Cashman and Big Woo standing over Mandi as she lay on the ground covered in blood. The two agents kept it moving, parking at the end of the block, they kept an eye on Big Woo's house.

¢ ¢ ¢

The distant wail of police sirens could be heard as they approached. Big Woo got Cashman's attention. "Ay Man, where that dope at? The police on the way!"

"That shit put up, so don't worry 'bout that," Cashman said, thinking of the kilos of coke in the back stash box of the mini-van.

The police arrived and quickly surrounded Cashman and Big Woo, badgering them with questions. They requested a coroner and told Cashman and Big Woo that they had to take a ride down to the station.

At the Bradley County Sheriff Office, Cashman and Big Woo were placed in separate interrogation rooms and questioned for hours before being released.

Chapter 29

Goldie sat in his study, sipping on a glass of bourbon while mulling over the conversation he'd just had with Jesus. It had only been two days since Goldie had sent Jesus his half of the 4.5 million that he and John Boy owed him, and Jesus was already requesting that Goldie return to Mexico. *Damn! Why the fuck I ain't use a rubber on her!* Goldie asked himself for the hundredth time.

So much shit had transpired in his life in the past three weeks. And because of the stress, he found himself becoming more and more dependent on Woodford Reserve. First Brown-eyed Ron and Lil Hezy got indicted. After that he had an unwelcome run-in with the DEA. Then, the night before, Cashman called him from Tennessee hipping him to the fact that his best mule – Mandi – had been killed by some got-damn gang bangers. Shit was just crazy!

Goldie drained the remainder of the bourbon from his glass, then refilled it. He took another sip, leaned back in his chair and began to massage his temples. *Fuck!* He bellowed before picking up his phone and calling John Boy.

After exchanging greetings, Goldie got straight to the point. He told John Boy about Lonita's pregnancy and Jesus' asking him to come back to Mexico. He also told John Boy that he needed to be hooked up with Dixie and Blair because he had a job for them. However, he neglected to inform John Boy of the Brown-eyed Ron situation and his run-in with the DEA, for fear that John Boy might get scared and slow down. Goldie had been spending a lot of money and he needed to make it back.

John Boy was undoubtedly surprised about Lonita's pregnancy, but was curious as to why Goldie needed to get in touch with Dixie and Blair. He hoped his young friend hadn't gone mad and was about to do something stupid. "Goldie, man, please tell me you ain't tryna have Jesus hit."

Goldie took another sip of his Bourbon. John Boy ignorantly took his momentary silence as an indication that Goldie was in fact considering having Jesus hit.

"Nigga, is you crazy?" John Boy barked. "Man, Jesus a have you and yo' whole family tree murked. Man, don't ev-"

Goldie cut him off. "Got-damn, ole *scead*-ass-nigga. *Jesus a have yo' whole family killed!*" he repeated mockingly in a whiny voice. "Man, get off Jesus' nuts!" he joked, laughing. "Nigga, I got somethin' else for them niggas to handle. I ain't worried 'bout no damn Jesus. Shit, ain't like I took Lonita's pussy."

John Boy sighed. "Oh, 'cause I was finna say…and nigga fuck you, nigga! I ain't *scead'*," he stated, laughing afterwards.

An hour later, Goldie received a call from Blair. After agreeing to meet him at the Starbucks off of University and Beach, Goldie got dressed and jumped in his Lambo. He arrived at the Starbucks twenty minutes later. Walking into the establishment, Goldie spied a pair of black dudes sitting at a table in the rear of the coffee lounge. One of the men – the one who sported the long dreads – waved him over.

These niggas can't be Dixie and Blair, Goldie thought to himself before taking a seat, facing the two men.

Blair, whose real name was Christopher Blair, was a tall dark-skin nigga with a mouth full of golds. He looked more like a pretty boy than anything else. And Dixie, the nigga with the long dreads, was of average height, brown-skin, with two golds. Goldie stared at Dixie, whose real name was Willie Foster, sizing him up. *This nigga don't look like he'll bust a grape,* he said to himself.

Yet both men were cold-blooded effective killers.

The three men introduced themselves, then immediately got down to business. Goldie explained Brown-eyed Ron and Lil Hezy's situation with the Feds and the need to have the informant that had did the controlled buys on them eliminated. He also told them that there could possibly be more work for them depending upon how things played out. Dixie and Blair agreed to kill Sherod Miller, the federal informant, for $20,000. Then they'd charge him

Capo Cat

$5,000 for each additional head that needed busting. A hand shake sealed the deal. Goldie went on to divulge to the assassins what Precious – Brown-eyed Ron's wife – had told him concerning Sherod Miller's potential hangouts, his ties to dog fighting and his insatiable lust for strip clubs.

¢ ¢ ¢

"Driver! Step out of your vehicle with your hands up," the officer barked over his loud speaker. Goldie was in his Lamborghini, trapped at the red light of a busy intersection. "Fuck!" he said aloud, thinking of the twenty kilos he had in his possession.

The cops had been pretty slick. They had been following Goldie in their unmarked cars all day. After seeing Goldie leave one of his mini storages, they decided to pull him over. Goldie glanced in his rearview mirror. Three unmarked cars and a Tahoe were behind him, blue lights flashing in their grills. There was about eight cops total, each behind an open door of their vehicle. Guns drawn.

Finally, the light changed green and Goldie floored it. He came out of first so fast that his tires barked. He was two miles up the road before the cops could get back into their vehicles. The chase was on! It all started at the intersection of St. John Bluff and Atlantic BLVD, but before the cops could get onto Atlantic, Goldie had already merged onto 9A. Seconds later he looked in his rearview and saw the blue lights flashing in the grill of the lead police car, it had also merged onto 9A.

Goldie looked over at the two duffle bags of cocaine once more and shifted his gear. The instant acceleration of the Lamborghini penned him to his seat. He looked in his sideview mirror a few moments later only to see that the cop cars had disappeared and in their placement was a helicopter. Shifting the gear once more, Goldie almost lost control as he rapidly approached the Dames Point Bridge. Shifting the last gear, he glanced down at his speedometer. It read 207 mph. When he brought his sights back up he realized that he was on top of the bridge and had a clear view of what was at the bottom.

"Got damn!" he muttered upon seeing the road block up ahead.

He was going too fast and had too much cocaine on him to stop. So he applied more pressure to the gas pedal and began blowing his horn. "Yeah, yall muthafuckas betta move yall asses out the way," Goldie said aloud.

But the cops did no such thing. Instead, they opened fire on the rapidly approaching Lamborghini. A slug struck the windshield, sending glass into Goldie's face. Another slug hit him in the chest a split second later. He lost control of the Lambo and hit the guardrail at 197 mph. The Lamborghini burst into flames before flipping over, leaving Goldie trapped in the burning wreakage to watch his own skin melt away like plastic.

"Mr. Jackson, we've landed," the co-pilot said while shaking Goldie. He was sweating profusely and moaning.

Goldie attempted to jump up, startled by the co-pilot's voice, but his seatbelt restrained him. His eyes darted around the jet's cabin for a few seconds before he realized where he was at. He let out a heavy sigh, laced with relief. "Thank God it was only a dream," he said under his breath.

¢   ¢   ¢

Lonita was standing next to a Hummer golf cart when Goldie stepped off of the jet. As soon as his feet touched the tarmat she was in his arms. "Oh, poppi, I'm so glad to see you," she said before kissing him. "I received the money you owed me when you sent father his money. Thank you."

"Aiight…then what Jesus wanna holla at me for? He know you pregnant?"

Lonita's smile disappeared and she lowered her head. "Goldie, I had no choice but to tell him. I'm keeping mi bambino, so there is no need of trying to hide it."

Goldie exhaled loudly then spoke. "What he say 'bout it?"

Lonita took a seat on the driver's side of the Hummer golf cart. "He's mad that I'm having a baby out of wedlock. He's also mad that I had sex outside of my race…my father…he's not a racist, however, he doesn't approve of race mixing."

"So this trip ain't got shit to do wit' business? Yo' daddy just wanna try to put his press down on a nigga?"

"Oh no, Goldie, he's going to discuss some business wit' you. But he's also going to ask you about your intentions concerning me and the baby."

"But me and you done already talked about that," Goldie stated, irritably.

"I know. And I've explained that to him, but he wants to talk to you himself," Lonita explained, patting the passenger seat of the golf cart. "My men will take care of your luggage," she said after Goldie was seated.

¢ ¢ ¢

When they arrived at the mansion, Jesus was in the great room waiting on them. When they stepped inside, Jesus excused Lonita from the room with a wave of his hand. He then motioned for Goldie to be seated. Silence occupied the room for about two minutes while Jesus stared into Goldie's eyes with a burning intensity that could have melted steel.

Jesus finally broke the tension in the room when he stood up and gestured for Goldie to follow him. He walked into an adjoining room, opened a door and left it ajar. When Goldie reached the door, Jesus had disappeared down some stairs. Reaching the bottom, Goldie realized that he was in a wine cellar. He heard Jesus call his name from somewhere in the rear. When Goldie reached the area where Jesus' voice had travelled from, his eyes grew wide with shock at the sight before him.

Jesus was standing next to a little Mexican man that was bound to a chair with chains. A small strip of duct tape covered his mouth. Goldie noticed that Jesus held a hammer in his hand.

"This man gets paid good money to take care of my horses...but," Jesus said, holding up his pointer finger, momentarily pausing before continuing, "He doesn't take care of his responsibilities... He takes all of his money and throws it away gambling, drinking, and going to the brothel. All the while, his wife and kids are at home starving. Goldie, what kind of man would neglect his family?"

This must be a trick question, Goldie thought to himself, but said nothing.

Jesus walked over to Goldie and stood next to him. Pointing the hammer he held at the bound man, he said, "He is a selfish man, who will betray anybody to save himself. He is a cancerous disease that must be removed before it spreads," he added before walking back over to the chained man and slapping him. The helpless man's head swayed from the force of the blow. "You see Goldie, you don't get my age by allowing a disease to linger. You have to eliminate it before it incapacitates you," Jesus said, squatting before the chained man, then bringing the hammer down hard upon his bare toe.

A bloody toenail went airborne, striking the wall, barely missing Goldie. The man in the chair passed out in shock. Jesus continued to relentlessly bash the little chained Mexican's foot until it looked like a pizza. Satisfied with his handiwork, he motioned Goldie over to him and extended him the bloody hammer. "Your turn," he simply stated.

Goldie reluctantly took the hammer, staring at it momentarily like it was some newly discovered tool.

"What are you waiting for? Hit him!" Jesus demanded.

Goldie struck the bound man on his good foot and paused as the man jerked awake in his chair. A muffled cry seeped through the duct tape.

"Again!" Jesus barked.

Hesitating for a few seconds, Goldie hit the man again. The stench of piss and shit followed the blow.

"What kind of man are you?" Jesus snarled. "You get my fucking daughter pregnant, yet you're afraid to get your hands dirty!"

Goldie glanced up at Jesus and released a sadistic chuckle. He turned his attention back to the bound man, imagining that he was Jesus, then began to savagely pound the chained man's foot unmercifully.

Boom! Boom! Two gunshots resonated in the cellar, surprising both men.

The chair in which the bound man sat fell backwards. Jesus and Goldie quickly looked behind them and saw Lonita holding a smoking .357. She lowered the gun and tucked it into her waist before casually walking over to Jesus. "Father, must you try to intimidate people all the time to get your way?"

Jesus looked like a kid caught with his hand in the cookie jar. "I was only trying to get an understanding with Goldie," he said, pointing. "But since you're here, I want to hear what Goldie's intentions are for you and the baby."

"Father, I've already talked to you about that. What yo-"

"I want to hear from Goldie, not you!" Jesus barked, cutting Lonita off.

Goldie locked eyes with Jesus. "Man, you ain't got to worry about me bein' a dead beat dad. And as far as Lonita is concerned, ain't shit I can give her she ain't already got. But I'ma be there for her anytime she need me."

Jesus exhaled an exasperated sigh, then mumbled something incoherently. "Goldie, I heard you when you said that you will be a good father to my grandbaby and that you would be there for my daughter, but why can't you be her husband? Why won't you marry her?"

"Wow," Goldie stated, taking a few steps back. "Husband? Yo' daughter? Man, I'm already engaged."

Jesus kicked the dead man in the fallen chair and got into Goldie's face. "What, do you think that you're too good for my daughter?"

"Father! Please, calm down," Lonita replied, stepping in between the two men. "I told you that I knew and respected that Goldie had a woman back in the states before I had sex with him. It's my choice to have this baby."

"Got-damn, you, Lonita! How could you do this to me? How could you have a bastard child on me?! What do you think our associates will think once they find out you're about to become an unwed mother? How do you think Manny is gonna feel?"

Lonita sucked her teeth. "I could care less about what our associates think. And Manny is of no interest to me. You're the one who wants me to marry him, so that you can get closer to Pedro and the rest of the Cali Cartel," she said while crossing her arms and shifting her weight onto her left leg. "Look father, I've already told you where I stand, so drop it."

"But Lonita w-"

"Don't but me, father! Just drop it. I don't need you calling Goldie to Mexico under the guise of doing business only to get here and be harassed."

Jesus' shoulders slumped in defeat. "I just want the best for you, princess," he said, looking into Lonita's eyes.

"No father, you want the best prices on cocaine and weed. And speaking of drugs, wasn't that the reason you wanted to see Goldie? At least that's what you told me."

Jesus knew defeat when he saw it. Lonita wasn't going to allow him to pressure Goldie like he'd sought out to. "Oh well," he sighed and turned to face Goldie, "Do you know anything about heroin?"

Chapter 30

Cashman stood behind Kismet and Goldie at the altar as they exchanged their vows. Pastor R.J. Washington presided over the wedding. The ceremony was being held at the Harvest Dome and was packed to capacity. It seemed like every drug dealer from Duval County and their mommas was there. And so was the Feds.

As Cashman passed Goldie the jewelry box containing Kismet's wedding ring, he saw one of the young flower girls out of his periphery and was reminded of Darshawna Davis. Guilt and sorrow ate away at him every time he saw a little black girl after crossing paths with the innocent child….

¢   ¢   ¢

Three Months Prior
After being interrogated and released from jail, Cashman and Woo caught a cab over to Woo's baby-mother's house. Cashman texted Goldie, using the coded numbers that he'd been taught, informing him that Mandi had been killed. Goldie texted him back telling him to get back to Jacksonville pronto. But Cashman was hard headed. He wanted retribution. He wasn't going to let some niggas shoot at him and leave without killing somebody.

"Who you thank that was that killed Mandi?" Cashman asked.

He and Woo were in Dona's – Big Woo's baby-mother's – living room smoking a blunt.

Big Woo exhaled loudly. "I thank the Bloods did that shit. One of my lil niggas got killed at one of my traps the other day. Niggas say a black Chevy SS stopped by there befo' another car came by wettin'."

"Well what's up, my nigga? We gotta do something! I ain't lettin' nann nigga shoot at me and get away wit' it."

Big Woo liked what he heard come out of the young Florida nigga's mouth. When Cashman said, *We gotta do somethin'*, Big Woo smiled on the inside. Cashman didn't know that Woo had started the beef with the Bloods, nor did he care. And Big Woo wasn't going to tell him either. It had been a while since Woo had gotten into some gangster shit, personally. And Cashman had him hyped up. Plus he was pissed that the Bloods had the audacity to bring him a move at his home. *Yeah*, Big Woo reflected internally, *heads is finna roll 'round this bitch.*

¢ ¢ ¢

Jimmy and Ma Cam's funeral was held at Mount Zion Baptist Church. There was a large turn out, as people from as far away as Kentucky came to pay their last respects to the fallen gang leader. Most in attendance wore red, symbolizing their affiliation or membership to the Bloods. Even Jimmy and Ma Cam's caskets were red. Teresa had them specially painted in the image of a red bandana.

¢ ¢ ¢

Cashman and Big Woo watched as the mourners entered into the church. They sat behind the dark tints of a chopped Camaro. Big Woo thought it to be a good idea to shoot up Jimmy Cam's funeral since he felt that the Bloods had been attacking him. He also knew that a lot of them would be in attendance at Jimmy Cam's homegoing.

"Aiight, my nigga, all you gotta do is pull up in front of the buildin', I'ma start wettin'. Then we out," Cashman instructed, then he added, "I'ma show you how we do shit in Duval."

Big Woo grunted, then smirked. He put the car in drive, cutting the wheel so he could get from behind the car he was parked behind. After Woo eased into the road, Cashman cocked the AR-15 he had laying across his lap and they both pulled on their ski masks.

¢   ¢   ¢

Meanwhile, Agents Tara Tate, Dallas Henry, Joshua Craft and Larry Groove were parked down the block from Mount Zion, snapping pictures and conducting basic surveillance on Jimmy Cam and Ma Cam's funeral.   After contacting the Cleveland, Tennessee DEA field office the day before, Agents Tate and Henry traveled there. They talked to a few agents and found out that the big guy on the pictures that Henry had developed was the largest drug trafficker in Cleveland, Tennessee and the leader of his own set of Gangster Disciples.

When Agent Henry divulged to the Tennessee agents that he and Tara had followed a DEA target from Florida up to Big Woo's doorsteps, they were elated. They had heard that Big Woo was being supplied by some major players out of the Sunshine State, but throughout all of their exhaustive surveillance – which included wire taps – they could never identify Woo's supplier. Now they finally had the break that they had been looking for.

Agent Tate put her two cents in, candidly informing her Tennessee counterparts about Operation White-Gold. Intrigued by the enormity of the case, Agent Craft contacted Assistant U.S. Attorney for the Southern District of Tennessee and lead prosecutor over Big Woo's investigation – Parker Anderson. When he told the government attorney what he'd learned from the two Florida agents, Parker Anderson was all ears. Especially when Craft boasted that the case stretched across the border. Parker was trying to make U.S. Attorney for the entire Southern District of Tennessee and being involved in a case of White-Gold's magnitude would surely make him a shoo-in for that office. Before the teleconference between the Assistant U.S. Attorney and the agents ended, Parker Anderson had become an official member of Operation White-Gold. Agents Craft and Groove followed suit.

¢   ¢   ¢

"So you're saying that based on what your informant has told you, you believe that a woman is now leading the Bloods set here?" Tara asked Craft incredulously.

"That's correct. We believe that Teresa is now calling all of the shots. And from what our sources are saying, she's put contracts out on all ranking members of the Gangster Disciples. ...Even the retired ones."

"Shit, pal, it looks like it's about to get real ugly up here. Too bad me and Henry can't stay for the fun. We're expected back at the Jacksonsville office tomorrow afternoon. We have a lot of paperwork to do back home. We're pulling out later tonight," Tara said.

"We understand, and we will definitely be in touch," Agent Groove added, watching the church through his spy-glasses. He continued, "Make sure-" he started to say before witnessing a grey Camaro jump the curb at the entrance of Mount Zion.

¢   ¢   ¢

Big Woo brought the souped-up Camara to a screeching halt in front of the crowded church, striking an old lady and her walker before coming to a complete stop. Cashman stuck the barrel of his AR-15 out of the passenger window and opened fire. Chaos erupted in and around the church as people scattered for cover, fearful of the thunderous claps from the assault rifle.

"Go! Go! Go!" Agent Groove barked to Agent Craft upon hearing the shots and seeing people running for refuge.

Cashman discharged close to fifty rounds before commanding Big Woo to hit the gas. The Camaro leaped forward, fishtailing as it sped down the street. It almost sideswiped the oncoming surveillance van as Woo thwarted an attempt by Agent Craft to cut him off.

"Got-damn! Who the fuck was that?" Woo asked aloud. He looked in his rearview and saw the van do a 180 in the middle of the road.

Slamming on the brakes and cutting the wheel, Big Woo made a sharp left turn onto a residential street. The Super Charger underneath the hood unleashed a distinctive buzzing sound as its turbines increased their revolutions. But the surveillance van's heavily modified engine made it impossible to shake.

"Man, it's some crackas in that van," Cashman informed Big Woo after glancing back.

Big Woo made a hard right. "Nigga, that's the muthafuckin' po'lice! You need to stop playin' anchorman and buss at them crackas!"

Cashman slid in another clip, leaned out of the window and peppered the trailing van with bullets. Of the twenty-nine rounds that were issued from the AR, one penetrated the van's windshield and the driver's side headrest, lodging itself into Agent Henry's forehead. Luckily Agent Craft had ducked under the wheel, but when he came back up the van clipped the side of a parked car, becoming airborne before landing on its left side, then sliding about thirty feet.

Big Woo witnessed the wreck in his rearview and smiled at Cashman. "Dog, you a wild ass nigga!" he complimented.

Moments later they were merging onto I-75 enroute to Big Woo's Uncle Weaver's house.

¢   ¢   ¢

Ambulance and police arrived at the scene of the overturned surveillance van. The surviving agents had already pulled Dallas Henry's body from the wreckage. When Dallas was placed in a body bag, Tara Tate released a floodgate of emotions. She could hardly maintain her composure while being interviewed by homicide detectives.

When she arrived back at the Tenneessee field office, Agent Tate placed a call to the DEA headquarters in Jacksonville. "Yes, could you get me Special Agent Ricks?" she asked the operator.

Seconds later, Ricks was on the phone. "Yeah, speak to me," he said.

"Ricks, this is Tara. You're not going to believe this, but Dallas is dead."

"What?! What the hell are you talking about?"

"He was killed about an hour ago as we pursued a vehicle that was involved in a drive-by."

"Let me get this straight, Cashman did a drive-by and you guys chased him?"

"Umm, no...I mean...Well, we don't know who did the shooting?"

"Okay, Cashman was on the scene when the drive-by occurred and was shot, right?"

"No...No, sir."

Agent Ricks sighed. "Okay, where was Cashman during all of this?"

"I don't know, sir. We were watching a funeral an-"

"A funeral?! What the fuck does a got-damn funeral have to do with our case?" Ricks interrupted.

Agent Tate advised her supervisor of the escalating war between the Gangster Disciples and the Bloods. She further explained that since she was almost 100% sure that Goldie was supplying the GD's, and that the gang was suspected of being responsible for the murder of the previous leader of the Bloods, the funeral was in fact relevant to Operation White-Gold.

"Well why didn't you just tell me all of this shit in the beginning?" Ricks asked.

"I-I," Tara stuttered.

"Never mind," Ricks cut in and continued, "I'll be flying out there on the next thing smoking, so stay put... Did you call Dallas' wife, yet?" he asked as an afterthought.

"No, sir."

"Okay, I'll handle it. See you later," Ricks stated before hanging up.

¢   ¢   ¢

Four Hours Later
"Aw, hell nawl, my nigga! Dog, I ain't mean to do that shit!" Cashman stated, pointing at the television.

He and Big Woo were at Woo's Uncle Weaver's house watching the 6 o'clock news. They were trying to see what the police were saying about the church shooting when a photo of a smiling little black girl appeared in the top right corner of the screen. The reporter said that she was one of the four people that was shot and killed by the same shooters a few blocks away.

When the reporter began to question the pastor of the church, Cashman really felt like shit. The pastor explained that Darshawna Davis, who was only eight years old, died while trying to shield her three year old sister from gunfire. Cashman turned the TV off after hearing the reporter quote a DEA spokesman as saying that things were about to get really uncomfortable for the City's gang members.

¢   ¢   ¢

Snapping out of his reverie, Cashman heard the pastor pronounce Kismet and Goldie *husband and wife*. Then they kissed and the church erupted in applause. It was a bittersweet moment…

Chapter 31

"Dog, I'm ready to buss that fuck-nigga head right nye'! Look at that nigga… In here flossin' like he a straight up gangsta when we just seen his bitch-ass walk out of the Federal Courthouse earlier today, snitchin'!" Dixie spat angrily to his partner in crime.

Blair nodded. "Shiid, you too? Man, a nigga tired of watchin' this fuck-ass-nigga. I'm witcha, dog, let's do this nigga tonight!"

Dixie and Blair had been on Sherod's ass for two straight weeks. Two and a half months had sped by since Goldie had given the two killers the contract on Sherod's life. Yet, they had not been able to track the elusive treasonist down for shit. It wasn't until Goldie contacted them with Sherod's new address that they got a bead on him. Sherod had moved his family and changed up his whole operation after fucking Lil Hezy and Brown-eyed Ron up. He had stopped selling coke, switching to heroin instead.

Goldie put his private investigator friend, Camila on Sherod's trail after Dixie and Blair kept coming up short. She found him in less than a week.

¢ ¢ ¢

Dixie shook his head in disgust as he watched Sherod and his two top trap lieutenants ball out of control at the Big Apple in Jacksonville. They were popping bottle after bottle of Dom, while tossing handfuls of cash over the balcony of their sky-box VIP booth, causing money to rain down upon the club patrons below.

The two killers exited the club to wait in the parking lot for Sherod and his trap bosses just as the DJ announced the last call for alcohol.

¢ ¢ ¢

Stumbling out of the club into the night, Sherod's lieutenants, TJ and Choppa, had to help his drunk ass into his Suburban. They did so gladly because they looked up to the big coward. Sadly, the two young thugs didn't know the kind of nigga their boss truly was. All they saw was a get-money, gangsta-ass-nigga. They were ignorant to the fact that they were not in Florida celebrating the success of their new heroin traps, but were actually there because Sherod had to render three days of testimony to the Grand Jury.

The only reason that Sherod brought the young hustlers along with him was because they were his most loyal soldiers and he was afraid to be in Jacksonville alone while snitching. Nevertheless, Sherod's snake-ass would be making up another lie the following morning, so he could leave TJ and Choppa at their three bedroom suite as he continued fulfilling his cooperation agreement with the government.

¢ ¢ ¢

After securing Sherod in the passenger seat, the two youngsters jumped in the SUV and drove out of the parking lot, making a left turn onto Norwood. Dixie and Blair was right on their asses. Oblivious to Agent Hogan and Ricks on theirs.

When Sherod's Suburban got caught at the light on Golfair BLVD, Blair ran the Buick he was driving into its bumper and watched as Sherod, TJ and Choppa jumped out to inspect the damage. He and Dixie then hopped out of the Buick, pistols tucked in their backs. Their initial plan was to gun Sherod and his people down as soon as they stepped out of the SUV, but it was foiled when Blair noticed Agent Ricks and Hogan's Maxima behind them.

"Hold on, some crackas behind us," he said in a hushed tone, still approaching Sherod and his two associates.

¢ ¢ ¢

Ricks unholstered his service weapon and turned to his partner as

Dixie began signaling for them to pass. "Hogan, there's something going on here. Something's not right."

"You know what, Ricks? I get the same feeling. And you and I both know that we can't afford for something to happen to Sherod. I mean, for crying out loud, the Grand Jury just convened."

The two agents had no choice but to jump out of their car with their guns drawn, "Freeze!" they both said in unison.

At that instant, Blair imagined himself in an orange jumpsuit and reached for his pistol.

"Hey! Hey! Hey, don't do it!" Ricks commanded, watching as Blair brought his gun up, leveling it. He opened fire, hitting Blair in his stomach, shoulder and chest.

Dixie had his pistol raised, but before he could get off a shot he caught two hot ones in his back, compliments of TJ. The slugs were meant for the two agents, but the scared youngster had his back turned as he ran away, busting without looking back. He only hoped that his bullets found their intended targets.

Sherod went down next. A .40 caliber slug slammed into the back of his head, releasing gray brain matter on the Suburban's back door and onto Choppa's face. Another one of TJ's rounds had found the wrong mark.

"Got-damn-it, get down!" Ricks barked at a horrified Choppa, who was frantically trying to wipe the gore from his face. Ricks squeezed off five shots at TJ, almost hitting him as the youth scaled the gate to Brentwood Projects. "Fuck!" he spat upon seeing the youngster land on his feet and continue running.

"I got this one," Hogan said, pointing his pistol at Choppa. "Go get that bastered!" he said, referring to the fleeing TJ.

¢   ¢   ¢

TJ was running for his life. He didn't know where he was going or if the two crackas that had started shooting was really the police or not. But he did know one got-damn thing, he wasn't trying to go to jail, especially in Florida! Shit, they had the death penalty and niggas was doing 85% of their time. No parole!

Now almost at the entrance of Brentwood, TJ saw a car

about to stop at a stop sign so that it could turn onto the BLVD. He quickly advanced on the driver's side of the vehicle and snatched the door open. He then heard Ricks yell "hault" from yards away. TJ paid him no mind as he forcefully removed the elderly lady from her car and jumped in. He stomped on the gas and fishtailed out of the public housing complex. Agent Ricks opened fire to no avail. TJ was on 20th Street Expressway heading north…

Chapter 32

Precious pulled up to the Chattam County Jail, got out of her car and ascended the steps with her three children on her heels. She hated to bring her children to see Brown-eyed Ron there. Moreso, she hated being there herself, but she put up with the inconvenience out of gratitude for Ron. He'd been a good man to her. Precious had three kids from three different baby-daddy's, and neither of which were Ron's. But he accepted and treated them like his own. He was actually the only father that Precious' children knew, since all of their biological fathers were either dead or in prison.

Ensuing a brief pat search, Precious was allowed to proceed to the visiting area. Brown-eyed Ron ambled out ten minutes later. The kids, happy to see their stepfather, ran over to him, hugging his legs. Ron picked them up one by one, giving each of them a hug and a kiss. Placing the last child down, Ron started for the table Precious was seated at. He noticed as he got closer that she hadn't stood up to give him a hug and kiss like she used to when he'd first gotten locked up.

He'd also started to notice a few other things lately. Like his mail getting scarce. And his visits dropping from twice per week to once. Then, when Precious did visit, she seemed distant and bored, like she wasn't as enthused as she once was to see him. Shit, Ron was a street nigga. He knew what the lick read. He was losing his bitch and although he had only been locked up for three months, he knew it wouldn't be much longer before Precious started looking for the next man. And the bad thing about the whole situation was that he couldn't get mad at the bitch when she did what was in her nature. She was a hoe when he met her and everybody knows you can't make a hoe into a housewife.

After exchanging greetings, Ron decided to let Precious know what the business was and what he'd been considering doing. "Baby, listen, I know I said that I was gonna take my time and lay down, but man… A nigga been thankin'… Shiid, I ain't tryna be gone for no twenty-five years. Them crackas came and holla'd at me and guaranteed me no more than three years if I help 'em."

Precious was bewildered. "Help 'em? Help 'em how? Boy, I know you ain't talkin' 'bout snitchin'?"

Ron dropped his head. "Shiid, it's either that or I take twenty-five… Or, I can go to trial, but if I lose they gonna give me life. Gurl, I ain't wit' this shit. I miss the hell out of you and them kids," Ron said, looking into Precious' eyes.

Precious was feeling Ron's pain. She wanted him home too. But she just wasn't sure about the snitching shit he was talking about. Precious had been faced with the same situation before with her first baby-daddy. He went to trial instead of snitching, lost and got a life sentence. So Precious knew the seriousness of Ron's dilemma.

Precious sighed. "Aiight, boy, I ain't sayin' I'm wit' this shit, but what them crackas want you to do?"

Ron took a few moments to respond. He exhaled an exasperated breath, then said, "They want you to plant some wires 'round Goldie's house. And the—"

"Boy, is you crazy?!" Precious interrupted loudly, drawing the attention of the CO at the officer's station.

"What?" Ron asked, shrugging his shoulders, palms up.

"What?! Nigga, what I got to do wit' yo' shit? Why they tr—" Precious paused, placing her hand over her mouth. "Boy, you been runnin' yo' mouth. You told them crackas I been stayin' wit' Goldie 'nem?"

"Yeah, I told 'em, but it ain't nothin'. They just tryin' to build they case. So what's up? Is you gonna help a nigga or what?"

Precious couldn't believe what she was hearing. She never would have thought ole' thuggish ass Ron would fall weak and start snitching. "I guess you really can't judge a book by its cover," she said to herself, but loud enough for Ron to hear.

"Damn, gurl, is you gonna help me or what?" Ron queried impatiently, desperation dripping from his voice.

"Ron, I don't know about this po'lice ass shit. Give me a few days to thank about this shit, okay?"

Not wanting to press the issue any further, for fear that Precious would get angry, Ron nodded his head and changed the subject. They chatted about happier times while Ron played with the kids until visitation was over.

¢   ¢   ¢

When Precious arrived back at Goldie's mansion, him and Cashman were in the kitchen having a private discussion. Precious quickly waved at the two brothers as she made her way through the great room enroute to the area of the mansion reserved for guests. Goldie was curious about her visit with Ron and called her name as she began to climb the stairs, kids in tow. "Ay girl, you aiight?" he asked, genuinely concerned.

Precious turned around and walked back to the kitchen. "Yeah, I'm scrate, just tired, that's all," she stated, now standing facing Goldie. She felt a slight pang of guilt, knowing what Ron had in mind, but not mentioning it.

"Well whe—" Goldie started to say but was interrupted by Kismet screaming his name. Everyone followed as Goldie quickly sprinted up to his bedroom. "Oh, shit! Baby, you okay?" he asked Kismet, who was standing wide-legged in a large wet spot in the plush carpet.

Her water had broke.

"Call the ambulance," she said, barely above a whisper, then fainted into Goldie's arms.

Chapter 34

A motorcade consisting of four Tahoes, three Crown Vics and three vans arrived in Swainsboro, Georgia's city limits at precisely 4:30 a.m. For the most part, the town was still asleep, except for the fiends and prostitutes that were up and about, not missing a beat. The convoy of vehicles split up into three groups after stopping at the Emanual County Jailhouse and arresting two deputies whose names were on an indictment handed down by a South, GA Federal Grand Jury. Afterwards, they all set out to round up the rest of the people charged on the indictment.

¢   ¢   ¢

5:30 a.m.
Slaughter pulled up to his heroin trap and smiled at the long line of fiends waiting for his shop to open. He had never made so much money off of drugs in his life. Dealing with the horse had truly got him on top. Goldie had given him an ounce of smack to see if he could move it, and not long afterwards the dope fiends started coming from cities as far away as Atlanta to cop. It was definitely true what they said about heroin money versus coke. Heroin money separated the boys from the men and Slaughter had become a giant. He was selling two kilos of smack per week in all dimes. And to top it off, each kilo could stand a seven, though he was only hitting them with a three.

Slaughter placed a call from his cell before getting out of his car. Seconds later, two men stepped out of the heroin trap carrying assault rifles. The gunmen pushed the thirsty fiends out of the way so that Slaughter could make a straight shot into the house. Stepping out of his car, Slaughter secured a duffle bag on his shoulder. He took two steps and turned around at the sound of a four-barrel carburetor opening up.

Suddenly, two more vehicles turned the corner behind the black Crown Vic. It didn't take a rocket scientist to figure out that it was the police. And they were coming to bust the spot! Slaughter had ten ounces of heroin bagged up inside of his bag. Unaware that he was already indicted for enough cocaine to sink a yacht, he jumped back in his car, started it up and stomped the gas. The Corvette came off the curb and cannon-balled past the approaching police vehicles. Slaughter glanced in his rearview mirror just as the Crown Vic did a 180 followed by the other two vehicles.

Putting his eyes back on the road in front of him, Slaughter made a hard left onto Main Street. His car was on two wheels. The once airborne tires made a screeching sound, like an airplane landing, when they came back down. With complete control of the wheel again, Slaughter pulled out his cell phone and pressed number two on his speed dial as he glanced in his rearview once more.

¢　¢　¢

5:36 a.m. Sheriff West's House
"Hello?" Sheriff West answered. "Got-damn-it, slow down! I can't hear a got-damn thing you just said!"

"Man, I pay yo' ass twenty G's a month and you let my shit get raided?" Slaughter spat, heatedly.

"Raided? Raided by who? I'm the sheriff of this got-damn town. Ain't shit going down here unless I say so!"

"Well, since you so in charge, why the fuck am I in a high speed chase right now? Man, they was comin' to kick my muthafuckin' doe' in… I thank it was them folks."

"What folks? Who in the hell are you talking about? Now you li-"

Just then a loud crashing sound emitted from the downstairs area of Sheriff West's house.

"What in the hell… Hold on," Sheriff West told Slaughter while retrieving his service weapon from under his pillow.

Mrs. West, who was next to her husband in bed, heard his

entire conversation, but said nothing. She'd learned a long time ago to keep her mouth shut and to stay out of her husband's business. She knew what the good sheriff was doing outside of the house. Hell the whole town knew. But the lavish lifestyle Sheriff West's criminal activities afforded her made it easy to turn a blind eye to his wrongdoings. However, the loud noise and the sound of seemingly thousands of footsteps ascending the hallway stairs caused her blind eye to open. Especially when two men wearing suits, followed by about ten men dressed in black tactical gear, barged into her bedroom flashing their badges.

"Got-damn-it, just who the fuck do you son-of-a-bitches think you are? I'm the got-damn sheriff," Sheriff West barked with this gun trained on one of the suited men. He didn't have his eyeglasses on so he couldn't read the letters DEA in large print inside of the agent's wallets.

"DEA. You're under arrest. Drop your weapon," one of the agents demanded.

¢   ¢   ¢

Slaughter held his phone in his hand, staring at it in disbelief. "How in the hell do the muthafuckin' sheriff get arrested?" he asked himself before using his speed dial once again. This time the call went to Goldie's phone.

"Yeah?" Goldie answered on the third ring.

"This Slaughter. It's some shit goin' down up here. Man, the Feds chasin' me and they got Sheriff West!"

"The Feds!? Ay, hit me from another phone when you get where you goin', yo' shit might be tapped!" Goldie replied, then hung up.

Slaughter tossed his phone in the passenger seat and looked in his rearview. The Tahoe that was once behind the Crown Vic and Econoline Van was now directly on his ass. Already racing at a speed of 110 mph, Slaugher got down on the gas a little more. He wasn't aware that the Tahoe was equipped with a twin turbo 8.1 liter Vortec engine.

The Tahoe got into the passing lane and seconds later its front bumper was lined up with Slaughter's rear finder. A second after that, they were side by side. The driver of the Tahoe cut his wheel, slamming into the speeding Corvette, causing Slaughter to lose control. The Corvette went into a half spin before flipping over, then wrapping around a light pole. Slaughter didn't stand a chance. He died on impact.

¢   ¢   ¢

Sheriff and Mrs. West were cuffed and taken to Machintosh County Jail. The DEA and GBI had been busy all morning rounding up the people listed on their indictment. Mrs. West had almost suffered a heart attack when she was placed under arrest. She was charged with money laundering. Ordinarily, the Feds wouldn't have wasted the ink it took to place Mrs. West's name on the indictment, but they wanted to use her as leverage against Sheriff West.

They were going to make him talk. And they wanted at least ten years out of his ass.

¢   ¢   ¢

Goldie woke up in the middle of the night. He couldn't sleep. Sliding into his bedroom slippers, he sat at the edge of his bed, looking back at Kisment, who'd also woke up and was staring at him through sleepy eyes. "Go back to sleep baby. I'ma go check on Sultan, Jr.," he said before getting up and walking to the nursery.

Sultan Jr. was sleeping peacefully in his crib. Goldie looked down at his son and said a silent prayer, in hopes that his sins wouldn't fall upon his only child's head. He wanted to see his son grow up. He wanted to see his grand kids. But with all of the shit going on around him he wasn't sure that would be possible. Shit was hot!!!

The arrest of Sheriff West, his wife and six other deputies had been one of CNN's top stories. Mostly because it stemmed from a corruption probe that started at the Governor's Mansion and trickled down to the Swainsboro Mayor's office and Sheriff's department. It was a mess.

¢ ¢ ¢

Governor Olen Hudson's, the Governor of Georgia, cell phone was tapped because his number had shown up numerous times on a DEA targeted street level drug dealer's mobil phone records. Already under scrutiny for receiving illegal campaign contributions and taking bribes, the DEA passed the information on to the FBI, who promptly began to monitor the Governor's phone calls. They'd received authorization from a Federal Magistrate Judge.

Olen Hudson was a good friend of Mayor Madox, the Mayor of Swainsboro, GA, so they spoke on a regular basis. During one of their weekly talks, the FBI heard Mayor Madox complaining about the declining kick backs he was receiving from his nigger *son-in-law* – who he'd given 95% of the city's cleaning contracts to. He then went on to complain about the measly $5,000 per month Sheriff West was giving him, accusing the Sheriff of making a killing off of the city's largest drug dealer and throwing him crumbs.

The Feds had hit the jackpot! A wiretap authorization was issued for Mayor Madox and Sheriff West's phone. Slaughter's was tapped shortly thereafter and although Goldie, Alex and Cashman's voices had been intercepted a few times, they changed numbers so much and never put phones in their names, they made it impossible to identify who they were. In fact, the only person who could have identified their voice in Georgia was Slaughter and he was dead.

¢ ¢ ¢

Goldie bent down and kissed his sleeping son's cheek. There was no way he was going to leave him. That's why he decided to sell his last 258 keys and take a long break. Especially after what Jesus had told him about John Boy. He really didn't want to believe it, but Jesus said he had secret documents as proof.

Goldie left Sultan Jr.'s nursery and ambled down to his entertainment room. He poured himself a shot of Woodford Reserve and took a seat at the bar. *Damn, I still can't believe my nigga snitchin',* he thought introspectively.

Goldie wanted to call and confront his mentor, but decided to wait until he came down for the Willie Gary Classic weekend in Orlando the following week. He'd confront him there – if Jesus didn't kill him first....

Chapter 35

Twelve professional killers emerged from three separate black cargo vans, forming a perimeter around a large historic mansion in the suburbs of Annapolis, Maryland. The two vicious pitbulls protecting the property were killed after trying to attack the first assassin as he came over the wrought iron gate surrounding the place. The muzzled cough of his silenced .40 caliber was inaudible in the night.

The assassins moved stealthily through the blue prints of the large home and the area around it.

¢   ¢   ¢

John Boy stood at the foot of his California king size bed, pounding Wendy's – one of his caucasion playmates – back out doggy style. As he did so, she had her face buried in Sasha's – John Boy's other caucasion playmate – twat, sucking and licking like there was no tomorrow. Suddenly, John Boy stopped fucking mid-stroke and pulled his boxers up. He heard his alarm system's computer generated voice announce that there was an intruder on the premises. It did this whenever the sensors buried throughout the mansion's yard picked up anything that weighed over 150lbs.

John Boy exited his bedroom quickly and shot to his basement. He turned on a sixty inch screen TV and flipped it to channel three. The screen split into eight individual monitors, all receiving images from eight different cameras placed at multiple vantage points on the exterior of the mansion. John Boy saw men posted at every entrance. He smiled before walking over to the closet in the right corner of the room. He was prepared for some shit like this.

Taking out his Russian made Z423 – a rifle that looked like

Scarface's but without the rocket launcher – John Boy glanced back at the monitors. The men were still there. He continued to remove things from the closet – mostly garments, some night vision goggles and a ski mask. John Boy quickly put on the dark clothing he pulled from his closet. When he was fully dressed he looked identical to the men outside of his door. He looked like a ninja.

John Boy ran back up stairs. "Aiight, yall we gotta get the fuck outta here, the Feds 'bout to hit," he lied to the two naked blonds laying in his bed.

Sasha was spooked. She had been to Federal prison twice and was still on paper. "Bitch! You need to hurry up!" she said to Wendy, who was taking too long to get dressed.

"When we get downstairs, I want yall hoes to run out the side door in the kitchen and hit the gate. I'ma pick yall up in five minutes on the next street," John Boy commanded.

"But what about your dogs?" Wendy asked.

John Boy smiled to himself. *These hoes ain't as dumb as they look,* he thought. He knew his dogs were already dead. There was no way the killers outside of his door could stand there if they weren't. "I already put the dogs up, nye' hurry up and go."

Sasha led the way down the stairs with Wendy close behind. John Boy, who had put on his ski mask and goggles, followed behind a distant third. Reaching the kitchen, John Boy told the two females to stop once they were at the kitchen side door about to open it. "When I cut off the lights, yall open the door and get the fuck outta here," he instructed.

"Okay, daddy," Sasha and Wendy said in unison.

John Boy did a silent count to six in his head, cocked his Z423, hit the light switch and ducked behind the kitchen island at the moment Sasha snatched open the side door and attempted to run out. She almost did a back flip back into the house when one of the assassin's shot her high in the chest with a riot pump. Wendy screamed, turned and tried to run but was shot in the back. She fell right next to the kitchen island, her dead eyes staring lifeless at John Boy.

Damn, I'ma dirty nigga, John Boy said under his breath before aiming his Z423 around the island at the doorway and squeezing the trigger. The high powered advanced weapon discharged close to 50 rounds in less than 4 seconds, hitting all four killers as they were about to enter the house.

Stumbling back, he regained his balance and ran towards the electric box in the hallway, killing the power. He did so just as another group of killers kicked in the front door, spitting fire. John Boy dove in the nick of time. Bullets riddled the wall where he once stood. He crawled on his stomach into his den, "Fuck," he barked, glad that he wasn't hit.

John Boy crawled back to the threshold of his den. Spotting the assassins as they advanced, he took aim and blazed his would be killers up like a blunt. The house was totally quiet when his finger came off the trigger. Nevertheless, John Boy knew there were more assassins and thought that it would be best if he made his escape.

Ejecting the 150 round clip from the Z423, John Boy crept to his front door, silently cursing himself for leaving his Benz in the driveway instead of parking it in the garage. He could have jumped in his car and backed it through the garge door without the assassins knowing what was going on until he was at the end of his driveway. But there was no time for crying over spilled milk. Besides, John Boy had spied three more assassins moving in on his left. He squatted down. Seconds later, he was in the bushes on the side of his front porch, watching as the killers inched closer to the entrance of his house.

"Fuck it," he said under his breath as the trio of assassins reached the porch. He jumped out of the brush like the boogie man, scaring the shit out of the three killers. With rapid fire from his *stick*, he made them contestants of the wet T-shirt contest.

Sure that he'd hit all three men, he ran over to his car, jumped in and backed out of the driveway. Reaching the end of the block, John Boy retrieved his cell phone from his pocket. He dialed Goldie's number and waited on him to pick up.

"Hello?" Goldie answered.

"Ay, my nigga, I thank that muthafucka Jesus put a hit out on me!"

Yeah, I guess so, if you 'round here rattin' on niggas, Goldie thought to himself. "What?" he asked.

"I said I –" John Boy uttered before seeing the masked man's head appear in his rearview mirror. The assassin had been hiding in the backseat of John Boy's 500 the whole time.

Bok! Bok! Bok! The gun sounded.

Goldie heard the gunshots. "John Boy…Hello?…John Boy!" Goldie called into the phone, but his mentor was dead.

Chapter 36

U.S. Attorney General Reecy Brown stormed into her office and slammed the door behind her. She was pissed that John Boy had been killed, and repulsed that there was a leak in her department. The Feds were supposed to be incorruptible, but somehow drug money had reared its ugly head once again. The attorney general had her suspicions about who was responsible for the leak, but without proof she felt there was no need to point fingers. However, she was damn sure going to investigate.

Reecy Brown took a seat at her desk, picked up her phone and punched in some numbers. "Yes, this is Reecy Brown, United States Attorney General, I need to be connected with the captain of the Mexican Federal police?"

¢   ¢   ¢

Sinoloa Mexico
Five burly men strapped with AK-47s climbed out of an armored Hummer and entered a popular Mexican restaurant. The patrons seated inside watched and listened as four of the men posted at each corner of the diner, and the fifth and last man demanded that everyone place their cell phones and weapons into the large black bag he carried over his shoulder.

After collecting everything that he'd requested, the fifth man exited the restaurant, reappearing moments later. His gun was replaced with a briefcase. He was also accompanied by his boss, Jesus Diez.

The restaurant's patrons began to clap as if the Pope had entered the eatery. Basking in the praise he was receiving, Jesus announced, "Everything is on the house," while enroute to the table of the man he'd come to see.

Peter Gibson stood and shook Jesus' hand before inviting him to sit. "Mr. Diez, how are you, pal?" he humbly asked.

"Cut the shit, Gibson. What's this meeting about? And why is it costing me a half-million dollars?" Jesus questioned, pointedly. He'd just, two weeks prior, paid Gibson $250,000 for information concerning John Boy becoming a cooperating witness.

Gibson's greedy ass took a deep breath and leaned back in his chair. He knew that what he was about to say could've been included in the info' he'd charged Jesus $250,000 for. Because he'd known back then what the Justice Department was up to. But he'd held back the information to make more money. "Well, Mr. Diez, there is a big problem. I'm sorry to tell you this, but as of today you're wanted by the U.S. Government."

"What? You can't be serious! I pay you go-"

"Wait, it gets worse," Gibson said, interrupting. "The indictment is only formal. You were declared a threat to national security."

"What in the hell does that mean?" Jesus asked.

"Well, for one, you've made the FBI's ten most wanted list. It will be announced tomorrow on CNN, along with your picture and a short biography. Secondly, the U.S. is not interested in bringing you in alive…"

Fear seized Jesus momentarily, then he smiled. "How much is this going to cost, to go away?"

"I'm sorry, Jesus. It's out of my hands," Gibson explained.

Jesus sat silently for a few seconds before standing. He snapped his finger and the fifth man placed the briefcase containing $500,000 on Gibson's table. "Call me on my satellite phone if anything changes," he said before turning on his heels to leave.

Four of his men escorted him out while the fifth man left, came back and placed the bag containing the restaurant patron's possessions on a counter before rejoining Jesus and the rest of his security team out front.

Jesus got into his Hummer and took out his cell phone. "Take me to the Fort," he said to his driver while listening for the number he'd dialed to be answered.

"Hello?" Lonita said.

"Baby, I need you to get to the Fort immediately."

¢ ¢ ¢

The Fort was a high security ten acre compound located in the Sierra Madre Mountains of Mexico. It was surrounded by a forty foot, eight foot thick, steel reinforced concrete wall. In the center of the cement and metal barrier was a mini-mansion that was protected by a fifty man army. The rest of the grounds were occupied by a thirty unit apartment building, a small private power plant, a helicopter and helipad, and a food storage facility with enough food to last three years. It even had its own water supply.

Arriving at the Fort, Jesus made a beeline for his home office. He picked up the phone on his desk and called Sergeant Santiago Garcia. "Did you know about the U.S. coming after me?" he asked the Sergeant of the Sinoloa State Police when he answered his phone.

"Mr. Diez, I was just about to call you. I just left a meeting with some FBI agents...We need to meet up as soon as possible," Sergeant Garcia suggested.

"You're got-damned right we do!" Jesus barked into the phone before hanging up.

One hour later, there was a knock on Jesus' office door, followed by one of his men peeking inside to inform him that Garcia had arrived.

Sergeant Garcia stepped in, bowed and took a seat. He got straight to the point. "Mr. Diez, the U.S. and the Mexican Federal Police want us to help bring you in."

Jesus laughed. "Is that what they told you?"

"Yes...Then there is the reward. Ten million U.S. There is a lot of pressure, sir."

"And people in the state government are going to help the Americans?" Jesus asked.

Garcia dropped his head. "They're considering it, sir."

Jesus slammed his fist onto his desk and stood. He was hot! "After all I've done for this town? For the people?! What is the-" He was interrupted by his phone ringing. "What?" he barked. Seconds later, all of the blood had drained for his face. "Got-damn-it!" he spat, slamming down the phone. He stormed around his desk and jacked Garcia up. "Who in the hell attacked my fucking ranch?!"

Garcia was scared to death. "I don't know. The Americans must have did it."

Jesus retrieved a .38 snub-nose from his waist, forcefully jamming the barrel of it in Sergeant Garcia's mouth. "You better find out what's going on, or you, your fat-ass wife, and your ugly little kids are dead! You got that?! ...And tell those cowards in the state police that nothing as changed. It's still silver or lead!" he threatened.

"Yes, sir, right away, sir," Garcia stammered, breaking free of Jesus' clutches.

¢   ¢   ¢

Unbeknownst to anyone associated with the Mexican government, Reecy Brown had instructed a high ranking U.S. General to assemble a special task force of military trained mercenaries to find and kill Jesus Diez. They stormed and destroyed Jesus' ranch while looking for him, only to come up empty handed. Lucky for Sergeant Garcia, Jesus' men had come and picked him up twenty minutes before the attack on the ranch.

In the weeks that followed, CNN's top story was on Jesus and the anarchy that had broken out in the streets of Sinoloa. Lazorito, the leader of the Commission, sensed that Jesus was vulnerable and increased his attacks on Jesus and his business interests. The bodies were piling up daily. Jesus was catching hell. On top of the attacks from the Commission, the Mexican Federal Police, under pressure from the United States, were seizing his cash and drugs during raids. The situation was costing him a fortune.

Jesus couldn't even leave the Fort for fear of catching a sniper round from one of the U.S. mercenaries or being riddled with AK bullets by the Commission. Shit really heated up when he made Forbes richest peoples list. He was ranked number 52 in the world. The President of Mexico was so embarrassed by the Forbes article that he called a press conference, denouncing all of the country's narco men, then pledging to delegate as many as 500 troops from the Mexican Army to help bring Jesus to justice.

Jesus was overwhelmed by the mounting pressure. He'd watched the Mexican President's press conference from his hot tub. However, being the eternal survivalist that he was, it only took him two weeks to come up with a plan to take some of the heat off of his ass. He enlisted the help of Sergeant Garcia to make it happen.

¢   ¢   ¢

Lazorito received a call from one of his top lieutenants, stating that they'd spoken to a state police officer, who for $1,000,000 U.S. would give them the date and time that Jesus Diez would be catching a flight from Los Cabos Mexico International Airport to South America. Realizing that it would be his best chance yet to kill the ever elusive Jesus Diez, Lazorito told his top lieutenant to arrange a sit down between him and the state police officer, who just so happened to be Sergeant Garcia.

A week later, Lazorito's whole world began to crumble. First an underground tunnel, stretching five miles from Mexico across the Arizona-Mexican border, was discovered. U.S. officials were tipped off by an informant that divulged information on the tunnel that Lazorito had constructed three years prior and had smuggled tons of cocaine into the U.S. through. Two days after that, following the information given to them by Sergeant Garcia, Lazorito's men riddled a limo thought to be occupied by Jesus Diez, with over two hundred rounds as it entered Los Cabos International Airport. However, it wasn't Jesus Diez that occupied the limo. It was the Archbishop of Guadalajara.

The people of Mexico took to the streets in mass protest in response to the Archbishop's death. Lazorito was named as the one responsible after two of his shooters were captured by police.

The two gunmen were taken to the station and questioned. At first they said nothing to the investigators who interrogated them. That all changed when one of the detectives stabbed one of the shooters in the thigh with an ice pick and tortured him by way of bone tingling. The Mexican government's focus shifted seemingly over night, from Jesus to Lazorito. The shift pissed the

U.S off to no end. The U.S. didn't give a fuck about the Archbishop. They wanted Jesus! But with next to no help from the Mexican government, the United States was fucked.

Chapter 37

Nayarit Riviera Mexico

Lonita lounged in the king size bed of her Four Season's hotel suite with a big smile on her face. She had to give it to Jesus, he was one clever son-of-a-bitch. The set up at Los Cabo's airport and the discovery of Lazorito's drug tunnel was a brilliant way to take some of the heat off of his ass. It was no wonder that Lonita grew up to become the scheming bitch that she was. She'd learned from the best.

Lonita began to reflect back over her demented plot to take over her father's drug empire. It had taken careful, strategic planning, but she was almost there. Thanks to her, Jesus was wanted by the U.S. and under heavy attack by the Commission all at once.

Jesus had unwittingly fallen into his daughter's trap. He'd purchased the heroin that John Boy had sold to Coval from an Arab man that Lonita had met a few years prior during a trip to Dubai. Shortly after meeting Bin Amin, Lonita found out that besides his family owning a few oil fields, Bin Amin was an international heroin trafficker that funded a terrorist cell out of Afghanistan.

Lonita had bided her time, waiting until the right moment to set her plan in motion. After finding out she was pregnant, Lonita convinced her father to purchase heroin from Bin Amin, knowing that he had terrorist ties and that it was a breach of Jesus' agreement with the U.S. to deal with terrorist. She had Jesus convinced that Bin Amin was just an oil baron with an Asian heroin connect. Bin Amin, oblivious to Lonita's plot, went along with her lie out of greed.

After Jesus took the first shipment of smack, the Justice Department received an anonymous call from Lonita informing them of Jesus' transgression.

Now, alone in her lavish suite, Lonita continued to ponder her father's situation. Sadly, she didn't feel one ounce of guilt for the old man. To be honest, she actually got a kick out of the fear she'd heard in his voice when he called trying to persuade her to come to the Fort. Jesus was worried. He knew that Lonita was a target of his enemies, but being the vindictive bitch that Lonita was, she wanted Jesus to suffer. She felt he deserved everything that was happening to him. After all, he'd taken her mother away from her.

Jesus married Lonita's mother, Rosa when he was 19 years old. Rosa was only 15 at the time. Back then Jesus was just a lowly cattle hand with a strong back and modest dreams. He worked hard to provide for his wife, and when she became pregnant he couldn't have been more happier. During Rosa's second trimester, a plaque fell upon the cattle ranch, almost wiping out the entire herd. Jesus lost his job and times became hard for the young couple.

Then one day after coming from the city looking for work, Jesus came home to see a sporty SS Camaro parked in his driveway. He walked into his house and saw a familiar looking man standing to greet him.

"Cousin," the man said, arms outstretched.

"Hyme, is it really you?" Jesus asked, checking out his cousin from head to toe. It had been ten years since they'd last seen each other.

"Yes, cousin it really is," Hyme said, excitedly stepping back.

Hyme had on heavily starched Wranglers, Gator boots, a silk shirt and a big silver and gold belt buckle with an AK-47 engraved on it.

The two cousins sat down and got reacquainted with each other.

"So, Hyme, what kind of work do you do? Is that your car outside?" Jesus asked.

Hyme told Jesus that he'd just bought the Camaro. He explained that he'd been making deliveries for a wealthy man, traveling back and forth between the U.S. and Mexico.

Digging deeper, Jesus asked, "What do you deliver? Do you think that you could get me a job?" he inquired, admiring Hyme's ensemble for the third time introspectively.

"Maybe I can, cousin. ...If you have the balls, that is."

"Hyme, I'll deliver dead bodies to provide for my wife," Jesus retorted half jokingly, looking over at Rosa.

"Would you deliver cocaine?"

"Cocaine? Sure, but what are you really delivering?" Jesus questioned, smiling. He'd always remembered his cousin as a prankster.

Hyme was smiling also, however his expression turned serious when he answered, "cocaine".

Speechless, Jesus glanced over at Rosa, who was staring at Hyme with her mouth gapped open.

"How much is the job paying?" Jesus asked after quickly considering his wife and unborn child's plight.

"Jesus!?" Rosa spat incredulously.

"Rosa...honey, let me handle this," Jesus said in a condescending tone. He continued, "If it will make you feel any better, I'll still look for honest work, but we need this right now," he said before turning his attention back to his cousin. "How much?" he asked again.

¢   ¢   ¢

Lonita was born three months later. Jesus made sure that she had everything that a baby could need. When she and Rosa were released from the hospital, Jesus took his girls to their new home, where there was a brand new pink Trans Am wrapped in a red ribbon parked in the driveway. It was for Rosa. The cocaine business was good indeed. Jesus and Hyme had been burning the road up!

As the years progressed, Jesus and Hyme were delegated more responsibilities by their boss, Felix Molina. They were in charge of twenty mules that transported cocaine all over the West Coast. They were also in charge of collecting the money owed to Molina by his West Coast clients. Rosa, on the other hand, had stopped complaining about Jesus' criminal activities altogether, having become accustomed to the finer things in life.

Everything was copastetic until tragedy struck. Three days after Lonita's fifth birthday, Molina and his second in command died in a plane crash. Jesus and Hyme had just returned to Mexico after collecting $2,000,000 from Dookie Dave, a crip nigga out of San Diego, when they learned of their boss' accident.

They'd stopped by Jesus' house before delivering the money they had collected to one of Molina's many stash houses. Rosa told them about the plane crash soon as they walked in the door.

Thinking of the money hidden in the hollowed out door panels of the cargo van outside, Hyme turned to Jesus smiling. "We're rich," he uttered.

"What?" Jesus asked, not hearing what his cousin had said, but wondering why he was smiling. Felix Molina had been good to the both of them, so Jesus couldn't think of anything to smile about at that moment.

"I said, we're rich... The money?" Hyme hinted.

"The money?" Jesus repeated, looking puzzled. "Oh, hell no! I know you're not thinking what I think you're thinking?!"

"Why not? You heard Rosa! Molina's dead," Hyme stated.

"Hyme, Felix was good to us. It's not right to steal from the dead. I think we should take the money to his wife."

"For what?" Rosa blirted, causing both men to look in her direction. "How much money are we talking about here?" she questioned.

"Two million," Hyme answered, ignoring the look on Jesus' face.

Rosa turned back and faced her husband. "That's a lot of money, baby. Jesus don't be foolish," she pleaded. "We need it," she continued. "Think, honey. How will we afford this house and sustain our lifestyle? Felix is dead... You're out of work..."

Jesus thought of all the bills he had and concluded that Rosa was right. They'd be in the poor house in no time without any income. *Shit, nobody else knows how much money is really out there. I'll just keep this little bit and make sure Molina's wife gets the rest,* Jesus said to himself.

He decided to keep the money.

¢ ¢ ¢

Ten months later, Jesus was down to a little under $500,000. Hyme wasn't far behind with $625,000. Without a cocaine plug, both of their bankrolls had dwindled significantly.

One humid Saturday night, as Hyme laid in his bed, bored, he decided to pay a visit to a local whorehouse in Sinoloa. He'd heard through the grapevine that there was a new whore there with head so marvelous she could make a dead man cum in a matter of seconds.

Hyme casually strolled through the door of the brothel, greeted the Madam of the establishment, then requested the new whore after paying the service fee. Moments later, a 6'2", olive-skin goddess appeared at the top of the stairs. Hyme grew an erection instantly.

Back in the goddess' suite, Hyme watched with great satisfaction as she stripped off all of her clothing, then sashayed over to her dresser. She retrieved a plate with three narrow rows of coke and a half a straw on top of it. She offered Hyme a taste, which he gleefully accepted. It was the best cocaine he'd snorted in months.

"Where'd you get this shit?" Hyme asked, face and throat numbing by the second.

The goddess smiled. "I only have two ounces left…but I can sell you one and that's it."

"An ounce? No baby, I need kilos. Lots of kilos. I will pay you if you help me."

¢ ¢ ¢

And so it began. The goddess contacted her cousin in Colombia, Pedro. He traveled to Mexico and after meeting with Jesus and Hyme agreed to sell them 50 keys for $250,000. The goddess received $1,000 off of every kilo sold.

¢ ¢ ¢

Ten years after the first shipment that Pedro sent to Sinoloa, Jesus and Hyme stepped their game up dramatically. 50 keys turned into multiple tons. They became the largest distributors on the West Coast. And with the demand for cocaine growing because of the crack epidemic, Jesus had to stay in the U.S. for weeks at a time. Hyme stayed in Mexico, receiving and distributing the shipments of cocaine to the mules.

Rosa, meanwhile, found a way to pass her time. She began sleeping with Hyme. She spent her days bonding with Lonita, showing her how to be a diva, taking her shopping and to salons. But her nights were filled with sin. She spent them drinking and getting her back blown out by Hyme. Some nights Lonita would hear her parents' headboard striking the wall and her mother's passionate cries of ecstasy. She knew what her mother was doing was wrong, but she loved her mother more than anything, so she kept quiet.

Lonita's whole world changed forever when Jesus made a surprise visit home one night. Lonita thought that she was dreaming when she opened her eyes to see a teary eyed Jesus standing next to her bed, staring down at her. He was holding a teddy bear in one hand and a velvet jewelry box in the other. Her parents' head board could be heard rhythmically striking the wall from down the hall.

Jesus cringed when he heard his wife cry out in joyful bliss in response to what another man was doing to her sexually. "Get dressed and stay here until I come back," he said to his daughter before walking out of the room.

Seconds later, Lonita heard the two gunshots that ended Rosa and Hyme's life.

¢   ¢   ¢

Lonita climbed out of bed, showered and got dressed. She figured that she'd get her feet done and do a little shopping. She arrived at a shopping center an hour later. Lonita entered the mall flanked by two body guards. She did a little shopping then stopped by a nail shop. Sitting in a chair while her feet soaked in the warm exfoliating solution, she thought about Goldie and how he played a part in her plans.

Lonita never intended to get pregnant by Goldie. She only wanted to control him with her pussy and her cocaine, once Jesus was out of the way. But shit happened. And being pregnant by Goldie wasn't so bad after all, she concluded. Besides, who would cross the mother of their child? Especially a rich and powerful one.

The manicurist finished Lonita's feet and was handsomely compensated. Lonita's body guards were in the waiting area when she walked back up front. They stood to escort her back to her SUV. The moment that Orlando, Lonita's most trusted body guard opened the passenger door for his employer to get it, a Lincoln Towncar came to a screeching halt behind them, boxing Lonita's SUV in. It was at that moment that Lonita thought of the warning her father had given her concerning her safety.

Although Jesus hadn't come out and said that he'd snitched on Lazorito's drug tunnel and tricked him into killing the Archbishop, Lazorito was still on the run and there was going to be some repercussions.

Orlando pushed Lonita into the open door of the Hummer, closing it behind her. He pulled his pistol from his waist just as the passenger of the Lincoln began shooting in his direction. The body guard on the opposite side of the vehicle opened his rear door and jumped in upon hearing Lonita's driver start the engine. Orlando tried to do the same but was shot in the back and calf as he attempted to do so. The other bodyguard had to pull him inside.

"Go!" Lonita commanded the driver once Orlando's door was closed.

They were boxed in, but the driver put the Hummer in reverse and stomped the gas, causing the SUV to wreck into the Lincoln. The shooter had to damn near jump into the driver of the Lincoln's lap in order to avoid injury. "Drive!" he barked, looking at the Hummer's brake light change from red to white.

The driver of the Hummer had shifted into drive, pulled up, then dropped it back into reverse.

The Lincoln pulled off just in time, avoiding another hit. Lonita's driver backed out of the parking space and gunned the Hummer across the parking lot.

¢ ¢ ¢

"Good bye, you bitch," Lazorito's top lieutenant said seconds before pressing the fire button on the rocket launcher he held.

Lonita's driver was about to turnout of the parking lot when the Hummer was struck from behind by a rocket propelled grenade. The Hummer was blown into the air and exploded, killing everyone inside…

Chapter 38

AUSA Parker Anderson sat comfortably behind the table reserved for government prosecutors. He had a satisfied smile on his face. Agent Joshua Craft had just rendered thirty minutes of damning testimony, so he was confident that the sixteen member grand jury was one step closer to returning the indictments he was seeking. Over the course of two weeks, Parker Anderson had questioned about fifty witnesses, from crackheads to Federal prisoners brought back on writs. He'd played taped conversations intercepted on wire taps and showed pictures of drug transactions and guns.

Now it was time to seal the deal.

The last witness to be called to testify was Agent Larry Groove. Agent Groove casually strolled to the witness stand and was sworn in. He took a seat and gave the Grand Jury a head nod before AUSA Parker Anderson began his line of questioning.

"Agent Groove, are you familiar with a woman by the name of Teresa Cam, or a man by the name of James Wooden, AKA Big Woo?"

Agent Groove nodded yes, then went on to explain that Big Woo and Teresa Cam were leaders of rival street gangs. He explained that they were both involved in drug trafficking, murder, racketeering, you name it. He continued to expose the evil that both gangs engaged in on the streets of Cleveland, Tennessee. He talked for close to an hour. By the time agent Groove was excused from the stand, the faces of the all white Grand Jury had turned beet red. AUSA Parker Anderson left the courtroom one hour later with signed indictments for Teresa Cam, Big Woo, and about fifty other gang members.

¢   ¢   ¢

Later that Day

Fat Tank, Bodywash and the new bomb-man were inside of their new place of business with a big pussy Chicana freak name Liz. They were taking turns getting their rocks off. After the driveby at the other trap, which left Fat Tank wounded and the old bomb-man dead, Big Woo moved his Gault Street operation six houses down from the old one. Gault Street was just too lucrative of a location to give up.

It was about 5:00 in the morning. As the three trappers smoked, drank and had their way with Liz, Agents Craft and Groove and about twenty U.S. Marshals were forming a perimeter around their drug den. The same thing was happening to about thirty other homes around the city. Big Woo, Wayne and Maine had been snatched up a few hours earlier coming out of Big Woo's baby-momma's house.

Fat Tank had just fired up the blunt he'd rolled and was about to pass it to Bodywash when a flash-bang came crashing through the window. It detonated next to the couch they were sitting on.

The new bomb-man was in the back digging Liz's guts out when he heard the explosion. "What the fuck?" he said, hopping off the bed, grabbing his pants. He rushed to the front room where he found Fat Tank and Bodywash dazed and bewildered on the couch.

After the flash-bang detonated, the Feds, who were split into two entry teams, tried unsuccessfully to kick in the front and rear door of the trap. Their plan was thwarted because both doors were made of solid oak wood with steel plates on their backs. They had support beams that were anchored into the floor, reinforcing them.

Fat Tank and Bodywash regained their bearings seconds before the police opened fire on the house, peppering the wall behind them with bullets.

"Oh shit, nigga, that hoe crazy!" Fat Tank said, hitting the floor. He reached back up and removed two SK's from underneath the cushions of the couch. He slid Bodywash one while the bomb-man crawled to the love seat in the corner of the room and retrieved a .357. All three youths thought that the Bloods were attacking them. The Feds serving indictments never crossed their minds.

¢ ¢ ¢

The day after Cashman and Big Woo shot up Ma and Jimmy Cam's funeral, Teresa Cam began wrecking havoc on the GD's. Gangsters were getting killed left and right. Teresa had lost her mind. She'd put hits on all the GD's. She didn't give a fuck. She even had her people leaving severed pig heads on the nigga's grandmother's porches. A block hugger was worth $2,500. A trapper $5,000. Even regular dope-boys were gunning at the GD's for the cash.

¢ ¢ ¢

The three trappers returned fire through the broken front window of the trap. Teresa had them all spooked. They saw men out front, masked up in all black. And even though "U.S. Marshals" was stenciled across most of the masked men's shirts, the three youngsters continued to shoot back. They were still under the impression that Teresa Cam had sent a hit squad at them. Especially after seeing all that black shit parked out front. Black Tahoes, Crown Vics and Suburbans. There wasn't a strobe light emitting red and blue lights insight.

¢ ¢ ¢

The gunfight continued for about 20 minutes. Just when the three trappers began to wonder where the police were and why they hadn't shown up in response to all the shooting, police cruisers came out of nowhere. They were leading the way for the police tank. Agent Craft had requested it. He was tired of the bullshit.

Fat Tank stopped shooting and turned to Bodywash and the bomb-man. "Dog, that's them muthafuckin' people out there," he said after seeing the Bradly County Police join in on the gunfight with who he first perceived as assassins hired by Teresa Cam.

The three youths crawled to the kitchen.

"Man, them crackas gonna give a nigga forever for bussin' at they ass," Bodywash commented, out of breath.

"Shit, nigga, we ain't know they was them folks!" the bomb-man exclaimed, eyes darting back and forth between Fat Tank and Bodywash.

¢ ¢ ¢

Upon noticing that the occupants of the targeted residence had stopped shooting, Agent Groove told the other officers to hold their fire. When they did so, he went to his trunk and grabbed his bullhorn. "This is the police! You have exactly five minutes to come out with your hands up! If you don't come out, we're gonna run the police tank up in there and drag your asses out!"

¢ ¢ ¢

Liz had hid under the bed after the flash-bang detonated. She stayed there during all of the shooting. She didn't know what the hell was going on. When she heard the police demand that everyone inside of the house *come out with their hands up*, she crawled from her hiding place, put on her clothes, then made her way to the front door to surrender. Passing the kitchen, she saw the three trappers inside, squatted down in a seemingly heated conversation.

Liz stood in the kitchen doorway with her hands on her wide hips, staring at the three youngsters in disbelief. "Ay!" she said, interrupting. "Did yall hear what them crackas just said?" Liz scolded.

"Yeah, bitch, we heard 'em," Fat Tank snapped.

Liz sucked her teeth, rolled her neck and swatted her hand dismissively. "Nigga, please, I ain't finna get killed in here *witchall* asses...I ain't come here for all this extra shit. I'm out," she replied, turning to walk away.

"Hold on, hoe!" Bodywash barked, choppa aimed at Liz's back. She turned around and faced him. The large weapon pointed at her chest scared her so badly that she backed up a few steps, turned and attempted to run away. Bodywash, on pure impulse, squeezed the trigger, shooting the frightened young lady in the back of the head.

"Nigga, look what the fuck you done did!" Fat Tank clamored, pointing at Liz's twitching corpse.

¢   ¢   ¢

Agent Groove heard the gunshot and got back on his bullhorn. "Okay, this is your last warning! You got exactly one minute left!"

"Man, fuck these crackas!" Bodywash screamed, succumbing to the pressure. He felt like a caged rat. Storming out of the kitchen, he went straight to the living room. After unlatching the steel reinforcements on the front door, he snatched it open and began firing at the police out front.

A sniper was hiding in a tree across the street. He had Bodywash's forehead between the cross hairs of his rifle's scope. Applying pressure to the trigger, he put Bodywash on his ass. The bomb-man unleashed a girlish scream after being splattered with brain matter, skull and hair follicles as he approached Bodywash from behind. He'd come out to try and talk some sense into the deranged young man.

"Oh, hell nawl! Not my nigga!" Fat Tank cried out after seeing Bodywash's brains on the floor. Him and Bodywash had played in the sand box together. So, it was only natural to avenge his partner's death. Fat Tank walked purposely to the door, passing the bomb-man on the way. He stepped over Bodywash's body and stood in the doorway as if he was bullet proof. But before he could raise his rifle to shoot, he was picked off by the same sniper who'd killed Bodywash.

"Okay, you bastards, anybody else that's in there and doesn't want to die better come out right now with their got-damn hands up," Agent Groove threatened.

The bomb-man easily saw that he was in a no win situation and surrendered peacefully. *Damn, that bitch had a nigga fucked up,* he said to himself as he was placed in the back of Agent Craft's Tahoe. He was kind of relieved to be going to jail. At least then he could rest. A few days prior, a pig's head had been left on his mother's doorstep.

¢   ¢   ¢

The Bradly County Jail was abuzz with activity. The Feds were bringing niggas in by the bus load. Teresa was arrested not long after Big Woo, Wayne and Maine. Her and Fat Boy were tossed into the back of a van by the Marshals after walking out of a local IHOP.

As soon as Teresa was placed in her cell, reality hit her with the force of a Mack truck. She had done a three year bid before, but that was nothing compared to the time she was facing at that moment.

"Goldy Locks, is that you?" a woman asked, standing up from the cement bench she was seated on.

Teresa turned to face the owner of the familiar voice. There was only two people that called her by that name. Mrs. Whitfield and her son Wayne. Teresa hadn't heard from Wayne since he'd tipped her off about Big Woo being responsible for her brother's murder.

"Mrs. Whitfield, what are you doing here?" Teresa asked, confused. She had known Mrs. Whitfield for about eight years. Her son Wayne, Teresa's first love, had taken her virginity and gotten her pregnant when she was only 14. Teresa suffered a miscarriage during her first trimester, a result of Wayne having rough sex with her. Crushed and angry from her failed pregnancy, Teresa quit fucking with men altogether.

"Child, you know how them crackas treat us poe' niggas. Them nasty muthafuckas kicked in my doe' and dragged my black ass to jail... Talkin' 'bout a muthafuckin' conspiracy," Mrs. Whitfield snorted.

Unknown to Mrs. Whitfield at that time, her and a couple of her son's phone conversations had been intercepted on a wiretap. AUSA Parker Anderson played the most incriminating of the two for the Grand Jury. On the wiretap, Wayne was heard telling Mrs. Whitfield to go into his stash and count out $50,000. He told her to have it ready before he swung through because he was about to cop some work. An expert slang interpreter was called to the stand after the tape was played. He explained to the perplexed Grand Jury members what Wayne had said and why.

Teresa sighed, "Yeah, I'm down here for the same thing. I won-"

Just then a male CO appeared in front of the cell. "Teresa Cam," he said, "There are some people waiting to speak with you."

Teresa was led to the interrogation room of the Bradly County Jail. Her and Wayne locked eyes as he was being escorted out of the interrogation room back to his cell.

"Don't be no fool, Teresa. Tell them folks who killed your brutha," Wayne said aloud, causing Teresa to look at him like he was crazy.

What in the hell?...Now that's some hot ass shit right there, Teresa thought.

But Wayne didn't give a flying fuck! Once he found out that his mother had been arrested he flipped immediately. The Feds weren't playing any games with anyone. They gave them two choices, Wayne's was tell to free his mom and take ten years, or life for him and twenty for his mother.

Needless to say, Wayne spilled the beans.

¢   ¢   ¢

AUSA Parker Anderson, Larry Groove and Joshua Craft stood to greet Teresa when she was led into the interrogation room. Parker Anderson wasted little time telling her what the business was. Thirty years or cooperate. Terese smirked at the three crackas across from her and told them to suck her dick. She told them to crank it up because she was taking her case to trial.

Agent Groove released a hearty laugh then pressed play on the cassette player situated in the center of the conference table. He watched with great pleasure as Teresa's smirk turned into a frown.

"What the fuck did I pay yall asses for, huh? I said kill Woo and yall done killed some white bitch!" Teresa was heard saying over the wiretap.

Teresa knew right then that she was fucked, so she did what most of the so-called real niggas did when the Feds stepped in.

She folded like a lawnchair.

¢ ¢ ¢

Goldie sat in his study smoking a blunt while sipping on a glass of Woodford Reserve. He was deep in thought. He'd just, a few days earlier, returned from Guatemala, attending Lonita's funeral. Two weeks before that he'd attended John Boy's.

Pulling heavily on the blunt, Goldie's mind wandered to the argument that he and Jesus had over his refusal to accept any more drugs. He'd paid the drug lord what he'd owed while in Gautemala. Jesus, in Goldie's opinion, was too hot to fuck with and he wasn't taking any chances.

¢ ¢ ¢

Jesus had lost his ability to reason since his daughter had died. He'd really gotten off the chain after recruiting a group of Chicano gang members out of Southern California to do his bidding. They were murking shit. First, they killed a Mexican journalist who'd been blasting Jesus in the papers. Then they killed a U.S. Consulate in order to send a message to the U.S. government. After that Jesus made world headlines. He had a Mexican presidential candidate assassinated after giving his acceptance speech.

The candidate was leading in the polls and had promised to partner with the U.S. to eradicate the Mexican drug cartels.

Seconds after the shooting, the trigger man was apprehended by an angry mob of supporters. They held him for the police and he was taken down to the station, where he was interrogated – Mexican style.

Unable to stand being electrocuted any longer, the assassin told everything, fingering Jesus as his employer.

¢ ¢ ¢

Exhaling the potent chronic smoke, Goldie's thoughts shifted once more. He began to ponder the bad feeling he had in his gut concerning Precious, Brown-eyed Ron and their kids. The day before, Precious and her kids left for Savannah to visit Brown-eyed

Ron in jail. When midnight came and they hadn't returned, Kismet called Precious' cell phone, only to find out it had been disconnected. Panicked and fearing something bad had happened to her friend and her children, Kismet called the Chatam County Jail to speak to Brown-eyed Ron through the Chaplain, pretending to have a family emergency. However, she was told that Ron had been moved to an unknown location.

Sighing, Goldie picked up his phone and punched in seven digits.

"Jerome Shay, speaking," a voice answered.

"Shay, this Sultan. Man, what's up wit' Ron?"

"Oh, umm, Mr. Jackson ...I was going to call you today. Uumm...I no longer represent Ron."

"Whatchu mean, you don't represent Ron? Cracka, didn't I pay yo' ass sixty stacks?!"

"Yes, b-but the DEA came to my office late yesterday evening and took Ron's files. They told me my services were no longer needed... Mr. Jackson, Ron has flipped. He's going to testify against Lil Hezy next week. He's also been to the Grand Jury on you. They have placed him in the witness protection program."

"What? He went to the Grand Jury on me?" Goldie asked, voice cracking with fear.

"Yes. It was about a week ago."

"Cracka, why the fuck you ain't call and tell me? Bitch, I'm the muthafucka who pay yo' ass!"

"I understand that, Mr. Jackson, but I was paid to represent Ron. Anything that he and I discussed was privilege information... The Grand Jury didn't indict you from what I understand, but a word from the wisc...The DEA won't let up until they do."

"Man you st-"

Goldie was interrupted by Kismet banging on the door, calling his name. He could tell by the urgency in her voice that whatever it was that she wanted was important. "Ay, let me call you back," he said, getting up and scurrying to the door.

"Goldie," Kismet said, stepping in. She rushed over to his TV, cut it on and turned it to C-Span.

Jesus was on the screen, shackled while being escorted into

a large building by police. Goldie turned the volume up to listen to the story.

"Reputed drug kingpin, Jesus Diez, a fugitive wanted by the United States, was captured today by the Gautemalan Army as he tried to board a private jet at an airport in Gautemala City. Ensuing a brief shootout that left three of Mr. Diez's bodyguards dead and two Gautemalan service men injured, Mr. Diez was taken into custody. He will be held in this maximum security prison," the reporter said, pointing at the building behind him, "until he is extradited to the U.S. to face drug smuggling charges."

"What are you smiling about?" Kismet asked when the news segment on Jesus' arrest had changed.

"Nothing," Goldie replied before hugging and kissing his wife.

Jesus' capture had taken a lot of weight off of Goldie's shoulders. Jesus was really pissed about Goldie's refusal to accept the ton of cocaine he was trying to front him. But with Jesus in custody and potentially never seeing the streets again, Goldie felt he could rest a little easier.

"Boy, let go of me," Kismet said playfully, pulling away from Goldie's embrace. "You smell like a wino," she said then smiled, gently grabbing Goldie's tool. "I'm gonna take Sultan Jr. with me to the store. When I come back, have that ass washed. I got an itch I need scratched," she said, turning on her heels and sashaying away, her butt cheeks jiggling through her sweat pants.

¢   ¢   ¢

"Did you get all of that?" Agent Tara Tate asked her new partner, Shericka Tobby.

They were in a surveillance van parked two miles from Goldie's residence.

"Yeah, I got the important stuff... He said sixty grand, right?" she asked rhetorically, scribbling in a note book pad.

They were listening to the bug Precious had planted in Goldie's study. The Grand Jury had granted the DEA permission to use wire surveillance on Goldie and everybody affiliated with him after Brown-eyed Ron made his appearance before the sixteen member panel.

"Ricks, come in," Tara Tate said into her walkie-talkie.

"Tara? Ricks here."

"Kismet is about to leave the house. Be on the lookout," she said, ending the transmission.

¢　¢　¢

"What in the hell?" Kismet said aloud, seeing the black Crown Vic in her rearview, blue lights flashing in its grill. She pulled over and glanced in her backseat, making sure Sultan Jr. was secure in his baby-seat.

Two casually dressed men emerged from the Crown Vic, walking briskly to Kismet's driver's side door.

It was Agents Rick and Hogan.

"I wasn't speeding, so what am I being stopped for?" Kismet asked, looking Ricks in the eye, holding out her license and registration.

"You're being stopped because of your drug dealing, murdering husband," Hogan scolded.

Kismet was caught off guard by Hogan's accusation. "What?" she was finally able to say after a few seconds of stunned silence.

"Mrs. Jackson, I apologize for my partner's rudeness, but we're DEA agents and we're investigating your husband. We want to help you. Wasn't your father a cop?"

"You leave my father's name out of this!" Kismet snarled.

"Okay, sorry, but this is a very serious matter… You need to take this," Ricks said, handing Kismet his card. "And call me if you want to talk. You don't have much time, so you need to think real hard and real quick on this, because when it goes down… And trust me, it's gonna go down," he emphasized in a grim voice, "there's a good chance you will go down too."

Chapter 39

Three Months Later

"I can't believe this is happening to our case," AUSA David Miller clamored, looking around the conference room at the solemn faces of the other law enforcement personnel that were present. There was another Grand Jury meeting scheduled for the following day, but there wasn't any newly discovered evidence to present to it.

Through all of the DEA's, as well as the other law enforcement agencies a part of operation White-Gold's exhaustive surveillance, nothing incriminating was intercepted over the wire or was seen being committed by Goldie or any close member of his organization after the Grand Jury authorized the wiretaps. Instead, Goldie, Cashman and Alex were observed investing heavily into real estate. They had begun to purchase businesses, cleaning up their dirty money as quickly as they had once made it.

"By law the Grand Jury can go on for 18 months. It's only been six. We have a whole year to get an indictment on these guys...we'll get 'em," Hogan assured.

"Hogan, you're always so positive, that's why I like you. But I don't know about this case here. I mean, I'm starting to think that Mr. Jackson has sold his soul to the devil in exchange for a lifetime of prosperity. Just think about... These guys have murdered, sold thousands of kilos of poison, and broke just about every other law known to man, yet everything they touch is turning into gold," David Miller complained, opening the manila folder before him. He pulled out a few photos, then placed them on the table. "Look at the long line of patrons waiting to enter Goldie's night club. Look at the parking lot, it's full," he said, fingering another photo. "All of Goldie's adult day cares are full also... All twenty of them," he added, pulling out another picture. Cashman's strip club, Ménage, was displayed. "Even Cashman has gone legit… Do you know how much money can be laundered through a strip club?" AUSA David Miller questioned rhetorically.

"Have we tried placing informants in any of the businesses that these guys own? Why can't the IRS get them for tax evasion?" Agent Shericka Tobby asked.

"Yes, we've tried to get a few informants hired, but we didn't get anywhere with that. And as far as the IRS getting them for tax evasion, that's not going to happen. Everything owned by these guys are held under one big corporate umbrella. Can you believe these slick son's of bitches sold 49% of their corporation to the public through a stock broker as an IPO?" Davis Miller stated, pulling another photo out of the manila folder. The picture displayed the strip mall where Alex's rim shop was located. "We have one last hope," Miller stated grimly. "And if this doesn't work I'm dropping this investigation. We have an informant in a shop next to Alex's rim shop. He's Colombian. Very smooth and flashy. He pretends to own a tint shop. We've supplied him with a few expensive cars to give off the impression that it's more to him than meets the eye, coupled with the flashy jewelry he wears, of course."

"Well how close has the informant gotten to Alex?" Shericka inquired.

"He hasn't gotten anywhere so far. Him and Alex hung out a few times and that's about it," Ricks interjected, speaking up for the first time.

Agent Tobby looked back to David Miller. "Give me a chance at Alex? I think I can get him. Maybe I can convince him to deal with our informant."

Everyone in the room looked at each other. After a few seconds of pregnant silence, David Miller spoke. "You know what? That sounds like an excellent idea. Give me a few days to think about it and we will set it up… You have one shot, rookie, so make it count," David Miller stated.

¢   ¢   ¢

Guatemala City, Guatemala
Jesus relaxed in his luxurious suite, which was actually the old

warden's office, puffing on a Montecristo White cigar and sipping on a bottle of Dom Perignon Vintage 1985. As he did so, he watched, uninterested, as three Dominican prostitutes danced and snorted coke at the foot of his king size bed. Jesus' mind was on bigger things. He was going back to his compound in the Sierra Madre Mountains at 3:00 a.m. – which was only a few hours away.

When Jesus was initially brought to the maximum security prison in Guatemala, he immediately tried to buy his way out. But the warden and a few other Guatemelan government officials were under pressure from the U.S. to make sure Jesus didn't move until his extradiction papers cleared the courts, allowing them to come get him. So it seemed, for a little while anyway, that Jesus had the key to every door in the prison except the ones to the front door.

The offer of $100 million U.S. dollars changed that.

¢   ¢   ¢

Three Hours Later
Stepping out into the warm fresh air, it was Jesus' first taste of freedom in as long as three months. He looked back at the maximum security prison as he descended the steps, shaking his head. An armored limo was at the bottom of the steps for him. The limo was to deliver him to his awaiting jet.

It took less than ten minutes for the limo to get Jesus to the Guatemala City Airport. As he was about to board his plane, the early morning darkness was suddenly illuminated by bright lights. Then, as quickly as the darkness had vanished, the two bodyguards that flanked him, carrying M-16's were knocked off their feet. They'd both received head shots from a sniper hidden somewhere in the distance.

"Jesus Diez," a man dressed in a black business suite stated as he stood at the top of the airstair of the jet. He descended the stairs with his hand outstretched. "CIA Director Walser," the man said after Jesus didn't shake his hand. "Look, I'm sorry about your men," Director Walser apologized, gesturing to the two corpses on the pavement. He noticed Jesus' eyes scanning his surroundings, possibly looking for an escape. "Mr. Diez, I just want to speak to you. Nothing more. You can board your jet as soon as we finish talking."

Jesus looked skeptical. "What's this about?" he asked.

Walser placed both his hands in his pockets, slightly bending his knees before speaking. "This is about getting rid of a common enemy. I want him to be a memory."

"And you need my help?" Jesus quizzed incredulously, but continued without waiting for a reply. "What about your government? They have me on their ten most wanted list."

"Yes, that's unfortunate, but if you agree to stop dealing the heroin you were dealing and never set foot in the United States, you will have nothing to worry about."

"So I will be removed from the most wanted list?"

"No. The Justice Department still wants you. You have an indictment. However, I'm the person who makes the decision to come to your country to get you. If you handle your business and take my advice you will stay free."

After Jesus was arrested, Lazorito went to war with the smaller cartels over the drug routes left behind by him. The violence was getting out of hand, spilling over into the U.S.—something the CIA didn't want.

"Mr. Diez, we liked it better when you were in power. Now what I need from you is for you to put together an army of men. We will supply you with the weapons and intel. Just make sure you kill Lazorito."

¢   ¢   ¢

Two Weeks After the DEA Meeting
"Got-damn," Alex muttered under his breath and grabbed his crotch as one of the finest bitches he'd ever seen stepped out of a brand new BMW, switching her wide hips into the tint shop next door.

Twenty minutes later, Oscar, the owner of the tint shop walked into Alex's rim shop accompanied by the woman Alex had seen getting out of the BMW.

"Alex, this is Shondra. Shondra, Alex," Oscar said, introducing the two. "Shondra is looking to buy some rims. She's good people, so hook her up," Oscar said in his thick Colombian accent.

"Aiight, I got her," Alex replied, glancing at Shondra's wide hips.

"Cool. I'll go finish tinting your window," Oscar said to Shondra before walking out of Alex's rim shop.

After convincing Shondra to purchase the new Davins he'd just gotten in, Alex asked Shondra out and she agreed. He picked her up in his Lambo later that evening. They ate at Olive Garden, caught a movie, then fell off in Cashman's club, Menage.

Seated in the VIP section of the club, niggas were coming up to Alex's table giving him pounds and saying what's up. Shondra was impressed. Alex ordered a bottle of Rosé, slipping two crushed up ecstasy pills into the bottle when Shondra excused herself to the restroom.

Ensuing the consumption of two glasses of Rosé, Shondra started feeling strange – freaky. Alex started up a conversation. He could tell that the ecstasy was starting to take effect on Shondra, because she kept sucking air through her teeth.

"You and Oscar seem pretty close. Yall ever fucked 'round?" Alex inquired.

Shondra was caught off guard by Alex's bluntness. "Umm…me and Oscar? …uh, no, we've never messed around. Oscar deals with my brutha. I-I mean is friends with my brutha."

Alex caught what Shondra had said, pertaining to Oscar dealing with her brother, before correcting herself. He also remembered that she'd told him that her brother had bought her the BMW and had given her the money for her rims. "I heard you say yo' brutha deal wit' Oscar before you tried to be slick and switch up what you said. But I wanna know what yo' brutha and Oscar deal in?" Alex questioned.

"No, I mean they're friends," she said unconvincingly.

Alex shot her a sarcastic look.

"Okay, you know that Oscar is Colombian. What do you think he deals in?" Shondra asked with a sarcastic look of her own, sucking in air through her teeth. Her pussy was wet and vibrating.

Alex smiled. "You ready to go?" he asked.

¢   ¢   ¢

An Hour Later

"Oh, Alex! Oh, baby! Why don't you put on a condom?! Oh, Alex, please don't cum in it! Oh God! Oh, God!" Shondra cried out as Alex pounded her pussy from the back.

But Alex was in his own world as he watched Shondra's ass cheeks jiggle each time his pelvis struck them.

During the ride to the Embassy Suites, Shondra told Alex about the hundreds of kilos Oscar was selling to her brother. She even knew the price. And although Goldie had said he was done with hustling, Alex wanted more. He never did want to quit, but he didn't have a plug, so he was forced into retirement.

Alex decided that he'd cut into Oscar about some work the following day when he saw him.

"Oh shit!" Alex roared, shooting his poisonous load into Agent Shericka Tobby's hot cum-catcher.

¢ ¢ ¢

One Week Later

Goldie sat in the office of his night club going over his receipts. The ring of his cell phone grabbed his attention. "Hello?" he answered without looking at his caller ID.

"What's happening, mi amigo?"

"Huh?...H-hey," Goldie stammered before taking his phone from his ear and staring at it like it was possessed.

Goldie had read about Jesus' prison break. He'd also seen the news coverage of Lazorito and his wife's car bombing. It *supposedly* left them both dead.

"Don't seem so surprised son-in-law," Jesus said, chuckling. "I just called to tell you that we are back in business."

"But I told you I was −"

"And I won't hear this nonsense about you being done either!" Jesus exclaimed threateningly before hanging up in Goldie's face.

"Hello? Hello? Man, how in the fuck did that muthafucka get my number?" Goldie asked himself, tossing his phone in the trash can next to his desk.

In a Van Behind Goldie's Club

"Oh my God! That call came in from Mexico. That had to be Jesus Diez," Agent Tate told Agent Tobby as they sat in back of their surveillance van.

"Huh?.. Oh yeah, you might be right," Agent Shericka Tobby said, snapping out of her daydream. She was thinking about Alex.

Every since the first night Shericka and Alex had fucked, Shericka couldn't get Alex off of her mind. She'd actually started to catch feelings for him. But because of her job and Alex's line of work, she knew that nothing could ever become of them.

Just thinking about her job made Shericka cringe. She couldn't have sex with the target of a DEA investigation. An investigation that she was a part of. But she'd already crossed the line. She figured she'd just deny it if Alex ever brought it up after his arrest. Besides, who'd believe a drug dealer over a DEA agent?

¢   ¢   ¢

The Following Day

"Can you believe this is finally about to happen?" Agent Ricks asked his partner, Agent Hogan, as they watched Alex pull into a Food Lion parking lot.

Alex had agreed to buy 20 bricks at $12,500 a piece from Oscar. The transaction was set up to be a 'drop off'. Meaning that Alex was to leave his car with the money in the trunk and hop into a white Ford F150 and drive off. The cocaine was supposed to be hidden in a hollowed out space wielded into the truck's gas tank.

Alex parked his rental car, leaving the keys in the arm rest, then casually walked to the F150. Before Alex could close his door good, he was swarmed by Feds.

¢   ¢   ¢

At the DEA headquarters, Alex thought that every question Hogan and Ricks shot at him was hilarious. That was until Oscar walked in followed by Agent Shericka Tobby, whose gold DEA badge dangled from her neck.

Up until that moment, Alex believed he had an illegal search and seizure defense. The truck wasn't his. He'd simply picked it up at the owner's request, to take back to his shop to put rims on it. It sounded far fetched, but that was his story and he was sticking to it.

Now his defense was shattered.

Hogan displayed a wide coffee stained grin as he watched Alex's shoulders slump. "We've got your ass now. There's no way you're getting out of this one. Now this is the deal. You go to the Grand Jury on Goldie and get five years, with the drug program you'll do a little under three. Play with us and I will personally guarantee you won't get a day under forty years. You have twenty minutes to decide," Hogan stated before walking out of the interrogation room with the rest of the agents in tow.

¢   ¢   ¢

One Month Later

"Jackson! Get ready for count," a C.O. barked, sliding a tray through the slot in Goldie's cell door.

Wiping the slob from his face, Goldie got up, got the tray, then sat back on his bunk. Glancing around his cell, reality set in. He was in jail.

The C.O. came back to the cell twenty minutes later and escorted Goldie to intake. There, two U.S. marshals were waiting on him. They drove him to the Federal Courthouse, placing him in a holding cell. It wasn't long afterwards that Cashman, Jay, Mike-Mike and Ernest were brought in. Ten minutes later, Sheriff West and Big Woo were brought in also.

"Damn! Man, that fuck-ass nigga Alex hot as fuck! Bruh, I told you that fuck-nigga was gonna snitch this time," Cashman spat.

Goldie couldn't say shit because Cashman was right.

Cashman had been telling Goldie that Alex was going to snitch ever since Goldie had told him about Alex's arrest. But there wasn't shit Goldie could do about it. Alex had disappeared without a trace.

"Got-damn-it!" Sheriff West interrupted. "I don't know any of you got-damn nig-. I-I mean, fellers. But these crooked sum-bitches just gave me ten got-damn years up in Georgia. Now they saying I'm part of a drug conspiracy down here. These motherfuckers gave my wife a year for signing for a house they done took from us," Sheriff West complained.

Big Woo stood up. "Cracka! Was you 'bout to call us niggas?" he asked, scaring the shit out of Sheriff West. "Man, them crackas up in Tennessee gave my blackass 36 muthafuckin' years! Now I get indicted way down here. Shit, a nigga fucked up! So cracka, I ain't tryin' to hear yo' bitch ass cryin' 'bout no ten funky-ass years."

Just then a marshal appeard at the holding cell. "Sultan Jackson? Your attorney wants to speak with you," the marshal explained when Goldie stood up.

¢   ¢   ¢

Five Minutes Later in a Room Down the Hall
"Look Sultan, I've talked to the U.S. Attorney and the plea is thirty years. Ten with cooperation. I think we should try them," Roy Black suggested. He'd become Goldie's lawyer because Marquis Wimberly couldn't defend him. Being as Mr. Wimberly had defended the government's star witness.

Damn, a nigga ain't even been to first appearance yet and these crackas already talkin' 'bout pleas and shit, Goldie thought to himself.

A detention hearing was held an hour after all of the co-conspirators had spoken to their lawyers. Goldie, Big Woo and Sheriff West were the only ones denied bond. After the last co-conspirator had seen the judge they were all taken back to the holding cell. There, they all agreed to go to trial.

During the six months leading up to the trial date, there was heavy media coverage surrounding the case. AUSA David Miller was offering time cuts to anybody with incriminating information against Goldie and his co-defendants. But niggas were too shook to talk. Especially after hearing about what happened to Brown-eyed Ron, Precious and their children. Even Goldie was spooked.

Brown-eyed Ron and his family's decapitated bodies were found in their new home in Portland, Oregon. Next to Precious' corpse was a note that read: *Talk and die, Alex.* An empty Tequila bottle was used as a paper weight to hold the note in place.

Needless to say, Alex changed his mind about testifying. So David Miller, with his case in jeopardy, offered plea deals – which the defense team being led by Roy Black, accepted after consulting with Goldie and his codefendants.

Goldie's guideline range was 10 to 12 years for the reduced charge he and his co-conspirators had pleaded to; but given he had no prior convictions, Goldie received seventy months because he was granted the safty valve. The safety valve authorized a judge to go up under a minimum mandatory sentence as well as the Federal Sentencing Guidelines.

Cashman also got the safety valve and the minor role reduction, receiving two years at sentencing. Big Woo was given five more years to run wild with the 36 he'd been given in Tennessee. Sheriff West got a nickel that ran wild with the ten he was sentenced to in Georgia. He could have gotten less time if he would have cooperated, but Sheriff West told AUSA David Miller to *suck his dick.*

Ernest, Mike-Mike and Jay received the most lenient sentences. They were all sentenced to a year and a day for facilitating a communication device to commit a drug offense…

To Be Continued in: CRUMBS TO BRICKS PART 2: RESPECT MY MILITARY

By Capo Cat Freeman & PLEX

About the Author

Christopher "Capo Cat" Freeman is a loving father of one and resides in Jacksonville, Florida. Besides working on his next two urban releases, he operates two local businesses and promotes some of the biggest shows in Jacksonville. To contact him please email him at christopherfreeman1978@gmail.com

BADLAND PUBLISHING
PO Box 11623
Riviera Beach, FL 33419
(561) 842-4746

,Shipping address

Name:_____

Address:_____

City:_____State:_____Zip:_____

Title	Author	Price
STREET RAISED: The Beginning	Mike Harper	15.95
STREET RAISED: The Raw Deal	PLEX	15.95
SUGAR	Mike Harper	15.95
BOO BABY: The Secret Of…	PLEX	15.95
SERVED: With No Regard!	PLEX	15.95
ONE LOVE	PLEX	13.95
BUCKIN' DA' DICE Vol. 1	BOOK GANG	15.95
NO TURNING…	Big Nation	13.95
GET IT HOW YOU LIVE	Big Gemo	13.95
CRUMBS TO BRICKS	Capo Cat	15.95
LOVE & THUGGIN'	Bo Brown	15.95
LIL ONE: Blood Investment	K-1 & Bino	15.00
EROTIC DESIRES	7 Supreme & BOOK GANG	12.95
PROMISCUOUS	Calvin Williams & PLEX	10.00

Please make checks or money orders payable to BADLAND Publishing. Shipping and handling is $3.75 for 1 to 5 books. For orders over 5 books add .75 to each book. Then allow 7 to 10 business days for delivery. We thank you for your support!!!

Capo Cat

PLEX PRESENTS:
NO TURNING...

Nathan "Big Nation" Welch

PLEX PRESENTS:
GET IT HOW YOU LIVE
Volume 1NE

Big Gemo

Capo Cat

Capo Cat

www.ingramcontent.com/pod-product-compliance
Lightning Source LLC
Chambersburg PA
CBHW060533260626
47161CB00003B/879